PRAISE FOR PATRICIA HICKMAN'S
FALLEN ANGELS

"A new book by Patricia Hickman is always an occasion for delight. She is a gifted author with a deft touch for all the elements of fine storytelling."

—T. DAVIS BUNN, AUTHOR OF *WINNER TAKE ALL*

"Captures the desperate joy and hope-filled sorrow of the Depression era to perfection. . . . Patricia Hickman's prose rings with gritty authenticity and stark, lyrical description. . . . A glorious story of grace, told with a skilled pen and an open heart."

—LO CURTIA HIGGS, AUTHOR OF
THORN IN MY HEART

"I love Patty Hickman's vivid language and rich descriptions. Her characters pop off the page, and in this latest novel, steal your heart."

—LISA TAWN BERGREN, AUTHOR OF
CHRISTMAS EVERY MORNING

"Hickman's story is as gritty as a plate of homemade hominy—and just as filling, just as sweet, just as true."

—NORRIS MAILER, AUTHOR OF
WINDCHILL SUMMER

"In a carefully and beautifully written story of home and family, Hickman reminds us that even when we hide, love finds a way."

—LYNN HINTON, AUTHOR OF
FRIENDSHIP CAKE

"Only Patricia Hickman could move from humorous simplicity to poignant epiphany on the very same page. FALLEN ANGELS will charm its way right into your heart."

—BRANDILYN COLLINS, BESTSELLING AUTHOR OF
DREAD CHAMPION AND *CAPTURE THE*
WIND FOR ME

"A haunting tale of innocence, greed, and spiritual awakening."
—RANDALL INGERMANSON,
CHRISTY AWARD-WINNING AUTHOR
OF OXYGEN AND THE FIFTH MAN

"A heartwarming read, both humorous and achingly real. A beautiful testimony to the truth of the human condition and the parts we play. Her characters are artfully unmasked to reveal ourselves."
—KRISTEN HEITZMANN, BESTSELLING AUTHOR OF
TWILIGHT AND THE DIAMOND OF THE ROCKIES
SERIES

"Inspired and inspiring, FALLEN ANGELS is a kaleidoscope of emotional hues—especially the emotions of laughter and joy. Can a story of the Great Depression lift your spirits? Can a con man teach you truths about life? Read this novel. It will make a believer out of you."
—JIM DENNEY, AUTHOR OF ANSWERS TO SATISFY THE
SOUL AND THE TIMEBENDERS SERIES

"Patty's innate ability to dish up a captivating tale with authentic Southern flavor is truly impressive! . . . This charming story is truly unforgettable."
—MELODY CARLSON, AUTHOR OF ARMANDO'S
TREASURE, LOOKING FOR CASSANDRA JANE, BLOOD
SISTERS, AND FINDING ALICE

FALLEN ANGELS

BOOK ONE IN THE
MILLWOOD HOLLOW SERIES

PATRICIA HICKMAN

A Division of AOL Time Warner Book Group

Copyright © 2003 by Patricia Hickman

All rights reserved. No part of this book may be reproduced in any form or by any electronic or mechanical means, including information storage and retrieval systems, without permission in writing from the publisher, except by a reviewer who may quote brief passages in a review.

Visit our Web site at www.twbookmark.com

W WARNER *Faith*™ A Division of AOL Time Warner Book Group

First Warner Faith printing: May 2003

10 9 8 7 6 5 4 3 2 1

Library of Congress Cataloging-in-Publication Data

Hickman, Patricia.
   Fallen angels / Patricia Hickman.
     p. cm.
   ISBN 0-446-69101-1
    1. Abandoned children—Fiction. 2. Brothers and sisters—Fiction.
   3. Depressions—Fiction. 4. Arkansas—Fiction. I. Title.
   PS3558.I2296F35 2003
   813'.54—dc21   2003041086

Book design by Nancy Singer Olaguera
Cover design by Beck Stvan
Cover photo by Hulton Archives/Stone

To my mother-in-law, Gaye Hickman, who reads every word of every book I write and makes me believe I should keep trying. It is for her and readers like her that I, with love and humility, dedicate this book.

ACKNOWLEDGMENTS

Writing a story set in the Great Depression in Arkansas was as natural to me as breathing. Although the characters from *Fallen Angels* in the Millwood Hollow series and the town of Nazareth are fictional, the mood of the period, and the color and pulse of the setting come from the stories told to me as a young girl sitting at my grandpa's knee. It was in my grandparents' home that I absorbed both the harshness of sudden poverty as well as the love of family that infused the Great Depression years. I am indebted to my family, mother and father, uncles, aunts, and great aunts who, although gone from this life, gave me a peek into a history roiling in change.

In interviewing those still living today who survived this period, I was surprised to find hardly any embittered people, and most lives changed for the better. From strife sprang stories of wonder and courage, faith and tenacity that left me with no fear of what may come. Whatever life may drop on the plains of American soil, always present is the courage to pick up our plows again and be transformed.

I'm thankful to my father-in-law, Kenneth Hickman, for providing the small tidbits here and there that make this story true. I'm indebted to Mrs. Lenny Betts and Mrs. Nelle Jean Dawson of the Camden Historical Society for their exhaustive facts and history of this era and setting in southwest Arkansas.

The meticulous care they lend to the history of their hometown is enrichment for the rest of us.

I'm also grateful to Rolf Zettersten and Leslie Peterson of Warner Faith for believing in this project. Also thanks to my gifted editor Lisa Bergren who, so far, hasn't tired of me. *Fallen Angels* is one of the most rewarding stories I've had the privilege of penning and it is due entirely to the community of friends and family who have contributed from the heart. I hope to pass this heartfelt wonder and love of story on to you, the reader.

He had never been sure but that there might be something to the doctrines he had preached as an evangelist. Perhaps God really had dictated every word of the Bible. Perhaps there really was a hell of burning sulphur. Perhaps the Holy Ghost really was hovering around watching him and reporting.

—SINCLAIR LEWIS, *ELMER GANTRY*

FALLEN ANGELS

A bit of trouble with attempted murder sent Jeb Nubey over the Texarkana border in the unfortunate direction of hunger. Everybody from the Texas side had gotten the wrong idea about the matter. If he had been a man of means, he would've been thought of as a stand-up guy instead of feller-on-the-run. That was all stand-up men were, he figured—the ones who could stand up with their pockets full of pay-offs and get fellers to see things in a new light. But now none of the itinerant boys—buddies he'd on many nights shared a bottle of the good stuff with—would talk to him. Once word spread of problems with the boss man, they just turned their sorry backs and walked away.

He'd never thought he would hear his name preceded by "no account," as in no-account scum, no-account filth-of-the-earth. Worthless. Shiftless. Twenty-two years after his momma had given him the good name of Jeb, he'd descended to the rank Leon Hampton had awarded him—Leon and his son, Hank, who could never keep a gal on his tight-fisted leash due to his alcohol-infused temper.

The gal, Myrna. The Betty Boop gal. Round hips. Red lips.

"Last night, I nearly killed a man. Maybe I did kill him. Now no one will talk to me," said Jeb.

"Hank got was coming to him," Jeb's brother Charlie said. "But you got to hide, lay low until things simmer down in Texarkana. Until Hampton forgets your name."

Hamptons owned everything in Texarkana, from the burlesque girls no one admitted worked for a nickel a dance down at the Biscuit and Bean, to the banking king who kept his doors open on Black Monday when the other Savings and Loans had closed.

"It's cowardly, Charlie. I ain't a running-away sort," Jeb said.

Charlie packed up two work shirts along with all the cash the two of them had earned picking cotton and handed it all to Jeb. "That's why Hank's laying near to death, because you don't run away. He came at you first. We all saw it. But you got them killer fists." Charlie gave the air between them a hefty punch and then handed him the bag he'd filled with the cash and such. "We don't have no clout in Texarkana. Without clout, you got no witnesses—not none that a-body would listen to."

Jeb wondered if Charlie had finally lost every bit of good sense. "Hank would have killed you, too, Charlie, if he had caught you with her. Don't give me eyes. I know'd you slept with Myrna, like we all did."

Jeb had memorized Myrna. Myrna, the girl that pretended she loved him when she loved most of the starving gaggle of sharecroppers' sons in Texarkana. Sweet skin, like the girls that posed for the better calendars. Paled by the blue of night, her hair spread against the hay bale, flaxen corn silk like the breath of moon and stars. Touched by Jeb. Myrna had her own perfume and the kind of girl's fragrant hair that wrapped her white dewy shoulders with an aroma like petals. Mind fogging. But not worth a killing. "It was you, Brother, that did the doing."

"I didn't, don't you see." Charlie's face gentled, faultless.

"We never. You know I got Selma waiting for me in Oklahoma."

"You expect me to believe you keepin' yourself for Selma? I believe that like I believe we's going to wake up a Rockefeller."

"Myrna loved you, Jeb. Said you cast a spell over her. Told me that over a bowl of beans. Now if that don't mean somethin', nothing does."

Jeb knew the truth. "She never belonged to Hank. Gals like her don't belong to nobody." He shook out the insides of the bag and stuffed Charlie's money into a leather satchel his grandfather had once toted across the plains. He listened to the bearish sounds of the sleeping itinerant workers, hard sleepers fallen on their cots from a week of picking. Blood dried on boll-torn fingertips perfumed by corn liquor. "You think Hank will die, for real?" He could not breathe himself.

"Either way his daddy's gone after the sheriff. You got to get out of here!" Charlie's face was wet with worry.

"If I leave, they'll believe I meant to do him in. I stay, they at least hear my side."

"You got no clout."

"Stop staying that, Charlie, like I got no name!"

Hampton's hound dogs bayed. The moon had a faded paleness, as though a candle inside its glass was melting before sunup.

"I never meant to kill him, Charlie. If he dies, I should be hanged."

"You listen to me, and you listen like I'm our momma! Give us some time, me and the boys, to talk to the sheriff. Otherwise they could string you up and gut ya before you can even whisper your own name. Hamptons, they got money. That sheriff listens to money. It calls his name. But if we all get to him, before the story gets turned around, blown into more than it was, I'll send for you."

"I don't know where to go, Charlie! Just where do cowards hide?"

"Find a big place with lots of people. Hot Springs. Little Rock. No, that's the first place they'll look. Best you don't tell me. But after you get settled, write."

"How you expect me t'do that?"

"Don't put your name on it, like, *Here I am, come and get me, police.*" Both of them stared at the floor, locked in place and out of ideas. Disgraceful shame. Good schemers, but between the two of them, kind of low on dependable means. "I tell you what—just draw a big X on the letter. Have the postman stamp it with the town name. Lay low. I'll find you when it's safe."

The whole desertion mess started in the Rialto Theater in Camden, Arkansas. The warm lap of summer brought out the townsfolk to the dance like they'd been spring-dosed with yarbs. Angel figured the Ouachita's old ballroom dance hall across the street had lured in the wrong kind of man to draw her Aunt Lana's wandering eye. Lana, who wasn't really her aunt anyway, only a conniving woman, of a mind to do her daddy's errands only so she could keep food in her belly. *Aunt, my hind foot,* her mother might have said—if she herself had stuck around.

Saturday night at the movies in Camden fed hungry imaginations a front row view of the American Dream. Pin-up girls lolled poolside on the big screen, California smiles as bright as morning light trickling across the Ouachita River. In the Arkansas movie theater, Angel closed her eyes to imagine the California sun warming her unshapely legs, tickling her calves until they turned heads, brown and never-ending like tall, elegant Sequoias. Forever legs, she imagined. Then she opened her eyes, palely thirteen again and deserted in the Rialto with her little brother, Willie, and her youngest sister, Ida May.

Two kids, a big girl with her younger brother, sat in front of them not in the least bit interested in Barbara Stanwyck or that glamour gal's rendering of a charlatan evangelist. With the movie screen for a halo, the girl turned around in the threadbare chair and stared at Angel and her siblings, curious and bored. The girl, her hair pigtailed to distraction, pressed another jelly bean between her lips that puckered when she spoke as though she had practiced the Shirley Temple pucker too long at her mirror. She glanced up the aisle and then back at Angel. "Where'd your momma go to?"

"None of your business," said Angel. She leaned right and slightly cocked her head.

"She ain't our momma. She's Aunt Lana," said Willie.

Angel gave him a sort of tap in the arm with her elbow. "Don't say 'ain't.'" She hated being marked an Arkie even though every farmer, bank clerk, and soda jerk in sight fit the type—the kind of people who drift into the middle of the nation, lose their wind, and stay. To Angel, saying "Ain't" was like saying "I give up and can't get no smarter." But worse was hearing Willie mix Momma with Aunt Lana.

Angel talked about everybody and everything. But not Momma. It was the kind of thing she kept to herself as though some day the secret would bring the two of them closer. Her momma, Thorne, had disappeared into a Ford with two women who traveled to Little Rock to try and find work. Angel had stared after her, held on to her eyes, a pair of exotic browns like the kind that belong to bronzy island girls. Eyes that set off her luxurious hair tendriling out of the window. With her momma had left the only opulence that lingered in Snow Hill. The only hope that Angel would some day be as elegant as Thorne, drove off to Little Rock with a promise to send money.

Lemuel, her father, had too often of late paid more attention to a neighbor divorcee named Lana than his own kin. With Thorne run off to Little Rock, he finally packed the kids all off aimed in the general direction of the town of Angel's oldest sister, Claudia—a place called Nazareth. But of all the foolish ideas Daddy had ever dreamed up, sending them off with Lana took the cake.

"Where is Aunt Lana?" Willie shared his popcorn with Ida May, trying to keep her in her own seat and out of his.

"She's not our aunt. How many times I have to say it?" said Angel. She knew that Daddy thought that if he had the little ones call her "Aunt" her every-other-day appearances at the front door would give her full authority over the youngens. But Angel knew better.

Daddy had underestimated his girl.

"I think she run off with that huckster nosing around the hotel and left us here. If Daddy knew, he'd bean her." Willie picked Ida May off his shoulder and deposited her on the other side of the chair arm.

"What's a huckster?" Ida May tried to curl up against her brother again.

"A peddler who ain't a bonafide person of worth." Angel disappeared into the screen again, into the sin of Barbara Stanwyck, *The Miracle Woman.* The motion picture had finally made it into Arkansas. When Willie tried to speak again, Angel shushed him, a slow hissing that seeped out of her as she followed Miss Stanwyck across the screen.

Angel made them stay until the last credit rolled up and away. The house lights brightened slow and easy, turning the wallpaper red as lipstick.

"Let's try and find Lana," said Willie.

Angel rolled up Willie's popcorn bag, tucked it under her arm, and herded the others out into the lobby. Once she thought she heard Lana's high, squeaky cackle—the same one she heard at night out on their front porch when Daddy sent them off to bed. But Lana was nowhere to be found.

Across the street from the Rialto a steady stream of couples clambered up the steps and across the mezzanine of the Ouachita Hotel to the grand ballroom, where a live band played. Most of Camden had turned out for the dance. The threesome headed out into the street and searched the crowd for what seemed like an hour. Finally, Angel turned to face the younger ones. The Rialto's neon marquis buzzed overhead. "Let's face it, Willie. Lana's gone. She ditched us."

Ida May huffed, "Did not!"

"Willie, you stay down here next to this couple. Make like they're our folks until I get back. For safety. Stop looking at me like that. I'll check out the dance."

Angel sidled up the steps to the landing. It led across the alley to the ballroom. She could see couples swaying across the hardwood floors, but no Lana. She met Willie and Ida May downstairs again and led them to Usrey's Drugstore on the corner of Washington and Adams, where she helped Ida May onto a stool. She made Willie stay with her while she crept past the faces reflecting back at her from the long ornate mirror behind the soda bar.

Moments later, Willie found her in the back and ran at her red faced. "That soda jerk told us if we ain't ordering, we have to leave!"

"Lana's not here either. Let's go," said Angel.

"Go where, Angel?" Instead of acting scared, Willie got mad. "Back to Snow Hill? To Claudia's? Where?"

"Hush! Don't be a rat, Willie! You got to give me time to think."

Ida May waited like a ghost in the doorway, jostled aside by paying customers. Her face was oval with brown eyes like her mother's. When upset, the oval got all long-like, hardening her eyes like penny candies. Her momma had always said, "Little Girl, you'll turn to salt and blow away makin' faces like 'at." Ida May stood in the doorway, her mouth an O. Angel hated the way the Depression toughened girl babies and made them old before their time.

Angel examined the town in front of her. First off, Camden was more electrified than Snow Hill. The Camdenites gathered in clusters in front of the movie theater, some in front of Usrey's Drugstore, and a lot of the people dressed for Saturday-night-showing-off. They clambered in and out of the ballroom, little ants spilling out of a thrown-away Coke bottle. The young women all wore hats that snugged to their heads like colored helmets. The whole place had a pace contrary to Snow Hill. By this time of night Snow Hill had rolled up inside of itself, an old man glad for the day to be over and done with.

"If we don't find Lana, where will we go tonight? Where will we sleep or eat? Lana didn't check us into the motel like she said she was fixing to do," said Willie.

"We'll find a room. I'm no louse when it comes to figuring things out, Willie. I can take care of things as good or better than Lana. I am thirteen, after all." Angel took Ida May's hand and led her down past the hotel and across the street to the Rialto. She tapped the counter to attract the ticket seller's attention. "Excuse me, Mister. I got something to ask," she said.

The ticket seller lifted his eyes and revealed a long, thin face with a chin that protruded like a potato. "Yes, what you chil-dern want?"

"I'm supposed to meet my aunt. She's getting us a room. Know where she might get us a room?"

Willie mumbled behind her.

The ticket seller pointed at the Ouachita Hotel. "Only one place."

With one graceful, popcorn-oiled hand, Ida May pointed toward the hotel. "I see her, Angel! Look, there she is yonder." Ida May bristled past her older sister, who had failed her as a stand-in leader.

Angel chased her across the street, through the gaggle of humans from the hills and lake that encircled Camden proper. Willie ran past her, charged up the hotel stairs, and barreled past the mezzanine.

"Angel, it's not Lana!" he called from the opening to the ballroom. The music blared above his nasal yell.

Angel reached the doorway and looked in at the mass of swaying bodies. A woman, blonde, bore Lana's posture—hips forward, shoulders slumped. The woman gingerly held up a cigarette for a man to light. She drew on it. The tobacco end warmed and kindled red like coals coming to life. The blonde leaned toward him and whispered into his ear. Then she turned and walked away from him as though she had excused herself to the powder room.

"It's not Lana, Ida May," said Willie.

Ida May had by now twisted Angel's skirt around her pointer finger. "I'm skeered, Angel."

"I'll get us a room. We'll get some shut-eye and then figger out what to do tomorrow." Angel led them across the mezzanine and down into the hotel lobby.

"I didn't like her anyway," Willie said. "Matter of fact she made me sick, come to think of it. She told lies about Momma."

Angel paused, remembering how Lana had said, *"It's a hard thing to hear. Your momma had to be taken off to stay with her sister who could keer for her better. Don't think that means she didn't love you kids. She loved you all right. But this Depression is enough to drive any person over the ledge."* She'd spewed it out inside the Rialto after pacifying Ida May with popcorn. *"Then strap on too many mouths to feed and you got trouble. Your mother went and leaped off the cliffs of insanity, that's what. They call it stark-ravin' mad."* Lana disappeared after that, Angel decided, to run into the powder room to smooth the bleeding rivulets of color on her lower lip.

"She tells lies, Willie, when it's easier to tell the truth!" Angel approached the front desk. She lied to the clerk about meeting her aunt. When Willie showed the clerk hard cash, he didn't seem to mind. He handed Angel the key. "Back up the stairs, down the hall, and third door on the right. You kids'd do best to remember we like it quiet after midnight."

Angel took the key and started up the stairs. Ida May took every step as though she expected Lana to appear and give an account for her delay. Willie beat them to the door and waited while Angel used the key and opened the door.

"I'm hungry again," said Willie. The first thing he did was to riffle through the nightstand drawer as though he might find a candy or two left behind by a former hotel customer.

"Ida May, you wash up in the lavatory and climb into bed with Willie. I'll take the extra bed near the wall."

Angel stopped for the first time and examined the lay of the room. The hotel room had wallpaper—genuine wallpaper, not magazine pages stuck to the wall—the first that Angel had ever seen. Her mother might have called it elegant, a swirl of gold and red that twinkled in the chandelier's light like a kaleidoscope. "This is a pretty nice place."

In the bathroom, Ida May ran the sink water until Angel yelled for her to shut if off and get in bed. After making sure Ida May and Willie were covered up good, Angel slid her mother's old satin nightgown out of the sack and pulled it on top of herself. She whispered twice, "Lana's a liar," and fell asleep.

She dreamed dreams of Barbara Stanwyck perched on a platform—the charlatan queen who touched her flock with her healing lies. The actress's features disappeared and Angel's face took Stanwyck's place. Her stomach was stretched full, satisfied with delicacies paid for by the faithful. She lifted her arms as though she possessed a power from above. The divine gesture caused the loyal to toss money onto the platform. She moved across the stage with her gown trailing behind her and dollar bills crunching beneath her slippers.

When she awoke to the sound of voices in the hallway, the first thing to draw her eye was Ida May staring out of the window into the alley below. Lana had never come back.

A deputy sheriff stopped Willie and Ida May out on the sidewalk. "I don't believe I know you kids. Who's your momma?"

Angel pushed through two people to get to them and lead Ida May away from the policeman before she gave away more than was needed.

"I'm calling Daddy," said Ida May. And then she yanked away from Angel and ran down the street away from the Ouachita.

Angel trailed behind her until she saw her disappear into a storefront. Inside, Ida May crouched behind a flour display.

"You can't call Daddy. You lost your mind?" Angel was entirely disgusted. Willie caught up with them, and the two younger children stood looking at the eldest. Angel hated to tell them but finally broke down. "He took off soon as Lana drove away with us."

"How you know that?" Willie's fingers followed the X's on the threads inside a basket of baseballs.

"I saw his things packed up. His job was spent. He's headed for work down in Texas. Lana told me. That's why she left— her gravy train was drying up. The only reason she hauled us off was because Daddy gave her a little money for it. He should have known she was brainless and likely to ditch us."

Willie fished around inside the bag Lana had left in the theater.

"What you think you'll find?" Angel asked.

"Lana hid a little money in here yesterday. Flighty gals like her forget their own names once they get their minds on other things, like that huckster." He fished out a scarf tied with string.

Angel untied the scarf and opened it. "Five dollars. Plus what Daddy give us. I'm glad she's gone. We can get to Claudia's by ourselves." Claudia should have gotten her letter by now, Angel decided. Her memory of an older sister was little more than a grown-up laugh in the kitchen with Momma. Claudia had not been one to write, but often enough she had dropped a note to tell Momma about her marriage to a railway man. She never said either way whether he treated her good. She just said the bills were paid and that was all the good in a man she needed.

"I don't think Daddy left at all. You're just saying it to get us to do what you want. I want to go home, Angel. We never heard nothing from Claudia. She doesn't know we're coming. What if she can't afford to feed us like Daddy couldn't?" asked Willie.

"Home's not home anymore and I'm not lyin'. Besides, Claudia knows about Momma. I wrote her a letter and told her. Daddy said he'd write and tell her we were headed her way, so stop complaining."

A lady with a natural smile counted apples into a basket next to them.

"Ma'am, we need to catch a lift to our sister's place in Nazareth. We'd be glad to pay you a dollar for the trouble," said Angel.

"Where would you kids get a dollar? Don't believe I've ever seen you around here." The woman's entire expression changed as though a cloud had all at once formed above her.

"Oh, we got it from our daddy." Angel backed away from the woman. She remembered the way the deputy sheriff had fixed his eyes on her as though he were putting her face to memory.

"Let's go over to that café and get us something to eat, Angel," Willie begged. "I'm starving."

Angel ignored her brother and studied a male customer who gathered food into a crate. He turned and glanced at them and returned to his shopping. "There's a man that looks like he's about to do some traveling. Let's see if he'll take a couple of dollars for letting us hitch a ride."

"Two dollars is too much," said Willie.

The man in denim bent over a stacked crate of canned goods next to his collected heap of flour and sugar. He looked a lot like the feller who broke ponies down at the auction barn in Snow Hill—nice face bones, but a little troubled around the eyes. He tapped each can, counting and recounting as though he could not remember the number of the items. Angel had not known many fellers with eyes so thread blue, like the stitches on her daddy's work pants. Sweet creases at the corners, but not so badly aged, although they made him look puckish. Angel gave her hair a combing through with her fingertips. It came to her that she should cast herself in the best light possible to Sweet Eyes.

She composed herself in the manner of a near-grown girl and said, "Excuse me, Sir."

"I don't have anything for beggar kids," he said.

"You don't know who I am?" She pulled on her earlobe whenever she lied, a habit her daddy had always called her on. Angel was not a name to give a girl who told her kind of lies. But anyone in her situation had to have resources or resort to invention. Through the storefront window she saw a Ford truck parked near the door and she noticed the decent set of tires, like Daddy always did. "My father is, well, he's the right-hand man to Henry Ford." The apple counter stopped her counting and stared at Angel. Angel spoke more quietly. "Matter of fact, Henry Ford's my uncle." She noticed how the man's eyes thinned, two rinds. He assessed her tattered green dress, the loose braiding at the yoke. She pressed the loopy part against her chest with one finger. "Our better clothes are at the hotel being—warshed."

"You're staying at the hotel?" Sweet Eyes asked.

The key was still in Angel's pocket. She held it up. "The Ouachita, of course. Nothing but the best, Daddy says. Anyway, Daddy sent us ahead to visit relatives and, truth be told, our mistress done got herself sick with the flu. Flu's been going around like nobody's business. Poor lady."

"What relatives?" asked Sweet Eyes.

"Our older sister, Claudia," said Angel. That was not a lie.

"She's married with a kid or two. Old enough to take us in, I reckon." Willie stood holding his hat. As though coached by Angel, he hung his head. Ida May bit her lip. She had been on the very edge of bawling all morning. So her lip quivered just by the very act of anyone looking at her.

"We're stranded as can be, but we got the money to pay our own way. If you think you could give us a ride to a place called Nazareth, we'll pay." She held out a single crisp dollar bill, considering Willie's caution that two dollars was too much.

"I don't know what you got for an angle but I'm traveling alone and I don't have any place to put kids." Sweet Eyes glanced up at the Ford pickup loaded with food and supplies. "Besides, if your daddy works for Ford, you should give him a call and tell him you're in dire need of his assistance." The man's crackling voice rose in pitch. His attention drifted, and then he lost interest altogether.

"Excuse me. Did I hear you say you're traveling to Nazareth?" A woman in a shapeless dress hovered near the apple crates, listening to everything Angel had said. Her skin had a pink cast blending into whiter eye sockets with feathery white brows for a topper. "I'm Winifred Mock. I'm a retired schoolteacher and I'm on my way to Bluff City. Appears to me Nazareth is a rock's throw from Bluff City. You say you'll pay for the ride?"

Angel held up the dollar.

"There's three of you?" She counted them with her nose.

Angel pulled out the second dollar.

"There you have it. A ride with a retired schoolteacher," said Sweet Eyes. He jerked a crate up and arched his back to brace the weight of the flour and sugar bags.

Angel watched him pay and leave. "We need to find a place to eat," she said to Winifred. "My brother and sister need some breakfast and then we'll be ready to leave."

"Best to grab some bread and apples then here at the store. You can eat in my car on the way, 'long as you mind not to clutter it up."

Small relief spilled over and Angel said, "I told you I could take care of us, Willie." She gathered a whole loaf of bread, a half dozen apples, and laid them on the counter, a paying customer.

✳

Winifred Mock whirred in a monotone. She droned instead of conversing and it occurred to Angel the woman had a terrible way of talking. She strung her syllables out, running words into other words until the whole of her sentence became a sticky lump of tedious slurs.

"How long did you teach school?" Angel finally asked her.

"Twenty years." Only it sounded like "twennyers." Winifred pulled a cigarette from her cumbersome black purse, a bag so deep it reminded Angel of Doc Campbell's medical bag in Snow Hill. Inside, beside a pair of red gloves, Angel saw a deck of cards.

"My uncle plays poker. You a poker player, Miss Mock?" Angel asked.

The woman reached and closed the bag with a snap. "Your uncle. You mean your Uncle Henry Ford, the millionaire?"

Angel tugged her right earlobe.

"You don't have to keep up the front on my account. You kids orphans or some such, I figure. You really got family in Nazareth or you just looking for the next meal ticket?" Winifred's cigarette pulsed in Morse code beats when she spoke.

"We're not orphans." Willie sat up from the rear seat. His annoyance blustered out of him and he grabbed the back of the seat to pull himself forward.

"Fine, fine. You're not orphans," said Winifred. "I guess you right about it. You got money. Least you had some before you gave it to me. How you come by the money for this trip?"

"We got almost ten dollars and we're not orphans," said Willie.

Winifred stared straight ahead. "I'm glad you got means. Shame to see chil-dern like you without means."

"Things'll pick up for us in Nazareth," said Angel.

"You must have a good little wad to be traveling on yer own."

"We don't have that much anymore. Our aunt—that is, the lady who dumped us—ran off with all our money," said Angel. It came to her they ought not to give out particulars that were nobody's business.

"Folks like that ought to be tied up and left for the crows," said Winifred.

Ida May huffed, an anxious dove's sigh that drew her sister's eye.

"You don't look old enough to take care of two little ones," said Winifred.

"I'm thirteen," Angel told her and it was true.

"Old enough to marry, they say. I guess you'll do then."

"I need to go bad," said Ida May.

"Course you do, honey. It's been a while since I been around little ones. Best to remind me of things like that. I'll pull over and you can find you a place to go out in this field. No one around. Your sister can take you."

The car rolled to a stop.

"Come with me, Ida May. Willie, you just wait here, I guess."

"Where are we?" Willie asked Winifred.

"Somewhere between Camden and Chidester," said Winifred.

Angel, who had kept the sack full of their belongings in her arms, opened Willie's door and handed him the bag of apples and leftover bread. "Ida May, let's go. You take too long."

Out of all of the Welbys, Ida May always took the trophy for being the household sissy. She had grown up around outhouses, but never wanted to go into one. Many nights Angel had stood outside the sharecropper's outhouse at midnight listening to her sister sniffle and complain about odors and wild things looking to grab a-body. This field, with its prickly weeds, offered Ida May a whole new crop of complaints.

"I hate this place. I can't go here, Angel. I want to go home," said Ida May.

"Ida May, you hate doin' your business back home, too. Just go." She opened the sack containing the money and counted the roll of bills again.

A faint sigh lifted from the bramble. Ida May emerged as though all her self-respect had been left in the weeds.

Angel pushed back a stock of goldenrod and let Ida May pass. When they entered the clearing, Willie waved to them from behind the car. "Miss Mock's car won't start. You all get in and I'll push it."

"Like you're the one with all the muscles." Angel helped Ida May into the backseat. "Hold on to this bag." She closed the door.

"Sometimes this car is hard to start up if I let it set too long." Winifred lit another cigarette. "You think your little brother can give it a push while I gun the engine?"

Angel climbed into the front passenger seat. "Give it a go, Willie!"

Winifred turned the key and pumped the gas pedal. Willie pushed against the rear bumper but the car didn't move. Angel opened her door and joined him at the rear bumper.

The car made a grinding sound and then an exploding roar. Angel looked up and saw Ida May staring at them from the side of the road. Angel yelled, "Get back in the Ford!"

The car engine turned over and Winifred took off.

"She's leaving us!" Angel saw that Ida May was empty-handed. "Where is the bag, Ida May?"

"In the car. That Miss Mock yelled and made me get out. You didn't hear it? She scared me half to death. I think she's lost her mind." Ida May watched the car disappear around a turn. "I'm glad she's gone."

Angel and Willie stared at one another.

"The money, Ida May! I knew something was strange about her the minute I laid eyes on her. Whoever heard of a poker playing schoolteacher? We're busted, don't you see?"

The hardness of Ida May's eyes dissolved and she cried.

"Angel, you got to stop yelling," said Willie.

"She even took our food. We don't have a blessed thing, not nary a thing to our name! And here we are stuck in the middle of nowhere." Angel started walking like she might just leave Ida May on the side of the road. She put on an I-don't-care face but watched from the corner of her eye to make sure the little chicks followed. The day was still new enough. She'd have to study about how they might survive through another ruinous day.

The outskirts of Nazareth sunned in the foothills of the Ouachita Mountains just a leap and a skip before Hope and Texarkana.

The road strung out like a dusty snake of clay and rock. Angel led them across a field and down a little road that paralleled the main road. Not too far down the road she found relief in knowing that other youngens had been put out. Three boys stamped along hurling rocks and fighting. She watched them knock on a door and beg for food. Knowing that about the road colored her ideas about Daddy.

"When folks are hungry, the first thing to go is the family dog," she complained to Willie. She did not mean to infer that they ate the dog, but Willie got a picture of just that in his head and told her so.

"That's what cannibals do, Willard. Don't be a goof!"

Willie said, "I don't want you to ever call me that again, Angel Minerva Welby. You know I hate it."

Angel smiled at him, owning everything that was said. "Here's the way it lays, Willie Boy—you can just stop feeding the dog and then he takes off to go and fend for himself. But the second thing to go is the ones who don't rake in the dough. I got this little deal all figured out. If you have too many mouths to feed, you send out your oldest. With John and Darrell dead, and Claudia married off, I was the next best choice to be put out. It's common sense. The way things go. Daddy did best he could by us."

"But me and Ida May saw how you cried and shoved your raggedy underthings into a paper bag. Daddy did wrong by us."

"I didn't cry."

Willie cocked his head to the side but he didn't argue.

Angel remembered that black crease around Daddy's eyes that coal miners acquire down in those caves of death. He had worked the mines down in Paris, Arkansas, until he had saved enough to get them back to Snow Hill where his momma lived. Even after he had taken the sharecropper job in Snow Hill, the black hadn't faded, and for Angel Daddy was forever fixed in her mind as a raccoon, a comic-strip animal with a headlight on his hat.

The sharecropper's shack was a lesser place even than the old crumbling miners' row house in Paris. Once they had settled in Snow Hill, Momma had lost all of her yearning to fix things up. Daddy didn't seem to notice a thing about her—not the way she stared out the window or left supper dishes dirty in the tub until sunup. As far as Thorne Welby was concerned, while Lemuel had stuck more magazine pages to the wall to cover the cracks in the pine, he'd hauled off and turned his back to the cracks in their everyday lives.

Lemuel Welby had stared at Thorne's picture the morning he had packed them all off with Lana. He had said no farewells, only how he wished that Momma had stayed to take on her share of the load. Angel had tried to keep everyone's mind off of Daddy and prattled about movie stars and life in California the morning they all gathered up their four belongings. But she saw the way he leaned against the doorpost with his face toward Little Rock. That was her last memory of Daddy.

Dew, their uncle, had wrapped cornbread wedges in newspapers, one for each of them, and one each for him and Daddy for their lunch that day. Dew had a stingy way of hoarding his money in a woolen sock he shoved into his pocket, even while he slept.

"That Dew, he would not part with a dime," she told Willie, "but he surprised me big time when he handed me two dollars' worth of change." Dew had gripped it in his field-blackened hand above her own hand and then finally released it as though it would be the end of his worries about them. But Dew's guilt had settled along the misty rims of his eyes, pink circles carved out of a dusty, cotton-picker's face. Like Lemuel, Dew had lost all of his childhood brilliance down in the throat of the mines, where little children laid aside notions of playthings and make-believe. The cotton fields had taken whatever was left.

Angel kept Claudia's last letter in a cotton drawstring bag on a string around her neck—the letter that told all of them she and her husband had settled in Nazareth with baby number two on the way. She said, "By now Claudia's baby must be, what, walking around, getting into trouble? That makes me Aunt Angel." She liked the sound of it.

Ida May did not answer.

Willie watched the drifter boys steal a chicken and disappear into a forest beyond a herd of skinny cattle. A distant train whistle spoke of too many young fellers that now lived, breathed, and traveled the rails.

Angel promised Willie and Ida May that it was a matter of an hour until they reached Claudia's house. But it only proved to be another of her inventions.

The rolling sky dumped rain onto their heads while great strains of thunder pounded from south to north. The sky let out its robes and dropped its liquid children to the earth, hard enough to pound the hollows and the creeks but not enough to lift the drought from the dry lips of the farmland.

Angel ran, yelling at her siblings to keep up. The long hot day had lasted longer than most other days, in her estimation. It would end with this drenching rainfall and cover the rest of the day like night. While she might otherwise have welcomed the wet respite from the summer heat if she had been in the cab of her uncle's truck, a muddy trek through a snaky field left her closer to tears than she dared to admit. Ida May was already full-blown bawling like a calf. If she herself lost it, they'd all end up sitting down and crying their heads off.

"I see a shack ahead. Let's see if it's unlocked." Angel slowed to allow Ida May to catch up. But Willie kept running until he disappeared entirely into the old one-room hovel.

"We got us a house," said Ida May. "I like it."

"It's not our house and it's not a house anyway." Angel

pushed back the tattered curtain from a window to let in what little light remained. "It's a shed or some such. But we can stay here and listen for the next ride. Then we'll hitch it all the way to Nazareth." She said it like a veteran of the highway.

The rain fell and Angel lost track of the time until night ascended. All three of them peered over the windowsill as a black automobile motored up over the hill with headlights penetrating the curtain of rain. She was about to shout, when Willie gripped her arm.

"Angel, the last person we hitched a ride with took everything we owned."

Angel watched the hulking vehicle slow, split a muddy hole in the road, and then pass.

"We can't stay here. What will we eat, Willie? If we can just make it to Claudia's before morning, it's bacon and fixings when we get up."

Ida May, for the third time, described her hunger in pictures like she was a little rabbit soon to be killed and forgotten along the roadway.

It wasn't long until Angel saw another set of headlights. "You two stay inside. I'll flag this next one down. If things look bad, I'll run off and hide in the woods. But don't come after me if that happens. Just wait and I'll be back."

"Angel Welby, you're just a big nut for doing it!" said Willie.

"I'm goin' with you." Ida May watched out the window next to Angel, but pinched Angel's sleeve as though she would not let go.

"Ida May, you stay here with Willie." Angel lifted the curtain rod and pulled the curtain off to take for a head covering in the rain. She left them behind to gripe to one another.

Lightning flashed and outlined the approaching truck. The cab had a smallish appearance. The lights drew closer to the shack, but Angel stepped behind a cluster of bushes. Willie's worry had unnerved her. But before the truck reached her, it slowed, careened onto an open field, and stopped. She watched the driver inside the cab. He appeared to dig through some items. Then he pulled out a blanket and laid down, apparently to sleep for the night. The truck bed was loaded with supplies and covered with a tarp.

Angel burst back into the shack. "Come with me! While this driver catches some shut-eye, we'll climb under his tarp and sleep. He's got grub, everything we need, I'll bet you a dollar!"

"He'll see us anyway. Why don't we just ask him for a ride and see how he takes to it?" asked Willie.

"If he turns us down it might be the last chance we get all night. We been here all day and seen only two automobiles. You coming or staying?"

Ida May headed for the door.

"I'll come. But if this feller cuts our throats while we sleep, you'll be the blame for it, Angel." Willie opened the door.

Angel led them down a shadowy path, through brush and trees until they were within a few yards of the truck. The driver had already fallen asleep. She lifted a corner of the tarp and helped Ida May hide beneath it.

"Apples. Oh, my! Apples!" said Ida May.

Angel peered over the crate of apples, the flour and sugar from the store in Camden, and the bed of the Ford truck. It had the same smell as her daddy's dirty wash on laundry day. Rain pelted the tarp, but it was dry underneath. She smiled. "You'll never believe this," she said. "We found Sweet Eyes. He'll be one surprised gentleman come morning."

2

The storm outside Camden steadied to a vertical shower, a soothing beating against the truck windshield, a hundred fingers drumming on the truck top. Jeb stretched out on the truck seat. He shifted to his right side, still bruised from Hank's lucky left jab, and turned his back to the night. The left side of his jaw was raw, but not from a lucky punch. Charlie had cut his hair away from his face and shaved him clean as a girl.

The storm quieted like a grandma's hum. The truck lurched beneath him. It felt like the wind had blown against the tarp and caused the supplies in the truck bed to tremble. Jeb pushed back the brim of his hat and lifted his eyes to the window. But the sodden field encircled him, empty of life. Not even the mottled patches of Depression-starved cows remained. All creatures safe in the distant barns, all hearts asleep in bed. Only a wanderer dared sleep in the rain. He dozed off.

The rain had taken Jeb's appetite from him. He slid upright, stiff from a night on the truck seat, and started the engine. He'd traveled five miles when he heard the cry of a child. It was a youngen's cry, he knew. It reminded him of his little sister back in

Temple, Texas, when, at the age of four, she'd fought her weaning. The subtle wail he heard through the open window grew louder and quivered, like a youngster chased by terror. He slowed the truck, although he had no interest in family entanglements. But children fell into wells or down old mining shafts, he told himself. *I'd be a sorry sort to ignore it.* Jeb slowed some more.

Black-eyed Susans smelled bitter along the dirt road, sloppy-wet with long green necks bent sideways from the all-night deluge of rain. A mongrel puttered past his door, glanced up at him, and then loped ahead at the sound of a boy's whistle on the wing of morning. The tires lumbered slowly over a slick road pimpled by stones. Jeb heard mockingbird and finch and the remote mutter of thunder as the storm moved away from western Arkansas. *But no cries. Musta' imagined it.* The storm had soaked every stick of kindling so the idea of cooking so much as a piece or two of bacon was out.

The truck shimmied. A thudding sound, louder than a spilled crate of apples, banged from under the truck bed tarp.

"Some animal has got into my grub," Jeb said. The earliest peep of sunlight made his eyes feel like two burned out headlights. He pulled to the side of the road. Behind the seat, Charlie had tucked a rifle. But at close range Big Brother's rabbit blaster would shatter a raccoon to ashes. He slid it out anyway. Untying a corner of the tarp, he lifted the edge with the butt of the gun with the same caution with which he might look into a snake hole.

Three pairs of eyes stared back at him with that trapped fox of a look. The youngest child, a girl about six, small like an understuffed rag doll, had smudges around her red eyes like little boys who play soldier. She jerked away from an older girl who bore a clear look of familiar about her.

"What's this? Kids? Get out of there!"

The boy in the group yelled, "Run, he's got a gun!" while the oldest girl continued biting into one of Jeb's apples.

"You hear what I say?" he said to the oldest.

The boy and the youngest girl scrambled over the back and ran down the road, slowing only when they realized the leader of their brood had lagged behind.

She shrugged. "You won't shoot."

The folly of a stand-off with an eighty-pound refugee caused Jeb to lift his rifle parallel to the ground and polish the butt with one hand. "Don't think I won't."

"You won't. I saw you back in Camden. You ain't the shooting type."

"Oh, that's where I saw you. Don't tell me you kids rode in the back all the way from Camden." Then he remembered stopping along the way for a dinner of beans and bread out of the truck bed.

"Angel, you lost your mind? Let's go!" the boy called to her.

"Angel. Ain't that a misleading notion?" Jeb said.

"Shut up, Willie! Don't you be giving away my name." Angel had a hoarse cough. So much of her hair was caked in road silt that the color had lost all sense of description.

"Angel, Willie. And who is the little one?" asked Jeb.

"Ida May. She's my sister. We need a ride only as far as Nazareth." Angel pushed herself up, her knees two dirty knobs, and hurled the apple core into the field.

"You been eatin' my grub. Them eats was supposed to last me for a good week or two. You heard of the Depression, I reckon. You think I got money to burn?"

"That woman you hooked us up with, she weren't no teacher. She was a con and she stole every penny we had on us."

"That nice teacher lady? I don't believe it." But he wouldn't take the blame for hooking them up.

"How else you think we ended up dumped on the side of the road?"

"That was the way of things. Had nothing to do with me. Now you eat up my stash and got the nerve to ask fer more. Back where I come from, we call people like you a mooch. You just climb out the way you climbed in and go beg at one of these farmhouses. Some farmer's wife, she's your best bet for help. I got places to go. No time for varmints."

"Where you come from?" Angel leaned over the back of the truck and helped Ida May back in as though she had no intention of leaving.

"Don't you hear anything I say?"

"You got a name, don't you?"

"Fine. I'll just haul your rear ends out myself. You, girl. Get your hands out of that sack of bread loaves!" He yelled at Ida May. She wailed.

Jeb hated the sound of her cry—a wounded girl sound, like a young one too long away from her mother.

"He didn't look mean at first. Maybe I was wrong about him." Angel lifted the hem of her dress and wiped her sister's eyes with no care for showing the hem of her drawers.

The boy stood at a safe distance, skipping stones, pacing.

"I never seen a man with so much trouble in his face. You in trouble?" Angel seemed to notice her dirty cuticles all of a sudden.

"I said get out of my truck. I've lost all patience with you, girl!" Jeb ran to the rear of the truck bed.

Angel clambered over the crates but Ida May wasn't fast enough. Jeb grabbed her by the collar.

Willie swore and leaped onto Jeb's right arm. "Let her go, 'fore I get mad!"

Jeb shook the boy loose and dumped him onto the muddy road.

"You's mean, that's what!" said Angel. "Like I figgered."

Jeb lifted the smallest girl from the truck bed. Before he could climb in after the oldest child, he saw a vehicle approaching. On the side of the vehicle were words he could not make out, but it looked to be the law. An idea came to him. "You two get in the cab and don't say a word."

"Don't, Willie! It's a trick!" Angel shaded her eyes and saw the copper's car, too.

"Go now or I'll leave you all on the side of the road. You said you wanted a lift. You takin' it or not?" He lifted Ida May over one shoulder and ran with her to the passenger side of the cab. While he tossed her inside, the boy griped at him for touching his sister. "Willie, if ever somebody offers you a handout, it's best you take it. Might be a long time before you get sech a thing again."

Willie stepped back and watched for his sister's response.

"Go on and get inside, I guess," said Angel. She climbed out and joined her brother and sister.

Jeb tied down the tarp again and jumped inside just as the law pulled up beside him.

"Everything all right?" The officer looked to be a deputy or some such, a portly man who stuffed ham biscuits into his mouth like everybody had plenty. He spoke with a jewel of Mayhaw jelly on the corner of his mouth. "You look like you got trouble, mister."

Angel would not cut eyes at the deputy as though she and Jeb had thought out the details of their story.

"I had a little problem with my supplies. I got it all back in place." Jeb kept his eyes straight ahead on the road.

"Purty kids," said the cop, like he didn't notice the grime around their eyes. "They yourn?"

"Mine? Why, yes. Sure, officer. They mine."

Ida May whispered, "Liar, liar."

"You passing through, I guess." The officer pulled out an etching of a bearded man, a wanted poster.

"Me and the kids on the way to visit my sister-in-law in Hope."

"Good melons in Hope. You just in time for the watermelon parade. Hope peaches is as good as they watermelons. They put on a big to-do, old timey picnics and sech."

"Thank you, Deputy. We'll take in the festivities while visiting the family."

"Just watch yourselves. They's a killer on the loose up from Texarkana. Least way, they's a man about to die after taking a beating from a cotton picker hired by his daddy. This man kicks the bucket, this Jeb Nubey feller, he'll be a murderer. You seen him?" The deputy held up the poster.

Jeb heard a ragged sigh next to him, but he didn't turn to see who made the sound. "Don't believe I've ever seen him. Why they think he's headed for Arkansas?"

"They got us looking from Dallas to Little Rock. We'll catch him. He's an itinerant worker. Vagrant. Hobo. You know the type. They pretty stupid."

Jeb held his words. With a turn of the key, the truck engine turned over. "I'll keep my eyes peeled. Kids, you help me look out for this feller," he said. He turned back to the deputy. "We could use the reward."

The cop watched him go.

As the truck made a turn, Jeb saw the smoke lift from the deputy's tailpipe before he disappeared from sight.

"You was that man in the picture, wasn't you?" Angel elbowed her brother to make room in the cramped cab.

"I'll have you know I'm a farmer. I drive into Camden for supplies and to get into town from time to time. Didn't know it was a crime."

"I guess you killed one man, you might kill all-a us."

"You going to kill us?" asked Ida May.

Jeb didn't answer.

"I knowed a killer once. A for real John Dillinger type," said Willie. "He was dangerous but I didn't keer."

"I know the one you mean, Willie. That man who lived in the shack not two miles from our place in Snow Hill. He hid out acting like he was one of us, but Daddy said he was shiftless. He just disappeared one night. We saw the law all over his place at sunup but no murderer in sight. I think I hear him some nights when I'm about between sleep and dreaming. It feels like prickles on my skin when that happens."

Jeb said, "Sounds like you're tellin' stories."

"He was evil and you could smell the devil when he came around. Daddy said to keep away from him." Willie sat up and watched the road ahead, like any boy seeking a diversion from a mind-numbing country ride.

"How you know what the devil smells like, Willie boy? You been sneaking around playing cards while your momma's not looking?" Jeb wondered where he might drop them off. But the oldest girl had a mouth that shot itself off too much. He'd have to find something to appease her, to make her want to keep a secret.

"The devil smells like coal dust mixed with blood," said Willie.

"I don't like this talk, Willie. You always tryin' to scare me," said Ida May.

"He smelled like you, Jeb Nubey," said Angel.

Jeb softened his eyes and allowed his lips to part. "I'm not him and you need to get it out of your head. How you feel if they string me up, a farmer, all on account of your mouth, girl?"

"Why else would you give us a ride—you the feller who

wanted to leave us on the side of the road?" Angel's voice lifted, convincing. Wise. A voice that anyone would want to listen to if she decided to squeal.

"I felt sorry for you. You're orphans, ain't you? Probably run off from some home. They beat you or something?"

"Jeb Nubey. What kind of name is that, anyway? Like some hick from Texarkana." Angel bluffed well.

"I figure you got somebody looking for you, like a orphan home. Maybe that deputy will show up with a poster of your face and say they need their three sweet potatoes back for the government money they missing out on."

"I ain't no orphan and I ain't nobody's sweet potater, neither. Me and these two, we was supposed to be at our sister's place by now. But that stupid Lana ran off and left us on our own. If Daddy hears of it, he'll come for us. But how he going to know if we don't make it to Claudia's and get him a letter?" Angel's bluntness made her look less pretty. "You get us to Claudia's and we'll just keep mum about you being Jeb Nubey." A bit of light came into her eyes and she added, "That and a little shuttin-up money."

"You can sing till the cock crows, little stray, but ain't no one going to believe you! If I drop you off at your sister's, it's 'cause I can't wait to have my peace and quiet back. Here I was feeling sorry for you. Now I just want you to be a memory."

Angel let out a girlish sigh, vulnerable. "A little cash, then, and it's a deal."

Jeb agreed with silence. She left him in peace until the noon hour when a road sign ahead read "5 Miles to Nazareth." Angel yelled it when she saw the sign. He had not believed up until then that such a place existed.

"Oh, Claudia, we're almost home! Sweet pudding and fried potaters. She's really the best cook in the family," said Angel.

Jeb realized this Claudia wasn't a drummed-up invention of the girl's colorful imagination. "Sweet pudding. Maybe I'll just hang around for a bit and see if she feeds me, too. She got a man?"

"Claudia got a good guy from Fort Smith. Not like you. They got a baby now, or maybe two. And number one, she would never look at you, anyway, what with you being a murderer. Number two, you being from Texarkana."

"What's wrong with Texarkana?"

"It's like living nowhere. You don't know if you're waking up in Arkansas or Texas, only cause you're surrounded by so many states you don't know where you live—Arkansas, Texas, Louisiana, Oklahoma." She counted them off. "Your whole life you're confused about things, like whose side are you on in a fight or how do you tell people where you live. People who can't make up their mind about things, well, they just live in Texarkana."

"You don't know nothing at all," said Jeb.

"You quit denying you're from Texarkana. 'Sides all that, you sound like one of them Texans. How come you're so easy to catch in a lie? Not like a real crook, are you?"

Jeb ignored her.

Honeysuckle bloomed along the fence lines all the way down the next three-mile stretch of road. It perfumed the air. Jeb remembered Myrna, how she wound honeysuckle vines through her hair and danced in her white dress, her shoes kicked off under the moon. The girl sitting next to her smelled like mud and soured apples.

"I want a ham biscuit," said Ida May.

"This Lana, how come your momma let you go off with her, anyway?" Jeb threw in a new question before the girls got off on a long list of things they wanted.

"Our momma wasn't about or she never would have allowed it. Daddy, he never had good judgment about women like Lana. Not that it was his fault. Granny, his momma, once told me that men was just growed-up boys. Granny lived with us 'til she died. She lost her place on account of her oldest girl and husband left her with nothing. I told Daddy not to put us in Lana's care, but would he listen to me? Like he ever listens to what I have to say." Another fissure opened in Angel's clapboard exterior. She sounded like a woman again, and sovereign. A girl that might stay home a year longer than others just to help out her family.

"So where's your momma?"

"Little Rock. Making money," said Willie.

Angel gave him a look.

"Your family's been split up by this Depression. Sad, but it's happening all over." Jeb saw a shimmer in Angel's eyes, but did not try and read it.

"If you ain't Jeb Nubey, how come you won't tell me your real name?" Angel paddled past Jeb's queries, the dogged rower that did not know she lagged behind.

But her question sparked a bit of hope. He picked a name that was not too far from his own, so he would not slip up and forget. "Fred Judson. I live in Hope."

"That's why you know so much about Hope, then, I guess," said Willie.

Jeb held back his elation. "That's right, Willie boy. You all ought to drop by the farm sometime and bring your sister and her youngens." Courage overtook his pack of lies.

"How come you let that cop tell you all about Hope, then, like you knowed nothing at all?" said Angel. "I'll bet you don't live there nor know a thing about it so it wouldn't do no good to look you up. Besides, after we get settled in with Claudia, we won't have no time for visiting. She knows everyone in Nazareth, I'll bet. We'll go to school and be very busy with our lives, I'm sure. Like normal folks."

"So you never visited her before?" Jeb saw another sign just as Willie yelled, "Nazareth—one mile away."

"This is our first time to Nazareth. It's our first time anywhere, besides Snow Hill and Paris," said Angel.

"Paris. France?" said Jeb. "I know that's a lie."

"Paris, Arkansas, further up than here. See? You don't even know about any place in Arkansas," she said.

"I got sick goin' through those mountains when we moved away from Paris," said Willie to Angel.

"But you know she's expecting you." Jeb pressed for an answer.

"'Course she's expecting us. I wrote her myself just before Lana hauled us off to Camden."

Jeb dismissed from his thoughts the way she looked so all-of-a-sudden troubled. "Look ahead. Nazareth on the border. I'll stop at this house and get directions to your sister's place. You got a letter, you say, with her address?"

Angel pulled the letter out of her pocket. "See, right here where it says 'Bo and Claudia Drake'?" She lives on Boll Avenue. The ink's kind of runny, but that's what it says. I remember Momma saying she lives on cotton boll once, just to be funny. Bo got hisself a good job working for the railroad."

Jeb read the year when it was mailed. Numbers he could figure out. "This letter's three years old." He opened the truck door.

"Has it been three years? I been saying two so long, I guess time has slipped past," said Angel.

He handed her back the letter and stepped out of the truck. When he stepped up onto the porch, he felt as though he should not allow all of his weight to rest on the steps. The clapboard structure had a sagging porch that gave the house a gray smile. Geraniums grew out of old, rusted lard cans stuck in the ground all the way down the length of the porch. But the blooms lay all around the pots as though stripped naked. He knocked on the screen door and the wood splintered soft around his knuckles. The smell of wet dogs and soured babies' things wafted from the one-room house. A woman, her face gaunt and drawn, stopped a foot from the door, shocked to see a visitor. Around her feet, twin baby boys who looked as though they had sucked all of the nourishment from her thin body banged on the floor with spoons. Their momma stepped over them as though to do so drained her of her last ounce of strength.

"Sorry to bother you, ma'am," said Jeb.

She didn't answer.

"We're looking for the family of these kids I got out in my truck. You know of a family by the name of Bo and Claudia Drake? They live in Nazareth. Got some little ones about your boys' age, I guess," he said like he knew the couple. He wondered if his smile looked truthful to her.

"Why, I lived h'yere, goin' on three yers." When she spoke, she showed that her shapeless face was fashioned from a tooth-less mouth. "I never heard of no Drakes. You say they live in Nazareth? Where 'bouts?"

"Boll Avenue."

"Now I heerd of Boll Avenue. We don't get out much, me an' 'ese two. Maybe I just missed meetin' up with the Drakes. Want me to tell you how to get over to Boll? It ain't fur."

"If you don't mind," said Jeb.

She took the letter with Claudia's address and made a primitive map on the back. "Does this make sense? I'm not a good explainer of things, my husband says."

"You're doing fine, ma'am."

One of the twins erupted in a fit of rage. His brother had grabbed both spoons.

The mother ignored them and was quite good at it. Jeb realized he was her amusement for the day. "I guess we'll be on our way, then."

"Won't you come in for coffee? We just bought new." The young mother smiled and it aged her.

"We best not stay, ma'am. These kids are anxious to see their family," said Jeb.

"I can tell you're a kind man. Lookin' out after three young-gens. My husband, he don't have nothin' to do with kids. Figgers it's my place to run after these two." She patted her abdomen. "And this other one that's on the way. Shore hope it's a girl baby 'is time. Boys eat too much."

Jeb excused himself.

Angel, by now, had his door opened and was sitting up on her knees with her hand bracing the steering wheel. "Did she know anything?"

"We're not far. Boll Avenue's a real place. But she said she never heard of the Drakes." Jeb studied the woman's scrawled, quivering pencil marks, his strained sight traipsing out on the tedious hard-to-read lines.

"Woman like her most likely doesn't know nobody." As they pulled away, Angel watched the woman and drew up her mouth, a sort of piteous pout.

Jeb wondered over the thought of a soul trapped in a country way of life. No other existence. He wondered if, when the woman saw the moon through the pecan trees, she thought it was a distant place or just a decoration for her prison.

He noticed Angel fidgeting and muttering as they followed the roads from one thin dirt lane to the next.

"What that lady said don't mean nothing, Jeb Nubey, you know. Claudia's on the porch waiting for us. I know she is and don't you try and say she's not."

Jeb remained quiet until Angel yelled out the hand-painted sign that read only "Boll." The truck turned onto Boll Avenue. The sun had melted into its own ebbing remains. The sky greened from the last storm, while the wooded land looked bleak, like a quiet place where no one lived.

3

If the youngest had not wailed while she held on to the door-post, Jeb might have thought the whole story about the sister Claudia had been concocted by Angel. She had a fast tongue and he knew she kneaded her words, massaged them to obtain the desired effect.

"If Claudia moved, why didn't she tell us?" Willie talked over Ida May and then shushed her, a bite in his tone. That made her yank away and run out into the yard.

"Not a stick of furniture inside, not nothing to tell us where she's gone to," said Angel. She pressed her hand against the front door, which looked as though it had a whitewash of paint over a turn-of-the century layer of blue. Paint chips feathered to the porch. She went inside.

Jeb watched her go room to room. He pulled out a flask; one Big Brother had won in a crapshoot, and closed his eyes as the Camden-bought whiskey washed over his tongue and down his throat. A truck motored down the same road that ran in front of the old house.

Jeb followed Angel inside. In one corner of the room lay a child's toy—a doll's head tossed against the baseboard, eyelashes missing, staring up open-mouthed with what was once blond strands of hair curled in the only two remaining wisps on its scalp. Jeb wearied of the littlest one's crying out on the porch. An old mattress lay against the wall in one small room.

"You all can sleep here tonight. Won't hurt you."

"You don't mean you're leaving us here?" Angel stepped out of the kitchen where she had picked up a discarded letter and two wooden spoons.

"I mean you got a roof over your head and it beats sleeping in the back of my truck. I don't have no room for kids if you haven't noticed."

"You is a plain mean man, a hateful killer." She moved around him as though he had a plague. "You're dangerous, that's what." She said the last part only so Jeb could hear.

"I can't let you ride no more with me, you kids." He hoped a dollar would appease her. The youngest, Ida May, pressed her face against the window, hiccuping through the smoky glass of the cab. She'd heard him tell Angel they had come to the end of the road and had climbed inside the cab to resist desertion. She closed the door and her head dropped. Her feet appeared in the window. She had taken to calling Jeb "Dud"—ignoring his Fred Judson alias. She'd made up a song about it that sounded like a cereal jingle. She sang it now. She ignored him when he yelled for her to get out.

"I'll pull you out by the feet, then!" Jeb ran through the open door. The whiskey made his face warm.

"Is that what you plan to do, Mr. Nubey, or whatever you call yourself?" asked Willie. "You going to leave us here? This place, it don't have a scrap for my littlest sister. Me and Angel, we get by, like we always do. But you can't mean you'd leave Ida May without food."

Ida May's feet clicked together at the toes to the beat of Dud's jingle.

"I'll leave you food, then. But don't ask me for nothing else.

Willie, you can be the lookout. You wait for a nice family to pass by, then you tell them you been left behind by your kin. That's what has happened here. I'm not to blame for your mess. This sister of yours, she was the one who left you all here. This Claudia, or whatever. I'm the good feller, the one who gave you a lift. That's all you honestly got to say about me. But this is as far as I take you. You think you can be the lookout for these girls, Willie?" He slipped him a buck.

"We all going to be the lookout, Jeb Nubey," said Angel. "Looking out for the law. When we find a law feller, see, we tell them everything we know about you—how you killed a man in Texarkana, used us for a front like you was our daddy, then left us here for bobcat food. Know what else? I'll tell him how you a shaved man now and they looking for the wrong face. That kind of lookout, you mean? The kind they pay a reward for, you know. Fix us up with some big bucks for your ugly head." She tore the dollar bill from Willie's hand and threw it in Jeb's face.

Jeb mulled over how the demon girl had ever locked onto him. It must have been that sympathetic smile he offered her back in Camden. He grasped for one last bluff. "Back behind this house is nothing but woods. I'll tie you up, you and your whining brother and sister, throw you in a hole. You want to see a killer. I'll give you a good taste." He took another drink, closed his eyes, and waited.

Willie flew off the porch and hied over a crackling stalk of last fall's mums. Wet at the mouth, he banged on the truck door. "Ida May, we got to run off. This man, he's wild, like Uncle Jack's ace of spades. Now get your hindend up 'fore I drag it out!"

"Your brother, now he got some sense. How about you, Angel? Am I going to have to throw you all down in those woods?" Jeb had a pocketknife he used for peeling apples. He drew it out and showed it to her.

"Go ahead, then! Cut my throat," she said.

"I will."

"Do it! You can't make me cry."

"Hold still." He wrapped his right hand around the back of her neck.

"No, please, Lord, save my sister! We know she ain't right, but save her anyway!" Willie fell to his knees.

Ida May's feet went down and her head appeared. A piercing soprano scream, like a young rabbit in a snare, split the quiet pastoral woodland.

"Willie got hisself religion, Angel. How about you? You a praying little gal?" He pressed his fingers around the sides of her neck. For a moment, he felt a notion rise, like he could snap her in two.

"You won't do it, I'll bet." Her voice quivered.

Jeb held her neck so hard she grimaced. He lost himself. That was the only thing he could blame on bringing the tip of his pocketknife close to her throat, just like he had took old Hank Hampton down.

"They'll find you. You'll be strung up," Angel said. Her face was softer, more childlike.

Thunder trailed from the southeast, from Texas. A black veil, thin but threatening, curtained the eastern rim beyond the hills. Jeb smelled rain. The knife tip touched Angel's skin. Her bottom lip tucked under the top lip like an envelope.

"I'll take you into town; let you ask around about your sister. If you find another way to get to her or if you don't, I don't care. You're not my charges. Ain't my responsibility. You think I know how to care for you kids? I don't, so don't be looking at me with those big sad ones of yours. I'm not the one to get you where you need to be."

"We're not riding with you no more!" Willie charged up

onto the porch and into the house. "Let's go, Angel! He's a crazy, done got let loose from the looney house."

Angel rubbed the pink markings around her throat. "I knew you couldn't do it. Let's take some of that stuff from out of the back. We can fix us a bite to eat then go into town. Don't look at me like that, Willie. I know what I'm doing. Bring Ida May inside. We're having us a dinner."

Jeb watched Angel lead the other two around, a miniature of her momma, most likely, parroting older women in the kitchen.

She found a bin that shook with a few matches. She asked Willie to heft Jeb's big iron skillet onto the top burner while she diced up potatoes. Once the potatoes sizzled nicely in a dollop of lard, the girl stirred up a pan of bread and got it ready to cook inside the oven. She took several trips to the truck and back before she addressed him again. "We need milk for the little one."

"You see a cow around here? I'll go see if your sister's old man dug her a well. Water's just as good." He wanted her to disappear from his life, but the potatoes smelled enticing. He figured she was good for at least one meal. He glanced over at Willie, staring hard at him from the corner.

"I guess water will have to do. Maybe in town we'll find someone with milk for Ida May. She has weak bones, and my momma always fussed after her with milk."

"You keep coddling her like that and she'll never grow up," said Jeb. "I don't know much about kids, but I know you treat a kid like a baby and they'll grow up to be a whining complainer of a person—no good to anybody."

"You right, Jeb Nubey. You don't know nothing about kids. My sister nearly died when she was born. That's why she's so small. Doc said she needed to be kept on lots of milk and meat every few days or so. I know those things about her. I don't need no advice taking care of my sister."

"That's what you tell yourself, 'cause you just a kid. Makes you feel bigger than yourself to think you can take care of Ida May. But truth is you don't know nothing more than me on raising that kid. If I hadn't of come along, what would you have done then? I can answer that for you. You would have starved like everybody else in Arkansas."

The kitchen was all grease and dust, a mash that smelled of old biscuit batter and milk gone bad. Jeb lit the fire inside the oil stove that had just enough kerosene for one night's worth of cooking. Angel slid the pan of cornmeal batter into the warming oven. "Don't know how this'll taste without milk," she said.

The sun had stopped shining through the glass. The storm from the east obstructed the glow of evening that settled on the outskirts of Nazareth. Night came early.

"Let's put this grub out and get to business. I don't plan on staying here all night. I'll be gone before tomorrow." Jeb opened the door to the rear porch to allow some of the smoke hissing from the overhead stovepipe to escape.

"You only got two plates," said Angel.

"One for me. One for all of you. I never said I was set up for company." Jeb watched her pile extra potatoes onto the plate. Finally the bread browned. He used an old shirt to pull the cornbread from the oven. The hot iron branded his hand through the shirt.

Angel seated herself, Willie, and Ida May near the door where the air was fresher. She had a nervous shake, a way that she tossed her head to make her too-long bangs part around her eyes. Often throughout the meal, she passed the plate back and forth between Willie and Ida May, tossing her head between the feedings. Her fingers, like everything about her, were long and brown. She might have been taught the way of grace had her mother stayed longer. Whenever she lifted her spoon to her lips, she did not eat with the same ravenous air as her siblings. Instead, she paused, a fraction of a pause that gave her the chance to study what she was about to ingest. Then she lifted the spoon as though she lifted a butterfly poised on her black little fingertips and tentatively deposited the food into her mouth. After that, she chewed as though every morsel gave her something to think about.

"I need to know what you think your plans might be if you can't find hide nor hair of this sister, Claudia. If you got it in your head I'm the passage back to your daddy or wherever you plan to go, you got some refiguring to do." The potatoes tasted fair to Jeb, something like what the cook fixed back at the cotton plantation, only without onion.

"Why you care what we do next?" Angel showed Ida May how to use the corner of her sleeve to wipe her mouth.

A wind blew in through the screens and across the porch, a cool breeze that smelled as though it had traveled from Alaska.

"We going to have us a storm again all right," said Willie.

"Even if it rains, we're going into Nazareth." Jeb wanted no more nonsense out of the Welbys. They were trouble enough in good weather, let alone the dead weight they would be in the bad.

"Good folks won't be out. We won't find a soul out in bad weather." Angel told Ida May to finish the last spoonful of potatoes. She nudged the bread in her sister's direction, too.

"Grab your gear. We're leaving now," said Jeb. "Don't dally. And you, Biggest, don't give me none of your looks. You must not have been slapped enough by your daddy or else you'd be respectful like girls is supposed to be."

"We're still eating," said Angel. "Ida May, you go on and finish your supper."

Jeb blew out a sigh. "Girl, don't you hear a thing I say? We're leaving now!" When he grabbed her plate, she held onto it. He yanked it. When she let go he could see the spark in her eyes. The greasy plate smacked up against his shirt. "Get your scabby selves out to the truck or I'll kick you all the way out there myself."

Angel marched. Her arms swung back and forth along with the legs that she straightened as though she marched on stilts, flouting his instructions. "How we going to have our food settle now? You carry on like your momma never said nice things to you."

"Mr. Jeb Nubey, I think I ought to say something right about now," said Willie.

"Say it on the way into town then."

"That's the thing, you see. We just lost our ride into town. See them fellers out in your truck? I think they's leaving with all your good belongings." Willie lifted a shiny finger and pointed through the front door.

"What fellers?" Jeb pushed the boy out of the way. A curtain of black sky blew wet wind across the porch. He slid out and leaped onto the overgrown grass and saw the truck lights brighten the rain that he could only feel smacking his face. "You, come back here! Those is my things!"

A big slack-jawed youth not older than his own brother drew his face back into the cab, laughing. "We's just borrying it for a while, bruther!" The thief manning the steering wheel gunned the engine just as Jeb reached the street. He chased them until the rain stung like mosquitoes. On and on he went, until his breath was long gone and his legs turned to rubber. His scalp was soaked. He heard breathless cries running up behind him.

"I see him!" Willie yelled. "Here, standing out in the rain."

"I'll say this for you, Jeb Nubey: you got some legs that can run. We thought we'd never catch you," said Angel. "We better call the police." Ida May finally chewed the potato she had saved in the side of her mouth.

"They took my rifle—my best hunting rifle! My hat. I never go without my hat." Jeb counted off every possession according to importance.

"Who cares about your stupid hat? What about the food? How we going to get into town now? How'd those boys take your truck, anyway? I'll bet you left the keys in it," said Angel.

"Hush it or I'll hush you with my bare hands." The wind hit Jeb smack in the face. "This is a bad one. Feels like the skirts of a Oklahoma sooner." He did not know if the Welby children heard him or not. The rain and wind howled, the ghost of wood and earth aroused by the tempest.

"Let's get back to Claudia's old house. At least inside her place we got a dry floor to sleep on until morning."

"You go back, take these two with you," said Jeb. "I'm going ahead. I'll find those two drunks plowing through the mud down one of these old roads and I'll nab them. Probably from around here, looking for trouble."

"We're going with you," said Angel. "You know how far we run after you? I'll never lead us back by myself."

Jeb wanted them to lose their way. But Ida May set to wailing. He heard his baby sister's cry again. "Foller me through the woods, if you have to. But I won't wait a step for any of you so you better move it like ducks behind they momma. We'll take the higher ground but foller the road alongside it. Maybe the woods will keep back some of the rain."

Rain plummeted to the leafy forest bed, still rotting the leaves from the past autumn. The woods smelled green to Jeb, like the marsh was given its daily drink offering from the sky.

But the thunder and the jagged knives of lightning pounded the winds from the tattered sky. The pines in the forest bent to the flouncing skirts of the storm. A seventy-year-old oak snapped off at the top about fifty feet from where they stood.

Angel shouted for Ida May to keep up.

Jeb slowed down in such a way to allow the vagabond trio to keep up but not in a way to make them think he cared a hill of beans about them. He didn't.

Blackness enveloped the last of the day. He had to rely on the sporadic lightning bolts to illuminate the road. The sodden trunks, black and dripping wet all the way through the backside of the bark, disappeared into the velvet black backdrop of stormy evening. Twice Jeb missed hurling himself straight into a thick trunk. The wind swirled freely and dogged them whenever they hit a clearing. Jeb thought he smelled a tornado. When three large oaks dominoed one against the other, he knew he'd surely seen the tailwinds of a bad one.

Lightning spit across the wall of rain and reflected against glass—two windows staring, blinking. "I don't know what I see. Maybe it's a house. Foller me this way."

As he led them toward nothingness, a bell sounded, tolling in the wind. He knew the sound and said, "It's a church!" The rainy twinkle of skylights illuminated the steeple, a white spire that glowed under the arc of lightning then fell gray again. Jeb ran up the front steps. Two doors hinged on each side and met in the middle, a heavy offering of hand-hewn timber locked on the inside with something as unmovable as a squared timber against iron holdings. "They bolted this door but good. Ain't no use trying to get inside."

"Let's try a window. Anything!" Out front, Angel made Willie bend over and give her a foot up. She pushed against the glass. "It's hard to open, but I swear it ain't locked."

"Out of the way then!" Jeb pushed against the window frame, joggled it back and forth until it slid an inch. He repeated the motion until the window opened. He grabbed the boy. "You're going in first. I'll hand you the littlest and you help her over the windowsill." He pushed Willie through the opening, rump last. He and the boy helped Ida May through the open window.

"Just a foot up, then," said Angel, who stood away from him.

"We're out in a tornado! Get yourself over here." He grabbed her and lifted her through the opening. She was lighter than he assessed and she went through too fast and thudded onto the floor. He ignored the way she screeched and with one arm pulled himself inside.

"You know you won't never find a woman treating them bad like you do!" Angel lifted her skirt and examined the yellowing bruise on her shin. "Not a good woman, not one that wants to do for you and bless your house."

Jeb lit the two lanterns with matches left on the windowsill by some blessed soul. "I don't know what you're jawing about, Biggest. Crawl up off that old dusty floor onto that pew by your brother and Littlest and get some rest. I need some time to myself." His eyes ran past the bruise again. "Did that happen when you came through yonder winder?"

Angel inhaled and blew out an impetuous little huff like a mare he once had that never took to its breaking. Her face turned to one side and she nodded obliquely.

"Look, I'm sorry. You satisfied? I don't think about being all polite and 'scuse, me, ma'am' and 'may I help you here through yon winder' when I'm about to get sucked away by a tornado."

"I never saw no tornado."

"You ever been to Oklahoma?"

Angel shook her head again, still showing the narrowed eyes that said she mistrusted him.

"In Oklahoma you know they's a tornado before it's upon you if you use your God-given horse sense. The whole air around you changes and you can feel something invisible pressing against the insides of your ears. That tells you, 'Hey, fool! Get yourself under the bed or down in the cellar.' I'm telling you I know a tornado. I once had a uncle lived in Oklahoma."

"They probably want you up in Oklahoma and Texas too, for killing somebody." She had lost all of her fight and sat down on the pew.

"What about you, Biggest? You on the run? You a runaway?"

"Stop calling me that."

"It fits. You got the biggest everything—mouth, eyes, big ears." He saw that got to her.

Angel touched both earlobes. "My granny says I got blessed ears. I can hear every little thing. Things that other people miss, I hear."

Jeb thumped the pew wood. "This'll be hard sleeping."

"Granny always talked about God and things being blessed. I didn't mind it. Daddy minded it some. Momma plain old made fun. But Momma is wise, too. They just had differences, my momma and Daddy's momma."

"Your granny a Bible thumper?"

"In a big way, big-time way. She could out-quote the preacher from Snow Hill and he is the biggest Bible thumper I know of."

"I think you should stay with your granny. Sounds like she could teach you a thing or two."

"She died. Last year."

"I'm sorry about it."

"Before she left us, she told me privately that heaven was just another country and that we would all be together again some day. So we visit when I sleep and she sees me when I dream. Granny's not gone."

"Where'd you say your ma is?"

"Little Rock. I think she wants to be a nurse. They make good money. When she gets everything lined out, I'll go back with her. Daddy's got some confusion."

"If your ma up and left, she must have some confusion herself."

"Don't say that! Lana said trash about her and it weren't true."

"Lana is?" He had already forgotten.

"The tramp that was 'posed to take us to Claudia's but left us and run oft. I don't know where. Once she talked about a place called Kennicut. I'm glad she's gone. Now she won't be sniffing around our place trying to steal Daddy's heart. That was all that was wrong with my momma. It was all Lana."

The wind outside the church squealed and whistled like a kettle going off.

"Biggest, you do a lot of blame-laying. I guess nobody ever told you that. Sounds like nobody's been tending to your upbringing. But you got all your family's troubles tied up in all the wrong boxes, every one of them labeled with the wrong name."

"Maybe no one told you nothing, neither. You don't know how to stay out of other folk's business, Jeb Nubey."

Littlest raised up. Her eyelids tucked slightly up from the centers, enough to show her irises fallen into the bottom lids, unable to focus. She fell back asleep. Willie snored in soft purrs that blew the smallest dark tendrils around his little sister's ear, making a sleeper's smile across her face. His stomach made slight fighting noises, like bats in a cave.

Jeb remembered his momma as one who saw good in him when nobody did. "My folks stayed together but I got notions sometimes that my daddy weren't easy to live with. I think when Momma died of a fever, she was just sort of willing herself on to the next place." Jeb removed his boots and set them right under the place he planned to sleep. "Maybe she knows your granny now. I don't know. Never understand things like that, don't pertend to. I do know Daddy never acted like he loved her until five minutes after she passed. Nobody ever put up such a racket as Daddy when Pearl Nubey left him all alone." His daddy had cried out in the yard like crying in front of his boys shamed them.

"Why is it men can't be good to women?" Angel asked. Her face appeared gold in the lantern light. Gold and soft instead of hard and insulting.

"Not all of us are bad. Maybe we just need a good woman."

"I knew you'd say that. I'll bet my daddy would say the same thing. But my momma, she's good. Every night when he came home from the coal mine in Paris, Momma had his supper fixed, waiting on him, everything just right so he'd not gripe and go on about his supper being too this or too that. She'd have it all just perfect for him. Momma read him stories out of the newspaper. He always wanted to know about the ballgames. He'd be real happy when she told him what he wanted to know. I think sometimes she just made up stories about who won and who lost so he'd go to bed happy."

"Maybe it's easier for women to be good."

"Stuff and nonsense! You think I want to be good? I never cared diddley about quoting the Scriptures or going off to tent meeting. I hated when the preacher came to Sunday dinner. Granny made me sit up and act right. If I didn't, she said she'd box my ears. Men don't have it no worse than us. They just never get away from needing their mommas. That's the way I see it."

"If you can't go live with your momma or your daddy, what you going to do?" Jeb asked.

"I just know I won't live off of no man. My sister Claudia wouldn't have it any other way. The only use she imagined for herself was in being married. I'm going to find my own way. Then, once I make my first million—I got Rockefeller whispering things to me about what do I think of this or that—then, if I feel like it, maybe I'll let a man marry me. But if he so much as lifts an eyebrow to me, out the door he goes, right on his sorry old keester."

"Saying you going to be kingpin and doing are two different things entirely."

"If I say it, I do it." She tried to suppress a yawn. "I am the queen pin, the bona fide belle. One day, no one will mess with Angel Welby. No one like my daddy, who tormented my mother, and no one like you." And then she said to herself, "Especially that."

This biggest girl had lived too long with her dreams, Jeb realized. No one to tell her right from wrong. No one around to shake the folly from between her ears. "How you going to work out your living just tomorrow then?"

"I'll figure it out. I'll rest on it and then when I get up, I'll know. I always know come sun-up."

"Well, I'll look forward to sun-up then. You take the pew behind your brother and sister. I'll sleep here in the back of the church."

Jeb watched out the window until he heard Biggest's steady

breathing. The rain battered every windowpane on the east side of the church. Leaves torn from the limb slapped against the glass and stuck. He watched dolefully through the drenching showers, hoping a truck would drive by loaded down with supplies from Camden. But no one drove down the roads of Nazareth on such a night—night of gloom, of empty pockets and growling bellies.

"Could you sleep behind us, Jeb?"

He did not try to hide his surprise. So she wasn't asleep. "I thought you wanted no help from a man."

"Not for me, silly. If Ida May wakes up, it will make her feel safe."

Jeb believed her like he believed she would wake up with all her answers. He stretched out one pew behind Angel. He turned his face several ways until the wood seemed to soften and allow him to close out the thundering drifts of rain and a single tolling church bell.

4

The pin light of sun streamed across the sawdust floor and straight into Jeb's eyes. Jeb never slept past dawn so the sunlight startled him first. The smiling faces peering all around him startled him next.

"You slept past your morning prayers, Reverend." The woman who spoke to him had a yellow pallor. Her dried-apple face and small, brown, seed eyes peered at him from a bonnet like his grandmother had worn years past.

"Wake up, Daddy. These folks has brought us food." Angel stood at the end of the pew where Jeb slept. She winked and that caused him to bolt upright.

Willie smiled so wide, Jeb noticed for the first time he had a front tooth missing. "That's right . . . *Daddy.*" He giggled and Ida May giggled next to him.

Jeb counted seven faces besides the Welbys smiling back at him. Each person held a basket of goods wrapped in cloths or newspaper.

A man wearing overalls with a stain of tobacco in the right corner of his mouth said, "We got all your letters and read every single one to the congregation on Sundays. We all been praying you could get free from your itinerating so you could join us. Nazareth is growing fast and we been needing a man in our pulpit that can stay with us."

"Your children are just as precious as you said they was, Reverend Gracie. What is it the little girl calls you—Dud?"

"It's her way of saying 'Daddy.'" Angel inserted herself into the conversation.

Jeb smelled fried chicken and started salivating. "Someone got something to eat? Two thieves run oft with my truck and everything I owned was in it."

"I told them we had everything stole, Daddy. This nice man here, Mr. Honeysack, he said they'll all fix us up with a place to stay here in the, what you call it?"

Mr. Honeysack filled in for Angel, "The parsonage, child. We built it with a room for you, Reverend, and a nice place with three little beds for your youngens."

"Fairly good-sized kitchen, too," said the apple-faced woman. "I'm Evelene Whittington. This is my husband, Floyd. He runs the Woolworth's downtown." Floyd had a bashful smile that made the center of his bottom lip jut out. He shook Jeb's hand while Evelene continued to make introductions. "Mr. Will Honeysack and his wife, Freda, run the dry goods store in Nazareth. She's down there now or she would have been here to meet you. Freda's the best baker in our town." Evelene stood with her hands clasped in front of her. "Here's her pie." She looked at Mr. Honeysack.

"Oh, yes, here's my wife's pie. Also, we filled up two bags of groceries for you and the children. But we got so many women around town that are concerned about your little ones. They know how we men don't cook." He winked at Jeb. "I doubt you'll ever have to cook again." Honeysack nodded at the others.

Everyone laughed and Jeb struggled to translate Angel's signals.

"I believe we've stunned the minister," said Evelene. "I'll bet you didn't expect such a welcome."

Angel spoke up. "No, ma'am. We normally don't get such help from the church. Mostly we just do for the Lord and then we just have to do for ourselves." She turned her back to Jeb.

"Can we eat? We had all our food stole yesterday and missed our supper," said Willie.

"My sister is weak and she has to keep her bones strong," said Angel. "She was a sickly baby."

"Let's take you all out to the parsonage, then." A woman whose hair was thick as steel wool drew Ida May close. "I'm Mellie. Your daddy never did tell us all your names. What is your name, baby girl?"

"Ida May. My momma's gone. This is Dud."

Mellie had a high, tinkering laugh that caused her elbows to squeeze into her ribcage. "I know, poor thing. I'll be your momma, your grandmomma, your auntie, or whatever else you need." She walked outside with Ida May, all the while calling her "Idy May."

Mr. Honeysack walked with the grinning Willie outside and the rest of the congregation followed them. "Church in the Dell was built in Millwood Holler back twenty year ago when the land was bought from the Millwoods—"

"Angel," Jeb yanked on her sleeve.

She waved at Evelene. "We better go, Daddy. They're going to show us the parsonage." Angel widened her eyes and stretched her mouth to form a frown that made her look frozen.

"We'll be right there," said Jeb. He waited until the one called Evelene ambled twenty paces away from them and then walked down the back steps outside with a skipping kind of walk, like an old woman spring-dosed.

Angel blurted, "I told you I'd have everything solved, Jeb
Nubey. You just keep quiet and keep your head about you and
we'll have us a meal ticket for a day or two until we figure what
we should do next."

"They think I'm a preacher! You don't see nothing wrong
with that?"

"I watched the preacher back at Snow Hill. They talk seldom and when they do, they just say things like 'Bless you,
child. God love you and keep you.' Stuff like that."

"They called me Reverend Gracie. What if this man they
been waiting on shows up today? Here I don't have my truck,
my gun, or my hat to make my getaway. I'll be trapped in some
hick town jail with three runaways and nothing to show for it
except a piece of old Mrs. Honeybaker's pie."

"Honeysack. You got to be good at names. That is a fact."
Angel opened the rear door of the church. "Look at that, will
you? We was not a hop and a skip from that house last night.
Here we were holed up on hard old pews. I'm eating my fill
then I'm sleeping on a cloud tonight. My own bed. I never had
one to myself."

"You don't hear a thing I'm telling you. We can't stay.
They're looking for a real widowed minister and his three, well-
behaved children. We don't fit the bill."

"You ain't got nothing to your name, not a cent, and here
you are complaining about what the Lord done give you. Me,
I'm thanking him for all He has done." Angel kneeled on the
lawn. She brought her hands together at her chin and closed
her eyes.

"Get yourself up. Don't be making a spectacle like that,"
said Jeb.

"Oh, Evelene, would you look at that sweet angel!" Mellie,
who still held Ida May's hand, turned red around her plum-

shaped cheeks. "Praying right here on the lawn and thanking Jesus. Yes, Lord, we all thank you for your blessings." Mellie pulled a white cotton handkerchief from out of her bosom. In front of her, she made an invisible bow shape with the scarf, waving it in the breeze like a ship's signal. "And for little Idy May."

"Sweet Lord, Reverend!" said Evelene. "You've done well with your ducklings in spite of not having a wife around. If you can get a young one to bow her knee to God, you'll have no worries with her when she's grown. I have to say, though, they all in need of some womanly grooming. You don't mind if we take them out to the washtub, do you?" Evelene grabbed Willie by the shoulders.

"Tell her no, Jeb," said Angel. She came off of one knee.

"Thank you, Sister Whittington. This biggest one, she needs it the worst, I'm afraid." Jeb bent and took Angel by the shoulders. "Bath time, Biggest."

"I got some good-smelling stuff you'll like. What is your name, girl?" Evelene asked Angel.

"This is Angel," said Jeb. "Angel, kindly go here with Mrs. Evelene. Mind your manners while you're at it."

"This is one I'm not worried about, Reverend Gracie. I hope you don't think I'm bein' too fussy. I never had nothing but boys. I love making over girls. You know, Angel, your name fits you to a T."

"I don't need no help bathing." Angel made a wide arc around Evelene.

"Please, let old Ev fix you up, curl your hair. I have a dress once belonged to one of my nieces. Pretty white collar. Petticoat."

"I'm not one for petticoats, Mrs. Whittington, if you don't mind. I guess you know the first thing I have to do is get my sister, Ida May, fed. After that, I'll go out later and wash myself."

"Ida May's inside eating. Why Mellie, she done fixed her up a plate of chicken and a glass of milk. I can tell you been having to care for your little sister. Now you got us to help."

Jeb watched as Evelene, with her long, plump arms, wrestled Angel into a tight clutch. Evelene laughed in a pleased manner and her eyes squinted. She looked pretty and giddy all at the same time.

"Angel, you know you got all your nice things stole. You let Mrs. Evelene fix you up with some of her pretty things."

Jeb saw Angel's antipathy for him coming out of her eyes—sharp blades. She lifted her face, and smoothed her hair. "Where's the washtub, Mrs. Whittington?"

"Reverend, have another helping of bread." Mr. Honeysack joined Jeb in the kitchen of the parsonage. "Now, Horace Mills—that's the banker—he's got a wagon that's old, but he'll sell it to you and let you pay it off as you go—don't want to owe him too much, though, if you catch my meaning. See if he'll throw in his mule and I'll guarantee you'll have some wheels that will get you where you want to go around Nazareth. When the deputy sheriff comes around again, we'll put him on the trail of those outlaws that stole your truck. In the meantime, you can have a means of visiting the folks around town that go to Church in the Dell. Our last preacher, he was a visiting fool. Never took a lot of stock in much else, though, like bringing in new people. Course we don't get many new folks, not like in Hot Springs. He seemed satisfied with things as is. But that suits us fine here in Nazareth. Now, this being Tuesday, you reckon you'll be settled in enough to preach us a good one on Sunday?"

The fried chicken tasted like the first time Jeb had ever tasted it. He took another bite of bread. It collapsed, almost as airy as cotton candy from the Texarkana Fall Carnival. "Sunday?"

"We been without good preaching for going on a year. That's why, when you showed up early, we was past ecstatic."

"Early?"

"We wasn't expecting you for months. When Evelene showed up at the church building this morning to check for storm damage and found you all safe inside, she ran and told all of us about it. We'd like to have a big picnic, if that's all right with you. Maybe Sunday after your preaching, we'll have us a dinner on the grounds. More fried chicken than you've ever seen."

"We'll aim for Sunday, then." Jeb thought about the mule and wagon, about how far he might travel before the Church in the Dell posse caught up with him.

Evelene drove Angel to her place. The two of them returned with a box that rattled with bottles and lotions. Petticoat netting draped from one side over Evelene's arm.

Three women in a matron's circle poured well water over Angel's head. Jeb could only see the crown of her head through the fried-chicken-stuffed female bodies. They lifted her and wrapped her in a blanket while the sun warmed them just outside of the shaded spire of the church. Evelene pulled the flouncy dress over Angel's head while the other two combed her hair out and helped her slip into stockings and a pair of leather shoes.

Angel looked up and saw Jeb, his smugness evident. She lifted her forearm and smelled the borrowed toilet water—essence of lilacs and honeysuckle. All at once, her hair was auburn silk, her nose and cheeks rubbed to a sheen. She pulled away from Evelene and twirled. The skirt billowed and for a moment in time, in the sun, Angel's name fit her.

"Now, I left you all plenty to eat. Then there's the pantry full of everything you need to get you started. I feel awful about you all getting robbed just as you was pulling into town." Mrs. Honeysack had shown up just before sundown with an evening meal. "This pot of beans will probably last you more than a day or two. It's full of ham. That corn on the cob's right out of a field just outside of town and they grow the best corn around. Sweet as nectar. Sweet and good by itself if you run low on butter or salt."

Jeb thanked Freda Honeysack for the eleventh time. "We thank you for your generosity, ma'am. Your pie is good eats. We had that this afternoon."

"You know when my husband, Will, read your letters to all of us, you sounded a bit, well, formal, in your writing. But now that I meet you, why I'd say you're just like anybody you'd meet. Not that there's anything wrong with it, but it's really a good thing. But you just never know. Some people are quite different in person than they are when they write. I guess it's 'cause we're taught formal writing but we talk like our ma and pa."

Jeb closed the door inch by inch as she backed out of the entrance. He watched her go, parceling out advice as she went, telling him where he could buy this or that and where the extra set of keys to the parsonage was kept hidden. When she finally climbed inside her husband's Ford, Mr. Honeysack waved from the driver's seat and hollered, "We're going to leave you good folks in peace." He made a delicate attempt to silence his wife, but her words were finally and only drowned out by Mr. Honeysack's engine.

"I'm satisfied as two ticks. How am I ever going to eat another bite? Long as I live I never saw people who could eat so much. You ever seen a dress like this unless it was on the movie screen, Ida May?" Angel fell back on the sofa. The petticoat inflated and then fell around her knees. "I feel like Miss Stanwyck."

"They give me these trousers. The legs are kind of short, but they nice," said Willie. "Ida May looks like she's wearing a doll's dress."

Ida May counted the polka dots on her skirt. "I like it."

"They're gone. Finally!" Jeb snatched up the clean set of clothes Mrs. Whittington had pressed and laid on the end table. "I'm out of this place. I'll take only as much food as I can put in one sack. The rest, you all can take. You kids are in good hands. If these folks don't talk you into a stupor, they'll love you to death. I don't need no more lovin' to death." Jeb calculated that if he hiked through the woods following the roads, he might be two towns away by morning.

"You're leaving? But why?" Angel parted the tulle and peered through the netting at Jeb.

"Didn't you hear the way that Honeyfat lady is already piecing together how I don't sound like my letters? She keeps putting two and two together like that and she'll have us figgered for cons in a jiffy." Jeb raked all of the leftovers into a tin plate. "I'll eat this later tonight. Dog, these women can cook!"

"Mrs. Honeysack likes us. You listen to anything she says and you'll know we got us a goldmine in this church business. Didn't you see Barbara Stanwyck in *The Miracle Worker?* There that poor woman's daddy was kicked out of his church and died of a broken heart. Next thing you know, she's dressing like a girl from California, all diamonds and furs and preaching for the Lord. They's money to be had, Jeb Nubey, in God's work. You let me give you all the hows and how-tos on this religion business and we'll make us a wad and then split town—split everything. Fifty-fifty. We go our way. You go yours. You think that sheriff is going to come looking for you when folks is bowing to you and three kids is calling you Daddy?"

"Ain't you afraid of nothing, Biggest? Like, being struck by lightning for one thing. Another thing, you aiding a murderer, don't that bother you none? That you might get thrown into the pokey?"

"I know that last night nothing came together for me, for us. Now everything is fitting like a puzzle come together and you want to throw it away. You know what I'm holding here in my hand?"

Jeb counted sacks of sugar and flour.

"This here is a letter. I got it a while ago from Mrs. Honeysack who brought us the mail. It is addressed by Reverend Gracie, namely you. They thought your letter arrived late and just gave it back to us—that right there is a sign. This letter from Reverend Gracie says he is months from being here in Nazareth. We're safe, Jeb. We got us a hiding place, a lunch ticket, and you even got income. You know about income, don't you? Folks is giving us things like we're the royal family. Never in my life have I ever heard tell of such things. I know you got the con in you and can smell pay dirt when you strike it. You run off in the night and that deputy sheriff, he'll find you and you'll be out breaking rocks—in chains. You stay here and you'll have these people eating out of your hand."

Jeb dwelled on everything she said. "Then I got to put up with you."

"I'll keep looking for Claudia. You got my word. I don't want to be tied to you neither."

"We have to keep calling him Daddy?" asked Willie.

Angel waited for Jeb to answer.

"Not only you going to call me Daddy, you going to do what I say." Jeb put back the flour and sugar in the homemade pantry cabinet.

"What we do is our own business—you ain't the boss! Let's just get things straight."

"You take your brother and sister and that frilly dress off to your beds. I need some time to think."

"Or some time to drink," said Angel.

"That don't mean nothing to you. What I do ain't none of your concern."

"People see us fighting and they'll suspect. They see you drinkin' now that's a whole new kettle of fish. They'll know we're cons for sure. You supposed to be a kind man and temperate, like my grandma said." Angel shook Ida May who had already fallen asleep with her head on the soft chair arm.

He still wasn't buying the whole preacher scam, but said, "They's different kinds of preachers. Maybe I'm the hard-nosed kind. I got to be true to my own self or I'll come across as a big fat phony. You kids don't mind what I say and folks sure as all get out won't think you're mine. Let's have us a little practice maneuver. All three of you—get to bed! I don't want none of your lip, neither."

"Maybe I'll just get me a helping of Freda's beans. You think you can just snap your fingers and I'll go running off with my tail tucked, you wrong about that!" Angel minced to the table, her on-loan shoe heels slightly too tall for a girl with a gangly gait.

"You want this con of yours to work, Biggest. You march your prissy self past that table and on into that little princess bed of yours. Otherwise, give me two minutes and I'll be out the door jackrabbit fast. You can explain my absence to the

good people of Nazareth in the morning. They'll have you
checked in to the closest sanatorium."

"Why you think they'd put me in the sanatorium?"

Ida May kept asking, "What's the sanatorium?"

"You're dead weight, Biggest. A nice family, they'd take
your cute little sister, figure she's still young, not yet ruint. Your
brother would fit nicely behind some old farmer's plow. But
you, you're too old to raise. Too thin boned to work. All the
children's homes is full. It's the sanatorium for you."

"Willie, Ida May, get to bed now!" Angel scuttled into the
bedroom with the three matching hand-cut beds.

"Good night, Biggest."

She slammed the door.

Night crept into Nazareth with crickets grating against tense
silence. Jeb pushed himself back in the rocker left on the front
porch of the parsonage. The storm had cleaned the night air
squeaky fresh, leaving behind only a few bluish clouds in the
sky. A transparent halo ringed the moon. An owl perched out
on a pine limb screeched twice until Jeb came close to knocking the bird off its roost with a pine cone. He reached into his
pocket for his flask. Then he felt a prickly feeling, like the hairs
of his head standing up on his neck. What if the good Mrs.
Honeysack returned to remind him of one more tedious detail?
Or, as the word spread that the Gracie family had finally
arrived, what would happen if more church people chanced by
to pay a visit? He made a circular motion on the cap of the
flask, as though he anointed it. His tongue pushed to one side
of his mouth, parched, deprived. He wondered how a parson
went seven days without a drink. Or did he sneak out into the
woodland to steal a taste? But then it came to Jeb that the min-

ister might run into trouble if he was so much as caught buying a pint or two of the good stuff.

Jeb's lips pruned. Thoughts of spending one more day as the town holy man gathered into his insides, congregating, bantering and milling in whispers about the destiny placed on Jeb Nubey. Another day as Reverend Gracie meant visiting the feeble, the elderly, listening to songs of elbow's complaint and gout. Once the visitation had wound down then Sunday would roll around. People would gather in the Church in the Doll with expectant grimaces, scrutiny making their eyes shine like the mad. Jeb had not called on higher powers before. It made him itch to consider it.

He had to leave before Sunday. He didn't know what kind of church to expect. Some congregations meld coolly into their pews, nursing silent, inward pain—biding the time until the final amen. He'd heard tell of how others heated up, roiling in a lather of brimstone-scalded judgment before marching away into the community to warn the sinners of their coming doom.

Searching back in the soft tendons of his childhood memories, he tried to recall the traditions of church. Jeb's mother had dragged him by the ear every Sunday until she was too sick to bother. He'd seldom paid attention to her prayers . . . until she got sick. Then he would've walked over coals if the Power from on high would just let her live. He figured it was him that caused the final curtain to drop on Pearl Nubey's life. Jeb felt cool metal against his lips. Something soothed his brow, like the young fingers of the sweet, plump girl in Texarkana, and then he tasted gin. He allowed it to slip over his uneven lower teeth and down the velvet length of whiskey-weakened tongue. Martyrs needed their sedative. He drank until his eyes turned back beneath red sun-parched lids, a calling toward sleep seeping through him.

His hand fell limp in his lap. Slumber drew him into rivers that swept over him, baptizing him in gin and fire. A bad sort of music faded in and out then turned into a grating rhythm as irritating as the clanking of chains and ankle irons.

"Angel, what's a sanatorium?" Ida May breathed out the words on her soft pillow. She wound her pointer finger around the lacey, embroidered edges of the pillowcase as though she stroked harp strings.

Angel could see the church ladies' handiwork all around the room—knitted dolls with pink and turquoise skirts. Plaid curtains with hand-sewn tie-backs. Embroidery tipping every gingerly sewn edge like delicate fingernails dipped in color. No one color dominated the room, but each item fought for attention. Loops of gold draped the plaid curtain; white and pink doilies battled a tablecloth of pale green. The Scottish monkey lolled next to a poodle made of dyed cotton bolls, all toys made from ragbags and dresses that could take no more mending.

"Angel, you hear me?" Ida May whispered.

"A sanatorium is a place where people rest. So let's play sanatorium, how about?" Angel rolled over and felt the fringe of the handmade quilt tickle her nose. It smelled of mothballs and something sweet.

"I'm tard. You two be quiet or I'll holler for Jeb," said Willie. "Nice to have a man around the house again."

"Don't get used to him, Willie. I have a feeling he won't be around no longer than Lana. People like that drift in, drift out. One day, they just gone. Nobody ever hears from them again." Angel listened for Willie's reply but heard only the soft sawing of his snores.

Ida May made a soft moan, turned to press her face into the pillow as though she expected it to kiss her good night.

Angel ran her hand across her sister's fingertips and watched out the window until the stars turned to a hazy glass. She closed her eyes and prayed that God would tie Jeb to his bed until morning.

5

Jeb allowed Evelene and Mellie to treat the Welby children to an ice-cream soda inside Fidel's Drugstore while he worked out the details of the mule and wagon with the banker.

"The mule, she's ten hands high and likes a good race so just watch yourself around other folks in wagons. Not too many on the road except for Ivey Long, who thinks automobiles are of the devil." Horace Mills ran his hand along the mule's flank. "I call her Bell. The kids gave her that name when she was a colt. We had to put a bell on her to find her when she ran off."

Jeb cocked his head and said, "She ran off?"

"That was long before she was broke. No need to worry about her now. She's a good wagon mule. I hated to see her put out to pasture with so many good years left in her."

"But you decided to sell her." Jeb studied her coat and her joints.

"The missus wanted an automobile. After that, every woman in town wanted her husband to buy one. I don't do much farming what with the bank to run and all. My brother, Freddie, he started a bank up in Hope. We learned it from our daddy. It runs in our blood, I guess you could say."

A black Ford truck motored past. A heavy-faced woman leaned forward in the passenger seat and smiled, her features stretched tight and shining. She lifted a hand that gripped a basket of honey jars and waved. The man seated next to her yelled, "Welcome, Preacher Gracie!" The back of the truck carried six children, the boys shirtless, the girls wearing clothes that were either too large for their slight frames or too small. All of the children waved and called out just as their daddy had done.

The banker lowered his tone. His eyes moved back and forth as though someone might hear. "That's the Wolvertons. Poor as church mice. Good stock. Just fallen on had times like the rest of the country. Lost their place to foreclosure. What's a banker to do?"

The Wolvertons greeted Jeb as minister. He returned the wave, a knot in his throat.

"Everything I owned was in the truck, Mr. Mills. You're sure you don't mind waiting for the money?" Jeb rubbed his palms against his trousers. An uneasiness traveled up his back while a bead of sweat trickled down and seeped into his borrowed shirt. Bankers made him skittish. Every citizen of Nazareth seemed to have appeared out of shops and automobiles to take a gander at him and the Welbys. Two young women with a bit of tease in their gaits smiled at him. He tipped his hat.

"Don't you give this transaction a second thought, Reverend. Will Honeysack is the head deacon of Church in the Dell. If he guarantees you're good for it, I believe it. He and his wife started that store out of the back of a wagon and built it up to the fine establishment it is today. You ought to count yourself fortunate to have Will as your deacon. His heart is as good as his money."

"Mr. Mills, I want to be sure I'm understanding you. Are you saying Mr. Honeysack is signing for me? He didn't tell me that if it's so."

"Signing on the dotted line. But we'll need your John Hancock, too. Just drop by the bank tomorrow, Thursday, and I'll have the papers drawn up."

A gnawing pang ate at Jeb's insides. He felt an inward drawing, as though something sucked him under.

"You all should enjoy living in Millwood Hollow. Good fishing and lots of land for a little hunting if you're of a mind."

"Church in the Dell's in Millwood Hollow?"

"That's what the old-timers have always called the place, even after a church was built on it. Wealthy man named Millwood bought it for his bride. When she died, he up and sold a big part of it, then gave some of it to be built for a church—Mrs. Millwood would have wanted it that way. Little history lesson. I've kept you too long."

"I guess I should be going now." He took the reins loosely and climbed onto the wagon and seated himself. He snapped the mule's flank with the tip of the rein.

The banker laughed. "You forget something, Reverend?"

Jeb had not shopped in any of the stores because he didn't need to purchase anything at all, not soap or bread or even a can of lard what with all of the pantry being stocked. "I don't think so, Mr. Mills. Why do you ask?"

Mills lifted his broad chin and glanced inside Fidel's. "You forgot your children."

Jeb climbed down from the wagon. His face blazed red. "My apologies."

"No need to apologize. It's hard for us men to remember such things. Must be difficult for you since your wife passed on." Mills excused himself with his white straw hat in his hands.

"Thank you, Mr. Mills." Jeb tapped on the window glass of Fidel's.

Angel was engaged in conversation with Evelene Whittington, who had introduced her to two other women. Jeb pushed open the door.

Evelene, eternally affable, gestured for Jeb to join the circle. "Here's our new minister himself, ladies. Reverend Gracie, I'd like you to meet Florence Bernard and Josie Hipps."

Florence had a wide face, big-boned, with a long neck that jutted out at an angle like a wild game bird—something red at the throat. "Nice to meet you, Reverend. We've been listening so long to Barney Hewlett's Bible readings we have forgotten what good preaching sounds like."

The pang grew to nausea inside of Jeb. He shook Florence's extended hand.

Josie had a fair complexion with a spattering of freckles across her nose that caused her eyes to stand out like a child's. "Reverend, I'm bringing your dinner over tonight. I hope six is a good time. Bill don't like to drive me around too late after dark."

"Six is fine, ma'am. But don't think you have to cook for us. We've been making do for a long time on our own." The lie sounded natural to Jeb. "We" and "our" came out of him with the fluidity of a natural father of three. While the falsehood settled itself inside of him, the nausea subsided. The back of his throat burned only faintly, tasting of fear.

"Of course we'll cook for you," said Josie. "Making do is not the way to bring up kids. They need a hot meal and fresh milk. Especially this little Ida May."

Ida May closed her eyes in ecstasy as she swallowed the last gulp of ice-cream soda.

"I guess we'll be going now. Nice to meet you ladies," said Jeb.

"See you Sunday." Evelene smiled out from far-set eyes, confident of every word she spoke as though each was a pearl.

"Sunday, then." Jeb poured out a breath so hard Angel warned him with a glance. He was done tired out over her nit-pickin', and ignored her. He opened the drugstore door behind him. "We got us a wagon, anyway, kids. May as well take a ride in it, see how she rides."

Willie and Ida May ran to pet the mule. Angel, who wore another of Evelene's collection of frocks from her niece, teetered past Jeb in stockings white and soft like jasmine, nothing like the bare-legged, mud-toed vagabond who'd stowed away in the back of his truck.

"You got ice cream on your nose, Biggest," said Jeb.

Angel rubbed the stain of chocolate with the back of her hand but walked around him as though he were the doorman. "Your oldest girl is blooming into quite a lovely woman," said Josie. "Better watch or she'll be turning heads in the shake of a stick."

"Good day, ladies." Jeb allowed the door to swing closed behind him.

Angel clambered on board the wagon seat with a box the size of which might hold one of Mrs. Honeysack's pies.

Jeb took a seat next to her while Willie helped Ida May onto a bench seat in the wagon.

"We're about to roll. Everyone hold on tight." Jeb stung Bell's flanks with the rein. The mule danced for a split second then moved forward. "Mrs. Whittington must have given you another gift." He gestured toward the box in Angel's grasp.

"It's for you. I told her your Bible got stole with everything else. You can't preach without a Bible," said Angel.

"I can't preach no way." Jeb tipped his new hat to another family who blew on the horn.

"It ain't hard, Jeb. You just stand up and talk at people. I never seen no one who could talk like you. Best of my memory,

I never seen you when you wasn't talking." Angel opened the box. "She gave us a nice one. Leather. Gold letters. Words of Jesus in red. My granny told me it's the sign of a good one if the words of Jesus are in red."

"You think I can talk, but what you think I plan to talk about anyway? Picking cotton? I can talk about that until sundown." He studied the scars on his fingertips. If the banker had noticed his rough hands, he had not said. "Or trouble-making women. I have known a few of them."

"I guess I'll have to tell you everything to do. You just talk on things like the Holy Ghost, getting baptized, and the Father and Jesus. Then just fill in with some 'a-has' and 'hally-lu-yers.' Stuff like that." Angel pulled the satin marker out of the Bible.

"I don't know nothing about no Holy Ghost, nor the Father, nor Jesus." Jeb tapped a fingertip for each member of the trinity.

"It's all in here," said Angel, relaxed. "You just read it and then talk about it."

Jeb turned the mule in the center of town, held up his hand so a driver would allow them to correct their direction. "I guess you going to make me say it."

"Make you say what?"

"I can't read. There. Now you know."

"Don't you tell me that now, when I got everything all laid out like some big grand plan, you're gonna blurt out you can't read!" Angel closed the Bible. It popped and made a hollow sound.

"First of all, I woke up to your grand plan. No intention, mind you, on my part of scamming a whole town of big-eyed church people out of food and everything else imaginable. This wagon and mule, for one thing. Free board for another. Fancy clothes on your skinny back."

Angel glanced down at her too-big dress.

"Every minute your grand plan sucks my life into the mud hole of yours. I had it made, wheeling my way to Tennessee with a little money in my pocket, a plug of tobacco, a flask of my favorite spirits, my hat—"

"You and your hat, your gun, and your truck! Everything you had was either stole or borryed. It wasn't like you owned anything. Those two lunkheads you lost your stuff to will most likely lose it to another lunkhead who will turn around and call it his things. None of you worked hard for nothing, you just stole it from each other and called it yours."

"You want to hitchhike back home, you just keep flapping your lips like that," said Jeb.

"In four days you have to stand up in front of these people and give them what they been salivating for—a big piece of God. What's wrong with that? Giving people what they want is not against the law." Angel adjusted her feet and recrossed her legs at the calf.

"It is against the law if you say you're someone you ain't."

"Did you ever tell anyone you was Reverend Gracie?"

He didn't answer. Too many lies to remember. Angel's voice sounded all at once soft. "I didn't tell them I was Gracie's oldest daughter. If thinking we're the Gracies makes them happy, well, then maybe we're just doing the work of the Lord after all."

"You're just nuts. They sure will take you off to the sanatorium. That I do know."

"The one thing I do know is that you got a lot of learning to do. Tonight, after supper, I'll pick out a story and teach it to you. But you got to say it differently, like, you know, everything coming out of your mouth is big news. Maybe, even if they've heard it before, they never heard it said like you're going to say it."

"I'm leaving. No way will I walk up in a pulpit and try and pull off the lie that I know somethin' about religion."

"First we got to pick a good story. You want to start with Noah and the ark, Daniel and the lion's den, Adam and Eve—"

"I'll head out of town on Friday like I'm going on visitation, see. Then I'll just drive on down the road. By Sunday, I'll be long gone."

"Granny told me this story once about a woman named Sapphire or some such, but I'll have to study on that one. I can't remember what she did, but it was bad. God struck her with lightnin' or rained fire down. That's what He does when He's mad." She raised one hand like lightning. The other hand wiggled her fingers for fire.

"She lied to God," said Willie.

Angel answered her brother with an imperious stare. "I don't remember asking your opinion, Willard."

"She lied to God and he struck her dead." Willie untucked his shirt and leaned far back against the front of the wagon bed. "You act like you was always listening to Granny, but you wasn't." He never won an argument with Angel, not that Jeb had noticed. But with that one statement carefully laid, a high-handed ease settled over him, one that caused him to cross his arms behind his head and smile. His eyelids made slits, almost smiling.

Jeb's gaze, the one that said he was suddenly interested, made his brows lift, to make seedy little arches over his eyes. Angel turned away from her brother. Jeb did not know who to believe. Nor did he care.

Ida May squirmed. Her face contorted as it always did when she had waited too long to do her business. "Dud, I need to go," she said.

Jeb stopped the mule before a bridge. The sign read Marvelous Crossing. "Angel, take your little sister down this path and over behind that rock to pee before she drives me out of my gourd." He had not seen Ida May use the outhouse once.

"Ida May, can't you wait until we get home? We got our own outhouse. It won't kill you to wait." Angel turned with one knee on the seat facing the rear of the wagon.

"I got to go," was all Ida May said.

Angel didn't wait for Ida May to crawl up to the front, but jumped down and made a puff of dust on the road. She flounced to the rear gate, let it down, and then pulled her sister out. "We'll be back." They disappeared down the grassy spiral of lane Jeb had pointed out.

Jeb noticed a family seated on the bank on one side of Marvelous Crossing Bridge. An older man held a pudgy boy in his arms, most likely his grandson. The boy's mother stirred lemonade and poured the older man a glassful. She did not look older than fifteen, although Myrna Lenora Hoop looked young herself and she'd been all of nineteen when Jeb took a turn with her on the cotton bale. Next to her, a young man close to her age in appearance touched her calf with a tickle weed from the water. A dozen other family members gathered in differing clusters of four and six, some pitching horseshoes. A few conversed on blankets and battled the invisible legion of bugs attracted to the water.

The cozy family scene coulda been a fancy painting of pink dresses and blue work trousers, tall human columns milling along the banks of the green water. The lemonade sippers looked much like his own family when they'd all lived in Temple, Texas. The face of the man took on his father's face; the pudgy child was his youngest recollection of his brother when they played near a lake, the name of which he could not remember. Deer ran along those banks. It seemed everything around them had smelled of rotting acorns and Indian burial grounds. Along that shoreline, he had picked a banjo not far from his momma. She had called it a sin, devil music.

Jeb's lids drooped and he felt his eyes sink into the cups of his cheeks. He could smell those acorns and the water, the brown and green algae, murky and wonderful. The sound of a hound dog lapping near a circle of sunshine and minnows stirred an inside circle of wanting, a giddy desire to find that green and happy place again—to replace that young man's face with his own and the young woman's face with some girl that held in her possession a higher plane of wisdom than that of Myrna Lenora Hoop. If he could have anything he wanted in a girl, he would narrow down the choices to such a person.

"Never, never again will I take Ida May to do her business," Angel loped back up the path. Ida May came walking up, moving sideways like a crab, holding herself with her dress tucked between her thin legs. Angel said, "She never will go out in the woods, like she's too much a girl, or I don't know what. But this is it, Ida May! Don't you say another word to me about needing to go. When we get home, you go to the outhouse A-lone!"

"Get in, then," said Jeb. The wagon squeaked only slightly, like a single mouse in a cornfield. The girls added almost no weight to the load. Jeb glanced at the family picnic again. Down on the bank, a hound bayed and loped after a rabbit while the sky cooled behind a cloud two hours past noon. He flicked the mule's ear, which caused the beast in turn to stamp, shake the harness, and then move ahead.

"I think the best thing for Sunday is Moses," said Angel.

Jeb grunted, "What do you mean?"

"He's this guy that did a lot with nothing. That's what we're trying to do with you."

"You'd look pretty floating under the bridge with pennies on your eyes."

"Well, actually, think of Moses floating along the water in a little basket. That ain't the worst way to start with him." Angel flipped back and forth between the pages of Evelene's Bible.

"He was dead with pennies on his eyes?" Jeb asked.

"You have to start listening. First, he was a baby floating down the river some place; I don't know where but I'll look it up. This is tiresome. I'll bet my granny is watching me over a cloud and laughing."

"You give her good reason."

"She always wanted me to know the Bible stories, now here I am teaching them to you," said Angel.

"Kind of like the blind leading the blind, you mean?" said Jeb.

Angel told him, "So first Moses was a baby in the bushes."

"I thought he was in the water."

"The bushes in the water. Jeb, you ever been serious with a girl?" Angel asked.

"I don't discuss my personal business with children. It sounds like you got the whole Moses story confused and can't get back on track, is what I'm hearing."

Angel dropped her shoulders back and clasped her hands atop the Scriptures. "I don't want to know nothing personal. Just if you ever got serious with a girl."

"I never said the word 'marriage.'" Jeb could not quite decipher her language, but he had found all females possessed a code he could never break. Angel was just another in a long line of them.

"Was she an older person?" Angel slid one hand under the Bible and closed it altogether.

"Older than me?" asked Jeb.

Willie lifted from his perch beneath the wagon seat. "She means older than her. Don't you get it at all, Jeb?"

"Shut up, stupid! You stay out of my business," said Angel.

"You know how you got names for different people, Jeb. Like you call Ida May 'Littlest' and stuff like that?" Willie stood and insinuated himself between Angel and Jeb.

Jeb nodded.

"Angel has a name for you, too. She give it to you back in Camden."

"Never mind," said Jeb.

"I said, shut up, Willie!" Angel turned away, her skirts rustling softly, her cheeks bright like persimmons in the fall.

"Willie, go find your seat again," said Jeb.

"Sweet Eyes," said Willie. He turned, satisfied at having saved the tidbit of gossip for just the perfect moment, delivering it like a sucker punch.

Jeb prodded the mule that had slowed. "That's not so critical," he said. "Kind of has a ring to it."

Angel's right hand came up and covered the left side of her face. She remained in that position all the way back to the Church in the Dell parsonage.

❈

Jeb reined the mule to a halt, allowed a Model-T to pass, and was about to turn into the lane that led to the parsonage when he saw the deputy sheriff's vehicle through the trees.

"It's the cops, Jeb! You think they're coming after you, that they know who you are?" Willie asked.

"I'm not sticking around long enough to find out." Jeb pulled back on the reins. The mule made a backwards step.

"Looky, it's that nice Mr. Honeyman," said Ida May.

"Maybe they just bringing the cops around to help you find your truck, Jeb," said Angel. "Reckon?"

Honeysack moved between two pine trees, stooped down, and shaded his brow with one hand. He pointed and the deputy turned around and acknowledged he saw Jeb, too.

"You're not going to get away whipping this old mule," said Angel. "May as well see what they want. If it's the cuffs, I'll see you get good food in jail."

"Could you stop rattling for just a minute?" said Jeb. "I need quietness to think."

"It's helped you so far." Angel kept moving her feet from one side to the next, crossing her legs at the ankles as though she practiced various starlet poses.

"Willie, you go run on ahead, like you just got a sudden need to stretch your legs. I'll slowly get this mule turned like I'm about to head on into the parsonage. Take this white handkerchief and if it looks like the coast is clear, like they don't know nothin' about me, then you just jump around and wave like you're playing a game and I'll know I can come on in." Jeb heaved a breath, his eyes still assessing the deputy's body movements.

"That's the stupidest idea I ever heard," said Angel. "Willie jumping around like a fool, what those men going to think— that he's lost his mind? No, most likely they'll wonder why you was afraid to come up to the parsonage like a man and give them a proper greeting."

"Willie, do as I say." Jeb handed the boy a handkerchief. "Go on, now."

Willie skipped all the way up the dirt lane, waving the hanky, never looking back. When he made it to the deputy's vehicle, Jeb saw them talk back and forth for a second or two.

Willie stood with his hands in his pockets, said a few things to Mr. Honeysack and then skipped around back to the parsonage.

"He didn't wave it, didn't wave the handkerchief," said Jeb, ready to bolt.

"Willie's a lot like that, acting like he's following everything you say. Then he can just walk into the next room and completely forget what you just told him." Angel sat straighter, restless. "Can we go now? That Josie lady's bringing supper by tonight and I want to change out of this dress. Maybe I'll wear that simple thing Evelene gave me, kind of a soft blue with little white petals every now and then along the hem."

"The deputy's walking this way," said Jeb. "You take the reins. I'm going to slip out the back of this wagon and run up through those woods. That's a big old heavy-set fellow. Can't be too fast on foot."

"How am I going to drive this wagon? Do I look like I can make this mule go? Not me." She stood up and waved at the deputy, who was halfway up the lane by now.

"I said take the reins."

She called out to the deputy, waving her arm in an invitation.

"Take them now."

"Quit telling me what to do."

"Fine. Just stand here looking like a fool then." Jeb leaped over the seat and landed on both feet in the back of the wagon.

"Reverend Gracie, you having mule problems?" The deputy called to him.

Jeb stopped when he heard the deputy call him Gracie. He bent over and picked up a board. "You think I ought to hit her up side the head, Deputy?"

"Poor old beast. Ever since automobiles came around, these poor animals don't know up from down. When I saw that

Model-T pass you I wondered if it would spook your animal."

"That's what it is, all right. It's spooked." Jeb jumped out of the wagon. After meeting the sheriff on the dirt road and shaking his hand, he took the mule by the harness and tugged. The animal moved forward.

"I'm glad you didn't have to give it a whack. Shame to punish it when machinery's to blame," said the deputy. "I understand you and your family is victims of a robbery. I hated to hear it, what with your just getting into town. Nazareth is a quiet place. Seldom do you hear of crooks in this part of the state. But what with this Depression on, they's outlaws comin' out of every nook and cranny. If you can give me a description of the boys that did it, I'll bet I can run them down for you."

"One had a skinny look about him, but they both had already climbed up inside my truck so I couldn't see all of them. I don't know how tall, but that boy by the window, he had a tall look, like the top of his head nearly touched the roof of the truck. He had light-colored hair, straw colored, I guess you'd say." Jeb tried to remember. It had been dark.

"I'll check with the sheriff back in Camden and the one up around Hope. If there's been a slew of crimes, maybe we got some real outlaws. But if nothing else is going down, well, it could be a couple of locals out for a joyride. Maybe from Hope or somewhere else. Now give me an idea of what kind of truck and the rest of your belongings and then I'll be on my way."

Jeb described the truck, the food supplies, the tarp that covered the goods.

"You got anything that says it was your truck?"

Jeb did not know how to answer.

"Truck in your name, Reverend Gracie? Free and clear."

Jeb knew that his brother had bought the truck off the Hamptons, but how it was transacted, he couldn't remember.

"It's mine." He felt the hope of finding the truck sucked from his grasp like a nickel down the well.

"That's Philemon Gracie," said Mr. Honeysack. "Good Bible name. Did your momma know you was going to be a preacher?"

Angel cackled and ran up the road toward the house. Ida May followed her, skirt flying like a paper parasol.

"How you spell Fi-le-mon?" the deputy asked.

"It's just like in the Bible," said Honeysack. "Right, Reverend?"

Jeb nodded.

When the deputy finally pulled away followed by Honeysack, Jeb marched up the steps to the parsonage and yelled, "Angel, out here front and center."

She failed to appear. He went inside and found her sprawled across her bed while the radio blared from the parlor.

"I don't need you running off like that. How in the world you expect me to spell a name like 'Fi-le-mon.' You pull another stunt like that and maybe you can just explain your-self without me."

Angel pressed the back of her head into the pillow. "Of all the names to give you. I mean, you can't read but you got to spell Philemon. That's funnier than the look on your face when Mr. Honeysack said it. I guess you're lucky you know your whole name now. Maybe you ought to practice saying it in front of the mirror. 'Greetings, I'm Reverend Philemon Gracie, at your service.'"

Jeb left her to her own devices—to laugh, wallow around in her own folly, anything she pleased as long as he didn't have to listen to her foolishness. He had an hour to himself before that Josie would show up with supper. He would spend it quietly drinking.

6

Jeb found Willie stretched out across the stream, one hand steadying his weight. The rivulet meandered an acre behind the house, clear water full of sun perch and a few trout. "Don't touch my trot line. I put it there for a reason. So no one would disturb it. I want to land a fish, not a boy."

"My daddy taught me how to do it." Willie, on all fours, looked blue in the morning light. Blue denims, blue eyes all beneath the blue morning sky.

"It's mine. I said don't touch it and I mean it."

"You'd make a terrible daddy," said Willie.

"Thank you kindly." Jeb saw Willie purse his mouth, his eyes dimming and disappointment coloring his face. "You know how to clean and cut up trout?"

"I do. You got three already, about yay long." Willie sat back on his heels and held out his hands, creating a measure of ten inches.

"Give it another couple of hours. Sun's just coming up. We might land another one if we wait." Jeb heard a faint rustle behind him, like soft fabric swishing against itself.

"Good morning," said a young woman. "Reverend Gracie, I assume."

Jeb and Willie froze like raccoons at the water's edge.

Jeb wondered how long she had listened to him and Willie. He turned and saw the woman, maybe nineteen, who smiled at him. Yet, her voice made her sound older. Twenty-two, maybe. The first rays of sunlight framed her in a yellow-white outline. She dressed simply, but the folds of the fabric settled on her round curves as well as any expensive fabric might do. Her dress was white cotton. A pink scarf tied softly at the neck blew across her chest. The scarf, pale like her cheeks, made the rest of her skin look white as linen.

"I realize it's early. If I'm coming at a bad time, I can make an appointment." Her posture was vividly erect, defining her shoulders while everything from the waist down disappeared into white fabric until her knees appeared beneath the hem. She possessed slender calves not lacking the same roundness as the rest of her. Her hands moved about often as though she searched for something to hold. She brushed her mouth with her fingertips and before she spoke her lips came together, an "o" shape that gave her a thoughtful look. The breeze caused her hair to flutter like petals. A strand of blond hair stuck to her lips, but she either didn't notice or didn't care.

"I don't believe we've met," Jeb finally said as he righted himself. He had clambered outside to scold the boy, still holding a cup of coffee and a newspaper, so he could not tuck in his shirttail or even straighten his slovenly tousled hair. "I'm—" He stopped, having forgotten that awful name but looking straight at her startled him. The sunlight behind her obscured her face. Jeb made a slight move left, found shade, and then started to speak again. By that time, he'd forgotten what he was about to say.

"Fi-lee-mon," Willie whispered. His prompting made the woman laugh. She laughed like a boy—easy, with high notes descending into low notes.

All Jeb could do was nod and mouth silently, "I reckon so."

"I'm Fern Coulter. I teach school here in town."

"She don't look like no schoolteacher." Willie said it to Jeb. When he felt bashful, he only addressed the person most familiar to him.

Jeb came to himself. "I'm the Reverend Gracie and this is my boy. Willie." He stuck the newspaper under one arm, rubbed Willie's head for the first time, and noticed the strawness of the Welby boy's hair.

"I met your daughters already. They cook for themselves in the morning. Never too young to learn," said Fern.

"You met Biggest and Littlest. I hope they used their manners," said Jeb, meaning what he said in the worst way.

"Quite mannerly. The oldest, Angel, said I'd find you out back. If it's all right with you, I thought I'd help you get the children in school when we start up again. Just a few weeks away, you know, and they'll need school paper, pencils and such. What grade are the children in?" Fern asked.

"Grade?"

"Sure, grade. You know, they matriculate up from one grade to the next. What grade will you be in, Willie?"

"Snow Hill had us all in the same class. I'm nine, though."

Fern kept addressing Willie, having found him the fastest source of information. "I can give you a test, if that's all right with your father," she said. "Figure out your placement. We've been using grades since I've been here. Keeps you up with the other students your age. You say you came from Snow Hill? I understood you all came down from Ft. Smith. We don't stand on ceremony too much here in Nazareth. But I can send a letter and see if your teacher would send us some of your grades."

"Ft. Smith is right. We did a little preaching, what-have-you around Snow Hill. Camden, you name it. We go all over."

Jeb placed himself between Willie and the teacher. "Maybe you ought to go inside and help your sisters with breakfast."

Willie stared up at him as though he had not a thought in his head.

"Go on, now. Do as your daddy says. Son." Jeb pressed his palms against Willie's shoulder blades to move him forward.

"Now, about the youngest girl, Ida May, is it?" Fern continued with the interview.

"Yes, she's the littlest." Jeb kept nudging Willie until he broke free and ran inside.

"She's not school age yet, I gather?"

"That would be right."

"I noticed she doesn't know her ABC's. You know it is a good idea to allow her to learn that early. She's five now but she is awfully bright."

"Her mother was bright, I reckon. Don't get much of that from me."

"I'm sure that isn't true. Your letters make you sound scholarly."

Jeb took a sudden interest in a fishhook.

"Regarding Ida May, though, we can work on all of that later. The school is not far from here. We don't have a new building or big schools like Camden or Ft. Smith. But it's a decent structure and we've managed to buy school books for most every student." She hesitated as though she wasn't sure how her presence was being received. "It's called Stanton School." Her lashes lowered, and then her whole face turned sympathetic, like Evelene had given her a boatload of benevolent facts. "I understand you got your truck stolen. But Willie and Angel, they can walk. They can join students from two families along the way. They probably make friends easily if you all have moved around a lot. Most students walk to school, what with no money for gas. When you and the children have the time, I can take you to the school building. My father gave me his old car when I came to work here, so I can drive you out for a look."

Jeb had never met a woman who drove herself. "We can do that later, as you say. I do thank you for coming by, Mrs. Coulter."

Fern's hand brushed over her empty ring finger, but she did not correct him.

"Very neighborly of you." Jeb took a few measured steps in the direction of the house.

Fern crossed her arms, one toe pointed at the house. "Your oldest daughter invited me in for coffee. But I don't have to stay if that's a bother."

Jeb raised his empty cup. "Time for a fill up myself."

Willie rushed ahead of them and sat down at the table. "Can't remember the last time I had bacon." He gripped his fork upright and stared over at his sister.

Fern stood over Angel, who stirred the bacon campfire style. "If you and your little sister want to go and get dressed for the day, I'll finish up."

"I usually do the cooking. I know how my little sister likes her eggs and stuff like that," Angel said, a flutter of irritation in her voice. She stretched her upper lip over her bottom lip and shook the pan by the handle.

"Angel, if our guest wants a turn at the skillet, you step aside and let her have a go at it," said Jeb.

Angel dropped the spatula onto the stovetop. She lifted Ida May out of her chair and led her into the bedroom. When she slammed the door, Jeb shifted uncomfortably and said, "She's tried to fill in for her momma for so long, it makes her a mite peevish."

"Don't apologize. For a man without a wife, you've done a good job with the girls." Fern shook flour into a bowl, added water, baking powder, and a pinch of salt. She bent down and checked the oven to see if it had preheated. "Mr. Honeysack put you a good stove in here, plenty of kerosene. I guess you're happy about that. I'm going to slow this bacon down a bit. We need time to bake the biscuits." She adjusted the burner knob.

"You know, Miss Coulter, on this school issue, there's no need to involve you with letter writing and what not. I'll take care of the schooling when the time comes." Jeb had to prevent her from delving into their past and finding Gracies of a different kind. They'd be gone long before the first day of school anyway.

"No bother. My family doesn't live here so helping others settle in is something I like to do." She rolled out the batter and cut out circles of dough with a snuff glass.

"Where are you from?" Jeb asked.

"I came here from Hot Springs, but that's not where I grew up. Good schools over there but I wanted to go where I felt needed. Nazareth is behind a lot of other towns so they don't always attract the experienced teachers."

"How experienced could you be? You can't be a day over nineteen."

"I'm twenty-five. I started working as a tutor when I was fifteen. I was in college by seventeen, graduated before age twenty. I guess I'll grow gray hairs at twenty-nine."

Jeb doubted that.

"I can make gravy with these drippings. You have milk?" she asked.

"I'll get it."

"No need to bother."

They both made it to the icebox at the same time.

Jeb reached for the icebox but touched her hand instead. He drew back as though scalded.

Fern clasped the handle and opened the appliance door. "You have milk from Lucy and Bill Dolittle's farm, I see. I can make real gravy with their milk."

Jeb returned to the table and seated himself. He clasped his hands in his lap and determined he should not stand again until Fern Coulter left the parsonage.

"I'm just seeing it all now. The longer I stay, the more tangled up I get in this place. Now duping those farmer folks is one thing, but that teacher gal, she's quite another. That girl's got a thinker on top of those shoulders and pretty soon she'll have us all figured out. I'm no saint and surely no man of the cloth. She'll be the first to know. Then you give her a chance to get a letter back from that school, wherever this Gracie family comes from, and our little con job will wash on down the river."

"We can tell her we use nicknames, you know. My name for sure sounds like a nickname. When we get hold of the real names, then we'll just give her that for an answer," said Angel.

"What if Gracie has three sons? Or two sons and a girl? This scheme of yours ain't going to fool nobody. I got enough food to last me a month; a mule and a wagon that will get me clear to Tennessee if I want. Come Sunday, I'll be somewhere, someplace you won't know about, but I won't be here."

Jeb heard a knock at the door. He climbed out of the rocker and answered it. Horace Mills and a man Jeb remembered from town greeted him. "Reverend Gracie, this is Tom Plummer, the tailor. I bought a suit for you ready-made but he won't have it any other way. He wants to fit you for it." Mills held up the suit of clothes, a dark gray suit with a faint pin stripe.

Jeb blew out a breath. "Please do come in, Mr. Mills. Mr. Plummer. Kind of you to drop by."

"I got to thinking about Sunday and it occurred to me you lost all your wardrobe." Mills stepped back, his toes pointing out, while Plummer lifted Jeb's right arm and measured it.

Jeb felt the house growing smaller, the windows squeezing shut and locking themselves from the outside in.

"I have to hand it to you, Reverend, you're a calm one, like a cucumber, you are. If I had all my clothes stolen, why I guess I'd just sit in the house and hide until the wife fixed me up again." The tailor moved to measure Jeb from the top of his leg down.

"He's a cucumber, all right," said Angel.

"Angel, you take your sister and go wash up those breakfast dishes." Jeb had had his fill of her. "Here it is noon and you have yet to make yourself busy."

Since the teacher had appeared at the parsonage, Angel had moped around sullen, answering him in short sentences.

"We already washed up. That Miss Coulter did it, actually," said Angel. When she said *Coulter* her voice faltered.

"Miss Coulter came by? Don't say. Well, now, that is a fine young woman, Reverend. I'm glad you had the chance to make her acquaintance." Mills handed the twine back to Plummer.

Jeb dropped his arms at both sides. "Mr. Mills, I'm feeling badly about you buying this suit for me. I don't think I can take it. As a matter of fact, I know I can't."

Angel studied him as though trying to see clean through him.

"The missus had me do it and I'm glad she did. Don't you give it another thought at all, no sir! Our two oldest children are off to school. Oldest boy, Matthew, is all the way up in a Chicago college. Daughter studies in Little Rock. Our two youngest boys will be going off to college in the next two years, if they ever start studying here, that is. Helping you all gives my wife things to think about besides growing old."

"I'll have this back to you on Saturday, Reverend," said Mr. Plummer. "You going to need some shoes. When you come into town, drop by Honeysack's. Or try Woolworth's. They keep shoes for men all the time."

Mills reiterated, "Sure, sure, you do that. I guess you know all the women done started cooking for the big church picnic on the grounds Sunday. My Susan, she's the best at potato salad, but I can't say that to anyone. Makes the others mad. Can't do that in a town this small."

"I appreciate you both dropping by," said Jeb. He followed them out onto the porch to be certain he headed them toward Mills's June-bug-green automobile. The men disappeared into the long vehicle, waved, and pulled away.

Angel appeared on the porch in a candy-red sundress. "They done too much for you now, Jeb Nubey. If you take off now, lightning will strike."

"If I don't take off now, lightning will strike. Willie, you go hitch up my mule. I do hear thunder."

"No use, Willie. He won't leave," said Angel.

"Do you mean what you say, Jeb? You really leaving after Mr. Honeysack signed for you on this wagon and mule? He'll be the one paying for it if you steal it." Willie had the corners of his shirt pulled up over the ends of his elbows.

"That's what it means when you take things don't belong to you, Willie—other people have to pay. Those boys took my truck and it didn't cost them a cent. Now I'm taking something that makes up for what I lost. It's plain and simple borrowing." Jeb saw his reflection in the window. His face looked shadowed again, as though his beard was coming back even though he had gotten a shave this morning.

"All them people are going to show up expecting to hear about all them commandments while you're off breaking them," said Angel.

"You got a confounded way of looking at things. All them commandments is for the good of the community. Just keeps governments orderly. You live on the road, you keep your own commandments. Do thyself a little good, feed thy face, and other ones like that."

"Mr. Honeysack is a nice feller. I don't think it's right." Angel seated Ida May between her legs on the floor and commenced rebraiding her hair.

"In case you haven't noticed, Biggest. One way, I'm lying. Other way, I'm a thief." Jeb tucked in his shirttail.

"Lying makes more money. How you think the big rich men like Rockefeller made it so big?" Angel's reasoning face emerged. Three wrinkles formed half circles on either side of her brows.

"You saying that me sticking around is going to make money? They give me five dollars and a month's supply of Mrs. Honeysack's pies. I ain't Rockefeller."

"Barbara Stanwyck preached, using big words, making all kinds of promises, and people just flocked to her with money." Angel tied off Ida May's braids with green satin ribbons.

Jeb sat slouched back in the rocker. He looked at Willie, "Why does she keep rattling about Barbara Stanwyck?"

"It's something she saw at the picture show, got her all goggly-eyed with big ideas. They're playing that one downtown at the StarLight."

The lights on the theater marquis buzzed and then came on just as the light of evening faded.

"Hand me the popcorn down," said Jeb to Willie, who sat two sisters away. "I still don't get what this Barbara Stanwyck has to do with Sunday."

"You talk too loud. Preachers ain't even supposed to go to the picture show," said Angel. "It's a sin." She sat on the other side of Jeb beside Ida May, who was none too happy to be seeing the same film all over again. She'd hated it the first time with Lana.

"How is watching this a sin?" Jeb dug into the bag and redeemed the remaining soft popped corn for himself, but then wished he hadn't said anything to her. He tired of her antagonizing him, feeding him little tidbits about preaching and Moses, like her superiority was all he had in his favor.

Angel sipped her Coke. "We should have gotten the giant popcorn. Movies is just a sin. Momma let us go if we earned the nickel for ourselves. Granny pitched a fit but we went anyway. She sang a song with words like, 'be careful little eyes what you see.'"

"That's just plain silly. If I preach, I'll tell people they can go to a picture show. What's the deal with that anyway?" Jeb watched Barbara Stanwyck enter a lion's cage and then preach from it. *The Miracle Woman* went from one unhappy part of life to the next, her money machine collecting offerings like a giant snowball rolling and growing out of control. She called people forward, daring the devout to buy into her theatrics, calling her malarkey faith. A blind man accepted her invitation for getting religion.

As he watched the film unfold, Jeb suddenly got the gist of the whole preacher business. Jeb watched her staging, the way she seized the platform, lifted her arms, and addressed the crowd. He'd never got any of it until now. "Some of those folks, they really believe all that show and put on."

"That's the point. Religious people get bored. They want

entertainment. You know—a big show. But they'll pay a lot of dollars for it," said Angel.

He watched Barbara's temple go down in a fire. "Big show. All an act. I'll study on that," said Jeb. "Willie, here's another nickel. Go get me some more popcorn and some of that penny candy." He hadn't had any in years.

"*The Lord God planted a garden eastward in Eden; and there He put the man whom He had formed.* Now you say it." Angel, standing behind Jeb, handed him the Bible. "Hold it up and kind of out in front of you.

Jeb wet his lips with his tongue, stretched out his arms and said, "The Lord thy God—"

"Not 'thy' God. The Lord God planted a garden. Can't you remember that?"

"No, I can't remember it. No more than I can remember Fi-le-mon. I'm telling you I can't memorize all the Bible and sure-ly not none of it by Sunday. What is this story about anyway? Since when did God do some gardening?"

"The Garden of Eden. Don't tell me you never heard of it?" Angel removed the Bible from his hand.

"It's coming back to me. That's when the two naked people was running about naming the goats and horses."

"You got to learn to read."

"By Sunday? I told you this wasn't going to work, did I not?" Jeb checked the necktie at his throat. "Willie, if this is the way you going to tie this, I might as well wear it around my head." He loosened it, lifted it over his head, and threw it onto the kitchen table.

"I'm tired of making you understand religion," said Angel. "I'd rather read a magazine."

"You're tired because you don't understand it yourself. Willie, throw me back that tie." He pulled the whole length of necktie out of the knot and drew it around his collar. "Now, Angel, you read me back that garden thing again. I'll give it a whirl."

Angel read it once more.

Jeb took the Bible and held it up to the mirror. "The Lord God planted a garden eastward in Eden. Yes, He did." Jeb tried to imagine a heavenly glow lighting people's eyes and loosening their pocketbooks. "I'm telling it right. He didn't need no other to plant it. He planted it himself." He dropped his hand down and said, "I sound like Barbara Stanwyck?"

"When you say 'the Lord God,' lift both arms up beside your ears," said Angel. "If you're talking about the Son, arms out in front like you're about to hug your momma."

Jeb gave the words a singsong beat in his head. "And there he put the man that He had formed."

"He got it, didn't he, Angel?" Willie asked.

"Let me see." Angel rechecked the Scripture. "You said it right, Jeb. Maybe that's the only Scripture you ought to use. Just fill in the rest with all that other business, the a-has and hallelu-yers."

"Halley-loo-yah!" Jeb handed her back the Bible. "Give me another one. How many am I supposed to read?"

"You can learn another next week . . ." Angel walked in her bare feet around the kitchen table and turned the radio dial to the evening serials.

"Here, Willie, you read me another." Jeb extended the Bible to Willie.

"I can't read much more than you, Jeb. Angel, she's the one with the learning." He hurled out a yo-yo and it came back to him.

"I thought you was going to school just like your sister. Isn't that what you said to Miss Coulter?"

"I was in the same room. But nobody never keered that I learned. I guess I don't give a keer neither. I learned enough readin' to get by is all."

"Willie has trouble in his books," said Angel. "I tried to help him but he just gets mad at me."

Willie formed his tongue into a fold and jutted it out at her.

"Someone's here," said Angel. She padded to the front room, walking on the sides of her feet.

A face appeared in the door glass. "Hello, I hope I'm not disturbing you all."

"It's that Josie lady. Maybe she brought our dinner." Angel let her in. She took one step back, surprised. "Hi, Miss Coulter. Mrs. Hipps, you, too. Nice for you all to come by."

"Josie told me she was bringing by a dinner so I thought I'd drop by some books. Maybe you two older kids can help Ida May with her alphabet."

Jeb turned around with the Bible still in his hand. "Miss Coulter. Josie."

"Don't you look nice," Fern said. She wore a dress, pale blue and that made her eyes more definably blue.

"Willie can't teach me the alphabet," said Ida May.

Fern pursed her mouth, but didn't reply. But her eyes held a question for Willie.

"I'm not good at reading. My trot line's better than . . . than Daddy's, though."

Jeb felt his tongue touch the dry top of his mouth. "You think you can run a trot line better than your old man. Maybe so."

"I'm going to set this dish on your kitchen table. If you all will excuse me," said Josie.

"Let me show you something," said Fern. She seated herself

on the sofa and patted the cushion. Willie joined her. "Reverend, if you want, you can come see what we're doing. Maybe you can help Willie yourself."

Jeb, still in his sock feet, pressed his heels against the linoleum that had a floral print just like Victorian wallpaper. He sat on the other side of Fern. As she read to Willie, he noticed the curls in her hair were tighter, held in place by some women's concoction. He resisted the urge to place his fingers inside one of the curls and pull it just to see it spring back.

Willie's face tightened when she tried to coax him into repeating a phrase.

"You just say it back to her, Willie," said Jeb.

"Not actually. If he doesn't see the word as a whole and then read it, he's not really learning anything. It's not any different than a parrot mimicking the teacher. Willie, I'll bet you're oceans smarter than a parrot," said Fern.

"He ain't, though." Willie pointed at Jeb.

"Your daddy's a wise man, Willie. Here, Reverend Gracie. You try reading to Willie." She laid the book in Jeb's lap.

Jeb looked down at the pages that were peopled with a farmer, his wife, and a cat.

"Daddy can read better stuff than that." Angel slid across the linoleum. She laid the Bible on top of the picture book. "Go on, Daddy. Read to Willie."

Jeb felt for sure his tongue needed to be pried off the roof of his mouth. He wet his lips and said, "The Lord planted a garden eastward in Eden; and there he put the man whom he had formed."

"Supper's on the table and everyone come now while it's piping hot." Josie opened wide the kitchen door. "Fern, if you don't mind. I got to be shoving off. My four children will be bringing down the roof if I stay gone too long."

Fern lifted the Bible out of Jeb's lap, slid the picture book out and handed it to Willie. "You keep trying."

Jeb smelled her hair when she retrieved the book and it smelled like canned peaches.

Fern said to him, "Enjoy your dinner, Reverend."

"You can stay, can't you? Eat with us?" Jeb touched her arm when he said it. Her skin was warm.

"I brought Josie out here. I should go back now." She pulled a pale brown sweater around her shoulders.

"I could give you a ride back." Too late he remembered Bell, his transportation. "Well, if I had my truck back, I could give you a ride back." He made her laugh. "I guess Josie doesn't drive, what with Bill to drive her around town. Thanks for coming by, Miss Coulter. Josie, you too. I'll see that Willie sticks with his reading." He ignored the way Willie lifted his wide nostrils, doubtful.

Jeb followed the women outside. The moon had waned to a thin crescent, sharp and shining like a woman's earring. "Kind of dark out here. I'll walk you both to your car." He lit the lantern he left on the porch every evening when he sipped his gin. With his right arm up, he led them back to Fern's old Ford. "You got a nice set of wheels, Miss Coulter."

"I didn't want to say anything in front of your children, Reverend, but most of the adults, they call me Fern. I wouldn't be offended if you did, too." Fern stepped back while Jeb opened her door.

"Fern." He closed her door.

Her engine turned over, rattling like something in a cage, and then settled into a purr. "Oh, I guess I'll ask. You all have so much to think about on Sunday morning. Maybe it would be best if I came early to the parsonage and made breakfast for your children, helped them on with their outfits. Unless you think it's a bad idea. I don't want to offend Angel. She seems kind of territorial."

"Don't mind Biggest. She gets over things fast," said Jeb. He couldn't tell if the faint hint of emotion in her eyes was attraction or just the moon giving off benign airs.

"Sunday morning, then?" Fern drew back into the automobile. Her eyes dimmed in the shadow of her father's old car.

Jeb could no longer read her mind. He nodded.

She drove away and he waited for a long time under the pines and calculated how far away he could have been if he had left with Bell this morning. It seemed like a dream.

7

I never liked standing up in front of the other kids talking in school unless I made them laugh. Wonder if church people like it when you crack off a good joke?" Jeb retied the necktie, bothered by the faint pattern of yellow that trailed in and out of the blue checks like a kite tail.

"Our preacher wore a bow tie. Maybe you should, too." Angel pulled up the end of the tie. "I heard you talking way in the night. Sounded like you was preaching at the owls from the porch."

"Many times as I slept in on Sunday, I never figured I'd ever wake up with knots in my stomach. Sunday was the day you always eased into. I'd sit up and look out the window from the men's house—the place they put us ol' Texas boys who came in to pick cotton. The sun would just be coming up and I'd see a whole line of women. Young, pert little gals, walking over the hill in they best clothes." Jeb remembered the colors of the dresses and how the women had looked like butterflies chasing after field daisies. "Every Sunday I'd get up just to see the parade. Over the hill they walked in those black lace-up shoes, the only day they wore those tight-fitting shoes. By Monday, those feet would be back in ragged-heeled shoes that barely covered a girl's foot. But Sunday, they all looked like Hollywood gals."

"Now they're parading to hear you," said Angel, humorless to the point that her lips pursed together, scarcely pink at all.

Her comment made him nauseous—the thought of every eye on him, expectant. He coughed. "If I were to tell them I did this only to get a meal, that'd be a sight to see on their faces. It would. Something I'd tell my brother about later and both of us would laugh."

Angel's forehead formed a ridge above the inward corners of her brows. "You do that, and you'll be laughing from jail. That's a funny if I ever heard one. Ha-ha."

He rubbed his palms, the lifelines moist and the fatty pillow at the base of the thumb almost hot. "I don't know what to do with my hands." He raised his arms up beside his ears and then lowered them in front of him. Practicing in front of the mirror might help.

Ida May entered the room, her nightgown so long she appeared to move as liquid, minus feet.

Angel demonstrated for Jeb. She had an all-day sucker poised in the right corner of her mouth as though it plugged a leak. "Maybe that's not right. When our preacher said 'Heavenly Father,' he pointed up, I'm almost certain. When you talk about the Son, spread out both arms wide."

Jeb bowed his brilliantined head in front of the mirror, lifted it, his eyes gray in the morning light. He mouthed silent prayers, creating an act to match the text he had memorized on Saturday, and then finished each point with a gesture. Father—hands raised. Son—arms open wide. Holy Ghost—a locomotive churning of his arms. He added a body swivel that made his shoulders gyrate. "Fern had me cut my hair yesterday at the barber shop on Waddle Street. That girl, she knows how to take care of me. You know a haircut is twenty-five cents now, but the barber threw in a shave just because I'm a preacher. If we don't make a dime, this business sure as the dickens hasn't cost me anything."

"Fern Coulter has big eyes. Kind of makes you nervous if you catch her looking at you—kind of a staring-at-you-all-the-time thing she does. Pop-eyed looking." Angel sniffed the air. "Willie! I told you to check the biscuits!" She left Jeb to practice alone in front of the mirror.

He grasped the tie at the knot. "Nobody told me I had to wear a bow tie. Nothing wrong with this little deal. Ida May, get up off the floor and go find your clothes." He heard Fern's Chevy Coup idling outside. He yelled into the kitchen, "What do you mean, big eyes? I think you're jealous, Angel, and it is quite childish, too, if I might say so." He watched Fern through the window just as he had watched the young women from his bunk. She wore a slip-on style of shoe, not lace-up, and they had thick heels that made her ankles look thin. Her rayon stockings were the color of a young doe he had almost shot once in Texas—tan, gleaming in the sun. Not wanting to break the stillness of his uncle's wooded acreage with a shotgun blast, he'd shaken the tree where he had sat perched for an hour and watched the doe lift its hindquarters and disappear.

Fern's legs were the color of the doe. She moved toward the house and he watched her, the thick heels wobbling across the stones, her black handbag tucked under her arm so that she could manhandle a basket with both slender hands. Jeb opened his mouth, feeling a desire to create the necessary noise to scare her away, but then swallowed it.

Fern knocked against the parsonage door and he opened it, smiling. "Nice to see you, Fern." It surprised him to hear his own voice, the first hint of authority punctuating his syllables. He sounded fatherly, felt preacherly, and liked the manner in which she addressed him, as though she spoke up to him from down-the-hill while he, the Jim Dandy, exuded coolness high on a summit.

"Reverend, I hope I didn't come too early. You're dressed

already, I see. What about the children? Ida May, I'll bet she isn't dressed." Fern set everything she had gathered up in her arms on the sofa and ran her hands through her hair. The pin curls were softer than they'd been on Friday night and lay flat against her shoulders.

"Ida May is not dressed, as you say," said Jeb. "Willie is in the kitchen with Angel. Biggest is dressed, however, and I do consider that a miracle." He noticed how she sniffed the air, the aroma of charred bread, without commenting. "It could be that breakfast is burned."

"If I run in and make a fuss over the biscuits, Angel will think I'm interfering, won't she?" asked Fern.

Jeb found it kind of her to notice.

"I brought breakfast by, already made. I'll see if we can make things right for Angel's sake." She left the basket on the sofa and soft-footed her way into the kitchen.

Jeb followed her.

"I see you're already dressed, Angel. I had a lot of food left over from my breakfast. I thought you all might want to add to what you already have." Fern did not go all the way into the kitchen, but left a wide space between herself and Angel.

Angel covered the black bread with a cloth. "If you want to you can, but you don't have to."

"I'll just leave it on the table for you all to eat, then," said Fern. Two willowy arms appeared around her hips. "Morning, Ida May. I guess you want help on with your dress."

Ida May smiled.

"Ida May, why don't you eat first and then dress? I'll help you with those troublesome back buttons." Angel slid the biscuit pan behind a canister.

Ida May slipped her hand into Fern's and then she smiled unevenly, insecure.

"You have a wise sister," said Fern. "Eat first and then we'll help you dress." Fern stepped around Jeb and fetched the basket. "Ham biscuits. Fast and easy to eat. While you all have your breakfast, I'll do the kids' ironing."

"I insist that you join us," said Jeb.

Fern set four places around the kitchen table. "I've already eaten. If you don't mind, I'm going to open up the church. Greta Patton wants to come early and prepare the communion cups. It's been months since we had a decent communion. I figured you would want to do that today anyway."

"Communion?"

Angel made gestures behind Fern. All Jeb could equate to communion rang distantly Catholic in his memory.

"We do need to take the Lord's body and blood," said Angel. She continued making signs with her hand until Fern followed Jeb's bewildered gaze.

Angel clasped her hands beneath her chin.

"Does Church in the Dell have communion at the beginning of the service or the end?" Jeb strained to hear any glimmer of enlightenment about this ritual.

"The beginning of the service, usually after the hymns. You can do it whenever you want, Reverend Gracie. You're in charge." Fern tore off a piece of biscuit and stuffed it in her mouth, careful not to rake it over the dark red of her lipstick. "I'll go and iron those clothes for you all. If you want, Reverend Gracie, I'll stay here and bring the children into church a little later so you can go early, that is, if you don't mind letting Greta in."

If he repeated her one more time with a question in his voice, she would see through him.

"To pray. Go in early to pray. You always look so lost." She laughed but it didn't sound threatening or as though the facts about him had somehow rose up from the fear behind his eyes.

"I'll bet you'll be glad when you get settled in so you can take charge of church matters."

Ida May and Willie joined Angel at the kitchen table—Ida May with her dress open at the back. All of them looked up at him. Ida May finally said, "You ready to preach, Dud?"

"You look nice, Ida May, for a girl who calls her daddy Dud," said Fern.

"He's just Dud," said Ida May.

Jeb touched the Bible that lay open on a stand with the same forefinger that popped the top of the whiskey flask. He closed the cover and took it under his arm, the biggest Bible he had ever seen. The first one he had ever touched. Across the living room, out onto the porch, the holy writ took on a heaviness, so much so that by the time he reached the back door of the church, it felt heavier than a dead body. Jeb remembered then how Hank had looked sprawled out under the moon with blood trickling out his mouth. The Bible felt heavy, like Hank's body when he had hauled it into the barn to check him under lantern light. Ducks had scattered that night and fluttered out into the barnyard, honking harsh complaint at the strange goings-on at the Hampton place.

The key to the church door was equally weighty but Jeb could not allow anything else to weigh on him before he preached. By nine he wanted every little shackle lifted off so he could have a moment of peace; clarity so he could say what he had come to say. The shackle idea might be a good point to pass on and leave with the sinners in the pack, though. He'd save it.

"I say skip the whole communion idea and go for the throat, Jeb. Before you forget what it was you wanted to say." Angel knelt next to the parson's chair on the church platform. She murmured, "Fern Coulter don't have no right telling you your business. Do it your way and she'll have her old communion when we say it's time."

"So I just take the grape juice, say a prayer, give us a sip. Everybody else just does what I do? That's the way it goes?" Jeb felt small inside the coat jacket, less at home than in the shabby jacket that had accompanied him out of Texarkana. He shut his eyes and rehearsed communion once more.

A woman with a purse that looked like a doctor's bag seated herself at the organ bench.

"That's Doris Jolly, the momma of Josie, the lady who come over with Fern Coulter on Friday night," said Angel.

"I need to know this or something?" Jeb asked.

"Sure. That's part of what a preacher does, know who is who and which person is another person's momma. I'm going to go and sit down with Willie and Ida May. You screw up and we'll stand right up and holler that you made us do what you wanted."

"I appreciate your honesty, Angel. Like I appreciate a burr in my saddle. Beat it, will you?"

She drew her bottom lip into her mouth. "Remember, the organist is Doris Jolly, but you call her Sister. Sister Jolly." She alighted from the platform.

Doris peered out from behind the sheet music at Jeb. "I picked a favorite of mine and thought you would like it, Reverend." She played several chords and then opened her mouth to sing. Her voice squealed, squeezing up through her spacious nostrils before flushing wide into a maddening, shaky tone.

Jeb rose. "Everybody stand up. We're going to sing here with Sister." He leaned against the lectern, his crutch.

"*Sister Joll-eee,*" is what Angel tried to mouth, but Jeb felt his mouth go instantly dry. When he'd come to his feet, his right hand had lifted. The congregation had responded. Every person had joined him and came upright. The idea that he had brought them out of their chairs with a feeble hand gesture unsettled him. The room tilted. His fingers, white at the joints, trembled so much that he turned his hands palms up on top of his open Bible.

Doris gave the chorus her utter attention and played it twice. That relieved Jeb since it gave him another chance to mouth the words more convincingly the second time through. But when she sang the third verse of "Shall We Gather at the River" he finally lifted his face as though deep in meditation. He stood frozen, wanting the song to end so that he could speedily dispense with the blood and body of Christ, go straight for the throat of his sermon, so to speak, and then end with a benediction. But Doris found a fourth verse and the organ pedal seemed to be stuck in a hellish song gear, driving Doris to repeat the chorus several times.

His memory ebbed and all at once he could see his brother's face. Charlie had a patched-together look, a wide jaw with a sort of egg-shaped forehead that fit down into the broad bottom of his face. He smiled at Jeb while Doris filled the rafters with squawking. Then, as suddenly as if Jeb had told him a joke, Charlie laughed. Jeb's fingers went to his mouth and all at once all he could remember was a dirty joke he had told his brother late one night as they lay upon their bunk.

Doris finished all at once and the organ keys dwindled to a soft gurgle, a funeral processional. Every eye returned to Jeb. A few church members placed their hymnals in the pew backs while others waited to see if Doris might perchance take them off into the next song. Jeb turned to Doris and gave her a nod that she responded to better than he expected. She lifted her doctor's bag and joined her daughter, Josie, on the third pew to the right from the front.

The silence gave him no cues, nothing but the sound of an old man's cough. He closed his eyes and when he opened them, everyone in the room had bowed their head.

He found his cue. "Heavenly Father, bless this grape juice which we are about to partake, and know that it is a symbol of your Son's blood. But we promise you, it is not wine, which is evil."

An older woman with a neckless head fitted into her body said, "Amen!"

Several other women agreed by a nod. A flock of pillbox hats was in sudden motion, an ebbing tide from front to back.

"Is someone supposed to pass this communion business around to the people?" Jeb asked of no one in particular.

Several faces stared back at him stunned. Angel closed her eyes and looked down as though she could hear nothing at all that he said.

Jeb saw the trays of broken crackers and cups of juice on the table just below where he stood. "They's plenty for all. God wants all of you to know that this is for every one of you, and He has plenty in His heavenly pantry. There's no Depression on in heaven."

Everyone laughed and made shifting sounds. The neckless woman lifted her hands and applauded silently but observably as a sign of approval for Jeb. Finally, two men came to their feet and marched forward. Doris hustled back over to the organ. She played another wheezing hymn while the ushers doled out the communion emblems.

Angel leaned over Willie and said something to Ida May, her posture suddenly relaxed.

Jeb held up a cracker crumb between his thumb and forefinger. The church members parroted him. He closed his eyes but before he did, he saw Angel slip her emblem representing the body of Christ into her mouth as though she had done it many times before. She held her hand to her lips to hide her chewing.

Jeb completed communion. The funny joke he had told Charlie came back to him and the Scripture he had memorized just as quickly vanished from his thoughts. It occurred to him that Fern Coulter was searching through her handbag, although she would give him a glance and then return to rummaging. Other eyes started to wander. Willie, who had a talent for having the best face for a boy with not a thought in his head, drew up all at once and lifted his brows, his expectation infused with anxiety.

Jeb said, "God was just the finest kind of feller about agriculture. As a matter of fact, he invented farming." Jeb saw Angel sit up and wondered if she knew that this was his way of merely stalling, waiting for the Scripture to slip back in under the door of his blocked mind. He stared down at the open Bible to the place where Angel had read to him just a few moments before the first family traipsed inside. The lettering might have been Egyptian, a series of dots and dashes, spaces, rounded formations possessing the mysteries of the planet, of God. All at once, he recognized the first letter in the very spot that Angel had underlined. The crossbow shape of the letter made a ta sound, he thought. His eyes lifted enough to see Angel mouthing the first word while Fern looked on, curious.

The.

"The Lord God planted a garden eastward," he said.

Angel leaned her head back against the pew, the top of her mouth folding over her bottom lip.

Jeb finished the Scripture satisfied that all eyes had returned to the written text that lay in their laps. "Adam had it made, a garden that watered itself, no lack of food, plenty of livestock, the sky for his roof. He didn't have no Depression breathing down his neck. None of it was good enough for him."

Doris fanned her face and nodded. She conveyed the contented look of a woman not to blame for the fall of the whole human race.

The words from Jeb's sermon, which was really more of a ser monette, according to a redheaded bag of a woman, felt like a cold coming into his chest, the kind that starts as a cough and ends in bed with a fever of a hundred-and-two. Jeb had imagined himself differently. The least he could do if he were going to act as minister—or lie as minister—would be to churn out a pew scorcher of a message. But the comments afterward made him feel more like he did when his older brother had coaxed him into taking a turn at hitting the baseball one afternoon when a few farm boys played ball in a cow pasture. Charlie had all the luck with athletics and women. That was how he got engaged to a girl from Oklahoma.

Jeb had squeezed the bat, really a broom handle Charlie had filched from his mother's kitchen, thought hard about Babe Ruth, then whacked at the air. The broom handle catapulted across the field and clouted Guy Bonet, a boy who waited his turn up next at bat.

Jeb's discourse on Adam and the creation story affected no one but himself and, he thought, perhaps Fern, if only because she gave off the impression that she rooted for him. The last radio address Hoover gave, awful and stinking with worthless words, had contained nothing useable to anyone. Jeb thought his sermon was on par with Hoover's last radio message.

Angel collected funeral fans left behind on the pews into a

neat stack in her left hand. Jeb ignored the fact that she was ignoring him, most likely because the only thing that had kept her from standing up and screaming fraud in the middle of the morning message was the fact that Ida May's sudden infatuation with Fern Coulter distracted her. Two women now surrounded her, taking turns touching her hair and asking her if she looked like her mother, to which she replied, "Most likely."

Fern finished up a conversation with a mother worried about her boy's arithmetic skills and approached Jeb. "We picnic on the east side since the west is full of ancestors."

Jeb could not stop the dark thoughts battering him. He tried to look at Fern, but only succeeded in looking through her.

"Ancestors, as in cemetery. You know, that's where all the families here bury their departed kin." Fern explained it very well but kept looking at Jeb's eyes, as though she examined him for bad eyesight. "I see that lost look again. You did fine today, you know. I had an uncle who preached and my aunt said he spent every Sunday afternoon beating himself up over his morning sermon. Really, you got everyone's attention and in Nazareth that is a real accomplishment."

"I preached *fine*?" Jeb kept his arms crossed, his hands fingering his forearms agitatedly.

"Better than fine, then," said Fern.

"I stunk up the place." Jeb saw how Ida May held so tightly to Fern's dress hem, she twisted it into a knot. "Let go of Miss Coulter, Ida May!"

"She's fine, really. A little insecure, but maybe that's normal considering all of the change that's come into her life." Fern pried the floral fabric out of Ida May's grasp and slipped a pencil in its place. "Draw me a picture, why don't you?" She pulled out an old grocery store receipt and showed her the blank back of it.

When Jeb moved away, Fern followed him. "You might want to move on out to the church grounds for the festivities. The minister always starts off the three-legged races."

"That would be me," said Jeb.

Fern meandered toward the front doorway. "If you stand out there on the steps and shake hands, people really like it. But don't stay long. Meet me in five minutes out on the lawn and I'll hand you the whistle for the races." She walked away, a strange laugh fluttering out of her.

Jeb watched her make her way through the hungry people. He followed the blue dress until it disappeared.

A group of white-hairs parted to allow Jeb through as though instinctively aware that the minister should already be at the entry shaking hands. He strode nonchalant to the double doors that were flung wide open, the sawdust floor ripe in the summer sunlight. Several men tipped their hats and shook hands with Jeb while the wives proceeded to the automobiles to retrieve baskets and dishtowel-covered bowls.

Angel stationed herself across from him, her back against the doorjamb. All morning she had walked around with her arms folded against her chest and this was how she now stood, watching Jeb, his every word spoken to each church member. At times her gaze wandered out to watch the locals' children. She watched them as an observer, distant and detached, as though she had lived two decades longer than those children her own age.

A woman, familiar to Jeb, extended her hand. "I met you the other day downtown. I'm a friend of Josie's. My name is Florence Bernard. I lead a boys and girls Bible class at the schoolhouse on Saturdays. Some of them I teach reading as well." She had a habit of lifting her handkerchief to her mouth after every sentence, touching the cloth to the right corner of her mouth.

"Oh, I remember. I met you outside Fidel's Drugstore the other day. Nice to see you again, Mrs. Bernard," said Jeb.

"Reverend Gracie, I'm pleased and delighted to know we have a new minister. But you know, I should tell you something." She lowered her tone as though she spoke in complete confidence. "Adam really did not eat an apple." She dabbed her mouth again. "You know the Scriptures don't really say what kind of fruit."

"Thank you, Mrs. Bernard. Is there a Mr. Bernard?" He used the grip on her wrist to pull her gently past, aiming her toward the open churchyard where she could roam freely.

"Mr. Bernard got up in the night to visit the out building not eighteen months ago. He never came back." She lifted the handkerchief and dabbed her eyes.

Jeb saw the flicker of pain in her eyes, a dour light that diminished when her thoughts retreated to Mr. Bernard. "I'm sorry for your troubles. You got means, I hope?" He found he meant it.

"I teach a music class, piano, at the house I was born in. My daddy left it to me. I give permanents and manicures down at Faith Bottoms Beauty Shop. The Lord helps me make do."

"That and tutor children?" asked Jeb.

"I'd never charge for that. I try and give back to God rather than take." She excused herself to go and fetch an apple pie.

Will Honeysack stepped up and cupped Jeb under the elbow. "Brother Gracie, we best move you on out to start the relays."

"I'll be right there." Jeb stooped to pick up the Bible he had preached from but could not read. He wanted to throw it at Angel for the way she stared at him. "What are you looking at?"

"I'm just keeping my eye on things." Angel, with her hands

behind her, pushed herself away from the doorway and followed the remaining people out into the sunlight.

"Oh, and one more thing," he said.

She turned back around again.

The last family joined the picnic and he said, "That Mrs. Bernard, she knows a lot about Bible things. You got to tell me details of the matter, like Adam didn't eat no apple. Important things like that."

"I thought he ate it." She was indifferent about the whole apple thing.

"We got to get things straight, watch them little details like that or women like Bernard will go sniffing around in places we don't want them to go."

"You got a whole nuther Sunday to worry about it. I'm hungry. You preached past dinner almost, rambling around trying to talk about things you don't know nothing about. If anybody thinks you're a fake, it's your own fault for talking too much. Like you talk too much to Fern Coulter. She was asking us questions after you left this morning."

He pretended not to hear.

"What our momma was like. Stuff like that. I just talked about our real momma and Ida May started babbling like someone had opened the lid on her mouth. I had to do some explaining and saying how Ida May gets her thoughts mixed up. Then Miss Coulter wanted us to go and visit the schoolhouse on Monday. I don't know what to tell her. How long are we staying anyway?"

"You go along with her. If she wants to tour you through the Governor's Mansion, what harm is it?" Jeb heard the whistle blow. Fern had pulled her hair back in a scarf and changed her shoes. She bent over a group of boys, her arms stretched out lean and athletic as she explained the rules of the relay.

"Nothing wrong with letting Miss Coulter help you kids out with things. Maybe that's just part of my plan." The need to join her, take the whistle from her hand, and exercise a dash of preacherly influence over her surpassed his desire to stand on the steps arguing with Angel. He waved at Fern. "Let's get this show on the road."

8

D ivining was of the devil, plain and simple,
    Whether or not the Mississippi flood of 1927 had
sloshed into eastern Arkansas as far as Nazareth was unknown
to Angel. But when the banks had emptied into the rivulet,
some high waters at one point had deposited an old table along
the shallow embankments. The table had no sign of any paint
or stain to its finish, but had the textured feel of weathered
wood that had somehow preserved its integrity. Having seen
the value of a quiet place to lunch, someone had left a straw-
bottomed chair beside it. Scattered around it were wood shav-
ings, curled remains of a whittler's happy hour.

The sun obverted its five o'clock face enough to darken
the hardwood shadow of pine and oak along the creek and
caused to arise the notion that spirits dwelled along the fringes
of the cemetery. Angel gathered three customers under her
seer's wing, including two younger girls dressed in store-
bought linens—Bea and her cousin, Winnie. Their presence
attracted three more. Angel's pack was growing nicely. "I'll
show that Jeb how it's done," she muttered under her breath.
Ida May, who feared her sister's hushed tone and squinty eyes,
returned to the adults situated on blankets on the safe side of
the church and far away from the ancestors. Willie, never far

from Angel's lead, posted himself next to her, holy man number two. Twin girls from a large sharecropper's family, Marcella and Johnna Lundy, looked on, one girl with a shriveled profile that appeared cut from newspaper, the other, less loved and overfed, moved side-to-side in the shape of a tomato. They kept a safe distance.

"Levitation is a gift from God," Angel said. "Superfied, mystical, and beyond human imagination, levitation takes a lot of practice, to get things just so objects obey your words."

Arnell Ketcherside, sack-race winner, sniffed. "Words. Like you know any words."

"Words is power. Power is words. All of you, come and lay your hands on this table and I'll give you a taste of my powers." Angel seated herself in the straw chair with the seat bottom scarcely attached by rope.

The smell of rain, long dried up along the creek bank, was a rotting mash of dead tadpoles and sucked-dry algae. The riverbed's decay, along with the retreating light, conjoined with Angel's spell.

She coaxed the Lundy sisters back to the table. "Everyone put your hands on the tabletop, pinkies touching." When all of the children complied, Angel told them, "It doesn't work right unless someone has gotten a sign from the spirits."

The two girls from the wealthy families, Bea and Winnie, averted their eyes. Unbelievers.

Marcella, the tomato-shaped twin, inquired with a degree of meekness, "What kind of sign?"

"Dead cats. Stillborn calves. Don't you know nothing, Marcella?" Angel drew in a breath and blew it out as though impatience and her superiority had found agreement.

"I saw a dead rat out in the barn, its mouth froze open." Arnell's youngest brother, Roe, who spoke ear-splittingly loud, received a box to the ear by his oldest brother for complying with Angel's entreaty.

"You've got the idea. For this to work you all have to close your eyes while I conjure the soul of the rat."

When Arnell snapped to say how stupid they all were, the others shushed him until he stepped into the ring and joined pinkies between Willie and Roe.

Marcella whimpered like an infant whose face has slipped under the blanket, a muffled sound that Angel disregarded as the lament of a mollycoddle.

She made them close their eyes, but peered through her lashes, pressing the toes of her reclaimed leather church shoes against the ground. Her knees abutted the underpart of the table. Squeezing her thighs together, she poised her knees and said, "OH, TABLE! MOVE!" The table, pushed against the compacted ground, jerked. The tabletop vibrated and moved a good two inches from its original position.

Johnna, who possessed the physical ability to sprint faster than most of the boys, did so. Her shriek ignited Marcella, who lumbered several paces behind her, terrorized. Johnna latched onto the low limb of a tree, swung up, and disappeared into the summer-laced branches. Marcella wailed, unable to either latch onto the limb or hope that it could hold her. She waited on the ground, sobbing and angry that her twin had left her behind.

Willie stared after the twins, open-mouthed, until a laugh fluxed out of him. Deep and throaty, an unbridled honk of a laugh, it drew the laughter of the remainder standing around the table. All except for Roe Ketcherside, who stepped back, fingers lifted as though scorched.

Angel, believing no harm was done, pushed herself away from the table and said, "I guess I made believers out of you all. Who wants pie?"

The Lundys, dishonored by their own histrionics in plain sight of their peers, might never have admitted they had tampered with the devil. But Bea and Winnie, daughters of overindulgent mothers, ratted at once—first to their mothers, who did not know what to make of the minister's daughter, and then to Florence Bernard, who could be counted upon to expunge evil from the portals of the church. Arnell Ketcherside, when interrogated, made more of the fact that he did not believe the preacher's daughter possessed one bit of supernatural power in her smallest toe and insisted to every person who asked that he had not for one minute bought into her spiel.

Florence Bernard had bobby-pinned a scarf to her head while the corners hung freely down the sides of her face. When she inquired child-to-child in her search for Angel, the flaps blew back from her face like a nun's habit.

Angel had cut a square of coconut cake and laid it next to a triangle of chocolate cream pie when Florence found her. "Ma'am, what's wrong, ma'am?" she asked.

"You come with me."

Angel stuffed as much of the cake into her mouth as was humanly possible and walked six paces behind Florence. The story of her levitation feat had traveled person to person until every eye followed her to the picnic table where Jeb and Fern conversed. Jeb had loosened his tie. His sleeves were rolled up above his forearm and he sat with both elbows on the table, hands clasped, as he chatted with the schoolteacher.

"Reverend, your oldest has got a thing or two to tell you," said Florence.

Angel feigned interest in the boys' race across the church grounds.

Jeb turned his gaze on Angel, but his lips pursed, cagey, as though mistrustful of what might come from her mouth.

"It's just silly, that's all," said Angel. "We was playing a game. It didn't amount to nothing."

"Stuff and nonsense! They were messing with witchcraft, Reverend, not a hundred yards from the church steps." Florence was ashen.

"I lifted a table with my knees. It was nothing," said Angel.

Fern's head tilted to one side as she said, "Mrs. Bernard, how was Angel involved in witchcraft?"

"She claimed to be hexing a table down by Long's Creek. Sent the Lundy girls up a tree, and that little Roe Ketcherside, who already wallows in confusion, is practically mute." She addressed Angel. "Now I know you thought you was funning, girl, but you start messing around like that and next thing you know, you'll have the children all mesmerized. You get that stuff started and there will be no end to the beguiling. We'll not allow it in our families."

Jeb's brow lifted as though he did not understand the nature of the complaint.

"Reverend Gracie, you cannot allow these kinds of games. If the minister's children run amok, then every family in Nazareth will pay the price." Florence sounded troubled.

"Yes, I understand, ma'am. Angel, you go apologize to the Lundys and see if you can't get Roe to say a few words." Jeb turned back to face Fern.

"Shall I accompany Angel to remedy her predicament?" asked Florence.

Jeb nodded without making any further eye contact with Angel.

Angel walked in such a way as to put some distance between herself and Florence Bernard. She rinsed her coconut-frosted fingertips in Josie's water pail and then saw the Lundy twins gathered with a group of church children. She approached them in the manner of a grown woman. "I'm sorry I scared you with my table trick. It was a joke, if you didn't know."

"Of course we know. Anybody could tell you was a fake," said Johnna.

Angel turned away to seek out Roe Ketcherside. She found him seated beneath an oak tree making a clover necklace. "Roe, if I scared you a while ago, I am sorry." She waited for him to respond, but he only linked another clover inside the stem of another.

Roe still offered no hope that he had recovered from his bout with silence.

"If you forgive me, then just give me a nod," said Angel.

Roe's tongue could be followed inside the right side of his mouth. Finally, with his eyes scarcely widening to acknowledge her, he nodded.

"Roe, could you let us know that you are able to speak?" asked Florence.

A shudder went through Roe. It caused Angel to stamp her foot. "Stop it now, Roe. You know you're not beguiled. Let Mrs. Bernard know you can speak if you want."

Roe fell backward and rolled his eyes back in his head.

"Oh, for crying out loud!" said Florence. "He's fine as rain. I know a possessed person when I see him. Roe, you ought to be ashamed." She padded away, Angel presumed, in search of chocolate pie and time with the adults, and joined the widowed women, her scarf knotted tightly behind her head, chignon hived up in a whorl of piety all the while, chatting and pointing back at Angel.

The religious had their notions.

❊

Jeb cut the brown substance with the side of his fork. It had a crumbly texture, very brown, like dark-brown sugar mixed with cinnamon. He delivered the load to his mouth and tasted the sweet-yet-still-indistinguishable flavor on his tongue. "What is it?" he asked Fern.

"Shoo-fly pie. My mother's recipe."

It tasted like nothing to him, as though the main ingredient had been left out of the filling. The dryness of it had the texture of flour, sugar, something once moist and now dried to a crumbly filler. "I've heard of shoo-fly pie." His mother must have hated it, too; to the best of his remembrance, she had never made it.

The slice Fern had cut for him looked to be a quarter of the whole pie. If there had been others around them, he could engage in picnic chat, baseball, fishing, or any number of things to keep his attention from the shoo-fly pie.

But Fern had a focused alertness, intent on the action directly in front of her.

Jeb ate another bite.

"It's made with molasses," she said.

The bite of pie crumbled inside of his mouth. "I like your biscuits, too." He wanted to say something truthful.

"Our last minister studied at a small school out west. I wonder if you knew him. Reverend Guy Holmbeck?"

Jeb said, "I never knew him."

"I don't know of any schools for ministers, really, though. I work to help the students find placement in other subjects."

"You went to school where?"

Fern accepted the diversion. "Oklahoma, where I grew up. I remember the loneliness of the first year. I missed my mother terribly and only a hundred miles from home. I suppose it is easier for young men."

Jeb cut another bite of the pie but left it on the fork.

"When you went away to school, did you miss your family?"

Credentials had not come up before. Jeb could not recollect if his mother's preacher had ever mentioned where he had pursued his education. He decided that it should not be in Oklahoma, at any rate.

Fern waited.

He could not remember the question. "I studied in Texas."

"Your family is from Texas or you studied for the ministry in Texas?"

"Both."

"Mr. Mills, the banker, did his studies in Texas, too. I'm surprised you too have not crossed paths. Dallas is a big place, though."

"Missouri, that is. My family is from Texas. I went to school in Missouri." Jeb handed her the plate. "I could never eat all of this. Please, if you want, you can finish this for me."

"If I eat one more bite, I'll explode," she said.

He placed the plate on the tabletop.

"Who is your favorite writer? For the life of me, I can't detect the influence in your sermons." Fern took the plate and laid it to the side of the pie.

"I write my own sermons. No influence."

"Reverend Gracie, I did not mean to imply that you stole your messages. But listening to speeches, like the president, or to ministers, I play a sort of game. I listen for quotes or philosophies. You know, like Pascal or some of those other church fathers."

Jeb saw the children laying in the shade with their mothers while the men congregated in packs to discuss farming methods. "Everyone looks bored. I think I should start another relay race."

Before he could pick up the whistle, Fern laid her hand

atop his. "They aren't bored, Reverend Gracie. Just tired. They're enjoying the peace of the afternoon. Rouse those children now and you'll get the evil eye from some of the mothers."

"Tell me who your favorite author is, Fern."

"Walt Whitman for poetry. Several writers for novels."

"Why do you like Walt Whitman?"

"His passion."

Jeb nodded.

"You might explain his work better than I do. What is your favorite Whitman poem, Reverend Gracie?"

"All of them," said Jeb.

"You're right. How would one choose?"

Jeb shrugged.

"So true."

Jeb fixed his gaze upon a sycamore tree. He thought Angel walked underneath its spreading shade to take a rest from trouble, but instead she hid most of herself behind it except for her face, which occasionally appeared around the other side. With Fern's back to her, she lifted both hands and waved.

Fern quoted a line from Walt Whitman.

Angel mouthed silently to Jeb words he couldn't interpret.

Fern now talked of the birthplace of the poet. Jeb pressed both hands against the picnic table surface and stood. "I'm sorry, Fern. Angel is trying to tell me something."

Fern looked over her shoulder at Angel. "Come join us."

Angel's agitation showed on her face.

"I'll be right back," said Jeb.

Angel drew up her fist and covered her brow. "You're in for it, Jeb. We have to leave—now."

"Now is not good. Fern is talking about Walt Whitman and slowly finishing off my shoo-fly pie." He smiled in Fern's direction. "I don't care for any of it but I'd like to watch her eat it."

"You know why everyone is still hanging out around the church, why the Lundys haven't started the walk home? Well, they just told me. 'Cause you got round two of preaching to go, that's why."

"Make sense, Angel."

"It's called the evening service. They're all waiting for you to ring the church bell and call them all inside."

The Mills had packed away their picnic inside the Buick Master. They joined Will and Freda Honeysack on the lawn. Several mothers combed grass from their offsprings' hair.

"How much time do we have?" Jeb asked.

"Fifteen minutes if we start five minutes late like we did this morning."

"Two messages on Sunday? That is surplus preaching, if you ask me. They're still digesting what I give them this morning."

Mellie Fogarty strolled past while removing her large sunbonnet. "Looking forward to this evening's message, Reverend Gracie."

Jeb watched her meander around three restless youths and chat it up with two women on the way inside the church. "We're sunk."

"We are for a fact."

Jeb had practiced for three days straight to memorize the Scripture about Adam and the garden. He had no time to remember a whole new passage. Angel coached him, saying over and over some verse her Granny taught her. But then she thought maybe it wasn't a Bible verse at all, just something that got told from one person to the next. "Don't tell them where to find this Bible verse or they'll be on to you for sure."

Jeb dragged Angel up to the church even though it caused the lingering families to set off behind them and fill up the pews. "I don't get what you're saying, Angel," he said.

"It's the only one I can come up with. Is it my fault you can't read?"

Fern had Ida May's hand. She settled her on the front row.

Willie ran in with his shirttail out and a dirty ridge of sweat across his brow. He took the back pew next to the Ketchersides, next to boys with grassy knees, although Mrs. Ketcherside was quick to sit in front of them and toss a warning glare.

Jeb said to Angel, "But I don't know why he did it. I don't get it."

"Same as why anyone else would. I have to sit down, Jeb. Everyone is staring."

With one hand, Jeb hefted the Bible and laid it on the lectern. He bowed his head and heard the corresponding shuffle across the sawdust floor. "Bless what I am about to say, O, God. O, God."

Ida May had already fallen asleep right in Fern Coulter's lap. Jeb wished for the same weariness to settle across the entire congregation, a sleeping sickness that would cause the heads to loll, fall back, and drop forward so he could quietly pad away. "They's a story about a friend, a good buddy of Jesus himself who got himself very sick. By the time word spread to the Lord about his friend, his good buddy had already kicked the bucket. So to speak. Now they's a lot of things that the Lord could have done. Something big he was about to do, in spite of the fact they all thought it was too late to ask anything of God," Jeb said. "But first thing's first. When Jesus came a-walking, walking he did, up to the tomb of his buddy, Lazarus, he was met by the old boy's sister. When she told Jesus Lazarus had gone belly up, the Good Book says, 'Jesus wept.'"

Angel's shoulders lifted and relief spread across her face.

"Why, people ask, would the Son of God have himself a good cry? He knew he had the power in his own two hands . . ." Jeb held up his hands in a vertical claw. ". . . to impress them all with a miracle. And that he was about to do. But first, Jesus wept."

Florence Bernard had a curious gleam, as though the twilight outside were coming straight in through her eyes.

"Because in spite of the bigness of God, he knows how all of us feel. When we smile, he smiles. When we laugh, he laughs. Where you think the good rain comes from so your crops'll come in? Got to be what happens when God is giddy. But when we cry, he cries, too.

"I was having a terrible day once. Well, not once. Many terrible days this old boy has seen. But on this day my mother had passed from this life. She was a lovely daffodil of a lady, my mother. I know of no sweet smell like that of a mother."

All of the women smiled at one another.

"Not just the way they fill the whole house up with the smell of cornbread, fellers. No, I'm talking about the smell that only a woman has, that aroma of love she has for an ornery boy. It is the smell of a distant sunrise on the lake just when the fish are biting. You know that smell, men. So when your mother passes from you, that aroma is gone. The cornbread skillet is cold and empty."

"The fish stop biting," said Horace Mills. He blew his nose.

"But it occurred to me when I read this Scripture that when I'd felt so sad, the worst day I ever knew, when my mother was carried away by the angels, God cried with ol' Gracie. I was not alone."

Florence, forced to dig through her handbag for a dry handkerchief, wiped her wet cheeks with the back of her hand.

"Sister Jolly, I feel the Spirit. If you would, I know we have an order to things, but if you could oblige us, would you play that song you played this morning? I kind of liked it." Jeb thought about what he had just said, part of it feeling serenely right and another part a stench in the heavenlies. "Jesus wept," he said again. "Let's all sing,"

9

Jeb did not sleep well between Sunday night and Saturday night for the next three weeks. The blanket on his bed somehow always wound up on the floor and he woke up uncovered. The pressure to memorize stuck in his head usually just before he got out of bed and remained until sundown. Every night.

On Sunday afternoon he paced down by the stream behind the parsonage and lost all interest in fishing or checking his trotline. He recalled and then analyzed the Sunday faces of that morning and always noticed if someone drifted from the message. The bored ones worried him since they were the church members who might sit picking apart why his preaching was no good. For drifting minds might ask questions such as "Why does this preacher only preach from one small text every Sunday?" Or even "Why doesn't he seem to have a preacher's history, all of his stories haling from the cotton patch?" Or in the case of the greater minds, such as Fern had been endowed with, "Why did he never correlate his message with what she called a church father, quoting Pascal?" Or that other guy she gushed about.

Jeb had gotten his schooling in the field. Mentored by sky and lake, he'd never thought of preparing for the next decade or equipping himself with learnedness. He had lived to eat and

have a good smoke, and not having the latter was on him like a
vengeance. The world continued its turn around the universe
while the rest of the country broke its back upon the plow. The
plow handles were his future, he thought. Someday he would
get himself a piece of land. He had looked at it from every
angle. He envisioned how he might turn the soil with the use
of a good blade, finish his day with a smoke and satisfaction.
But a lesser vision had kept him back in another man's cotton
field. It was the crossing over from one life to the next that
bewildered him. Getting to the other side with his name on the
deed was the hardest piece to unravel.

Fern had a whole cockeyed view that he could not decipher,
either. Whereas he pondered how he might get the next meal
ticket, she wondered how she might feed the world.

Six trout glistened on the line. Their tails waved gently
now, soft and agile, but earlier on, each shining fish must have
put up a fight. Over the hours the hook had weakened their
resolve. One large fish with passionless eyes opened its gaping
mouth, slow, slow, fast. Its fins moved only with the current,
translucent wings beneath the surface, subservient to another
will. One glistening moment the trout hunted the next meal.
The next, it became the meal.

Jeb wanted to ask Fern about the whole idea of a man
hooked by his circumstances. But he liked her assumption of
him that he had deeper thoughts. But if he asked her, she would
see him as plainly ignorant. He could not let that happen. Nor
could he give up her image of him even if it meant never
obtaining legitimacy. Her respect for him had fed the new
image he'd gotten of himself in the mirror. For a moment, he
could almost smell his soul rotting.

He left the stringer of fish in the stream as though to do so
might mend his hypocrisy.

*

Inside, Angel paraded in an old borrowed dress in the kitchen, dissatisfied with it, but not unhappy enough to change out of it. Mellie Fogarty had loaned a box of clothes to the girls if they promised to return anything they would not use. The idea of returning anything was what caused Angel to find use for every article in the box.

Ida May walked out of their room in a dress two sizes too big. She flopped the sleeves that fell over her fingertips. "This'd fit you, Angel."

"Ida May, you will grow into this in six months. Put it in the closet and you'll be glad you have it later." She watched over her sister unhappily.

Ida May stripped out of the dress and left it on the floor.

"You act like the bless-me bird is going to just fly in here with a box of clothes every other week. It don't work like that."

Ida May, enjoying her shirtless folly, made checkers out of Coke bottle tops. "I don't want to try on clothes, Angel. I want to play."

"Jeb, tell Ida May she has to do as I say," said Angel.

Without a cigarette to his name, Jeb rifled through every kitchen drawer. If he found so much as a butt, he would take a drag on it. "Any of you kids seen the matches?"

"The preacher can't smoke nor drink, Jeb. If anyone sees you, you may as well take yourself down to the jail and lock yourself inside." Angel held up one last dress in front of Ida May.

"If they'll let me have a smoke in jail, I'll go willingly." He slammed a drawer shut. "Not a match, not a smoke in the whole joint." He had stolen a pack from Honeysack's when the clerk wasn't looking and tucked it, he thought, into a drawer. "It's like someone came in and robbed me of my smokes. Now who did it?"

Angel folded up the last dress and shuffled off the heeled dress shoes, the long shoes too wide for her slender tomboy feet.

"If you know anything about the sudden disappearance of my personal belongings, you'd do best to speak up," said Jeb.

"You'd never catch me touching your old things," said Angel. "The way you light up one right after the other down by the fish stream, it is no wonder you eventually ran out."

"I'd better not find out differently," Jeb thought he saw a pinch of tobacco in the corner of a drawer but it was nothing but crumbled bread crust.

"Other people go buy their personal things at the store. If you need something, just go down and buy it. Better'n pacing around me like a cat," said Angel.

"You know I can't."

"Don't bother me with it, then, like I did it to you. Nobody is out to get you, Jeb Nubey." Angel had Willie grab the other side of the clothing cast-offs box. "Let's take it to our room, where it's quieter."

She and Willie disappeared.

Ida May gathered the Coke bottle lids into her hands and ran with the load to follow Angel and Willie. Dropped lids made a trail all the way into the children's bedroom.

Jeb's mother once said that Charlie was given to tantrums, but Jeb was given patience. But the very idea that he could not get a smoke whenever he pleased raised up the soul of Charlie inside of him. For an instant, he felt like him. "Is it too much to ask that I'm allowed a pack of smokes?" During the tirade, his voice rose into the loft and bellowed down into the root cellar. "I think there is a funny joke going on here but it ain't funny to me!"

Angel hollered at the exact moment she slammed the bedroom door. "Stop yelling!"

"If I don't get smokes here in the shake of a stick, I'll tear this place apart looking for them!" He picked up a kitchen chair, thought about throwing it, but then just allowed it to fall back, enough to make a nice slamming bang against the wooden floor.

Angel had stopped yelling.

"Next thing you know, you'll be hiding my liquor. Then my poker cards. There'll be no end in sight!"

"Nobody has your pack of cigarettes or your gin! We don't have your poker cards, neither, and who would you ask into a game anyway?"

"I tell you what you'll do! You take this money in my pocket on down to Honeysack's grocery and you bring me back a new pack of smokes! Anything else I want, you get that, too!"

"Reverend Gracie?"

The face pressed against the screen door was too dark to render precisely. Jeb only knew the voice to be feminine.

"I'm sorry if this is a bad time. Miss Coulter said the children might need help with some school things. I have a few extras I keep around if you all could use them."

It was Florence Bernard. If she'd heard his ranting diatribe, her polite nature would not allow her to say anything.

"Mrs. Bernard! Now is fine, just fine," Jeb lied.

She waited outside with a shoebox.

Jeb's feet were frozen to the floor as if she would just leave the box out on the porch if he made no move toward her.

"I don't have to come inside," she said.

"No, no, where are my manners, Mrs. Bernard? I'm sorry as sorry can be! Come inside." After Jeb opened the door for her, he called out to the children.

Only Angel emerged. She had a sour face and wore another of Mellie Fogarty's hand-me-downs, a pleated dress the color of pickles and at least one size too large.

"Don't you look all grown up?" Florence made no comment on the oversized dress, no more than she addressed Jeb's ranting about smokes and liquor.

"None of them fit. But I have to wear them or give them back to Mrs. Fogarty." Angel did not address Jeb. Only Florence. "My mother sewed like everything, but I never had the chance to pick up her skills."

"I sew, too. You want me to fit that dress to your frame, I'll do it. If you have some other things, I'll alter them for you. It doesn't take long and I have the time before school starts."

Angel's body stretched from the toes up to her shoulders. She expelled the elation and said, "I'd really be grateful."

Florence told her, "We'll have at least a few of your things ready in time for school. Only two weeks left. Now you take this box of pencils and paper to your brother and divide it with him."

"I will. Thank you," said Angel.

"You got some pins; I'll start with this green dress if you like it."

"Mrs. Bernard, you've done so much, I hate to impose," said Jeb.

Angel said to Florence, "I'll get the pins, ma'am."

"Pleats are a specialty of mine. You'll need a good pair of stockings to set that off." Florence called out to her. "But I don't know what to tell her about shoes. I'm never clever about picking out children's shoes." A bit of reticence settled in Florence's voice.

"The girl has a pair of shoes," Jeb interjected. "If this isn't a good time, you can do this later. I feel as though I've interrupted your whole day."

"Actually, Reverend, it is I who have interrupted you."

Jeb could not prove the insinuation in her tone. She kept

her back to him the entire time she spoke with Angel. But he felt the heat of what she didn't say.

He excused himself and wandered out onto the porch. Angel and Florence could be heard exchanging polite girl banter. Florence commented upon how Angel should not allow such a small matter to distress her.

Angel's reply could have been directed at him or not. "One day I'll be good as you, Mrs. Bernard, at not allowing petty things to get the best of me."

Jeb chopped wood even though the night was warm. The very act of aggression against an inert object eased his tobacco jitters. Angel braided Ida May's hair on the front porch and sipped orangeade. She pretended, as she had all day, not to see him.

"You act like this scam is all me when most of it is you. I been watching how you sit in the middle of the church ladies with your orphaned face."

"The things I say about my mother are all true." Angel twisted her sister's shoulders three quarters to the right.

"But what they believe is a lie. When they find out about me, you're the one they'll hate. Ida May, well, they'll believe she just did as she was told. Willie, he's a boy, and most boys lie. But you've painted yourself as the near-grown motherless orphan they all dote over. Don't think they won't find a punishment for you, too."

"I didn't haul off in front of Florence Bernard and throw a fit, foaming at the mouth like a mad dog for a cigarette. If they find out your nasty secret, it won't be me they blame."

"This is like waking up and finding out you're someplace you know you wasn't at when you went to bed. Am I hearing you right? Wasn't it you that begged me to go along with your plan? Best as I remember, you even called it that—your plan. *Just for the night, Jeb. Then, just one more day.* Now look at me, I'm the Big Preacher Boy now!" He made a brazen motion in front of him with the ax, a figure eight. "Charlie, he'd laugh a big one if he saw me behind that pulpit with my shiny tie. Might even give me credit for the best little hidey-hole this side of Texarkana. But I can't take credit for it. You know why? Because I give you every bit of the credit." He leaned over the porch railing and pointed at Angel with the ax blade. "You, Biggest."

"You just keep flapping that big mouth of yours, Jeb, and let Miss Coulter know who you really are. Here she comes right now in that old car of hers. Maybe she'd like to hear what else you got to say, like what Mrs. Bernard heard this morning."

Fern's Chevy Coup motored down the dirty lane toward them.

Angel continued to rant, "Or maybe she's already heard from Mrs. Bernard. Maybe the whole town knows. Church in the Dell has itself a tobacco-addicted preacher. Maybe they'll just call you Smoky Joe."

"Quiet!" Jeb told her.

"Fires of hell, Jeb. That's what you smell like!"

Before Fern could open her door, Jeb met her and helped her out. "Fern, glad you could drop by."

"Reverend Gracie, I wanted you to know that I'm having trouble locating the children's last teacher. Here's the letter I got today," said Fern.

Jeb pretended to read the letter. He thought of coaxing Angel off the porch, pretending he needed glasses. But Angel, he figured, would not cooperate. "Let me know what I can do to help, Fern."

"Maybe if you used the phone up at Honeysack's store? He'd let you. Call this number here." She circled the telephone number at the top of the school's stationary. "Let them know you're the children's father and ask for these three things." She pointed to three lines of cryptic language. "They don't have to have it to start school but it would help me out to know a few things about their schooling."

"I'll do my best," he said.

"What are the three things we need, Daddy?" Angel asked.

Fern turned the paper around. "Your grades mostly. At what level you last tested at. And any letters from your teachers. It helps to track your progress."

Jeb blew out a breath.

"It's like the letter says, they don't remember your children at all."

Willie ran around the house, no shirt, just overalls and a streamer of fish trailing behind.

"Reverend Gracie, I'll bet you can clean those fish, can't you?" Fern asked.

"Like a thousand before them."

"I can't clean them, but I can cook them. Angel, you all have cornmeal and salt?"

"Last time I checked, yes," Angel answered her.

Jeb remembered the shoo-fly pie. "You don't have to cook for us again, Fern."

"I insist. Ida May, you go get some shoes on. The ground is getting chilly with dew." Fern disappeared into the house.

"If I didn't know better, I'd say you aren't wild about Miss Coulter's cooking," said Angel.

Jeb knew better than to answer.

❊

The biggest trout, too big to be pan fried, had lain tail out of the pan, coated in cornmeal and seasonings but not touching the grease. The other pieces had cut up nicely. But Fern, in an effort to have at least one whole trout laying wall-eyed on the plate and festive, had left it whole. When Jeb cut into the middle, the insides were still pink and moist. He forked a smaller, crispy piece onto his plate and said, "It sure smells good."

While Fern walked around child-to-child, adding potatoes and cornbread to their plates, he choked down as much as he could, careful for the bones and remembering the simplicity of trout cooked along a streambed. Maybe it was the rushing stream, the spray of fresh water in the air that made the trout taste better. Fern's recipe tasted sooty, like the bottom of the skillet. He doused everything in ketchup and drizzled the fish with extra salt. All the while he lamented over the waste of a good trout. He wanted to apologize to the largest fish, repent of it having made its way onto his hook. He poured on more ketchup to atone.

But he liked the cornbread and the way Fern looked when she served it, slender and round and bent over the table, nurturing and faintly smelling of whatever perfume she had sprayed on that morning.

"Ida May tells me that every night Angel reads the Bible to her daddy," said Fern.

Jeb drew in his bottom lip, did not look either at Ida May or Angel, and said, "Yes, it's a tradition."

"I don't want to interfere in your family customs, but if it's all right, I'd like to stay and listen."

Angel, with her fingers tugging at her earlobe, prepared to offer up a defense, but Jeb interjected before she made a lame excuse. "Sure, Fern. Please join us."

With the front door still open and the screen door the only barrier between the parlor and the outdoors, the crickets started a song that set all of the forest in motion. Owls, katydids, toads, all in a ruckus. Willie sat on the floor cross-legged and listened to the night music while Angel read.

"This is from the book of John," she said. "'Abide in Me, and I in you. As the branch cannot bear fruit of itself, unless it abides in the vine, neither can you, unless you abide in Me. I am the vine, you are the branches. He who abides in Me, and I in him, bears much fruit; for without Me you can do nothing.'"

"You have a nice reading voice," said Fern. "Willie, you want to tell us what your sister just read about?"

"Vines and branches. Growing grapes, I figger."

Jeb figured on how to get Angel up and Fern seated closer to him.

"The vine is Christ. We are the branches. We can't bear fruit unless we are attached to him." Fern explained it but Willie did not get any of it.

"I wish I could make fruit. I'd make lemons and then make lemonade. We never buy lemons. How much could they be?" Willie asked. "Arnell Ketcherside's mother always has lemonade waiting for him when he gets home from school."

"Willie, you're off the track now, son," said Jeb. When he tapped the back of the sofa, his intention was to make a point with Willie. But his finger touched the back of Fern's hair, soft, blond circular strands. He left his hand on the back of the couch.

Fern said to Jeb, "Maybe you can explain it better than me, Reverend Gracie. How do you all do this? Read a bit and then explain?"

Willie piped up, just as though for once he knew the answer. "Angel reads a Bible verse over and over until I'm about ready to scream, then *Daddy*, here, says it back to her."

Jeb took the Bible from Angel and closed it up. "You explained it well, Fern. We probably need you over more often, what with you being a teacher. I'll bet your explanation is more on their level. More for children. I probably talk way over their heads."

Angel watched him lift the Bible over her head. She dropped her hands in her lap and sighed.

Fern said her good nights and walked more slowly toward the Chevy. "Any more news about your truck, Reverend?"

Jeb pressed his lips together and shook his head.

"I hate to see you all riding back and forth to town in that wagon. I had to explain to one lady it had nothing to do with your religion. Funny how rumors can spread. If I didn't have to have mine every day for school really soon, I'd just let you drive the Chevy."

"Please, we're doing fine. You already do so much, Fern. I feel guilty about all you do." Jeb saw Angel waiting at the screen door. She opened it and came out onto the porch. Her habit was to call out to him if he got as much as six inches from Fern. But this time she just watched. "Good night, and thanks for the fried fish," said Jeb.

"Anytime. I don't know how much I should come over here. Or if I should. You never say if you need anything. Or if you need for me to drop by."

"You're always welcome." When she turned, Jeb thought he saw the faint hint of disappointment. He wanted to take back whatever had caused her brows to sag. But she climbed inside the Chevy and started the engine.

As Fern drove away, Jeb listened to the sounds of croaking and hooting, which made as much sense as a woman's thousand-and-one shadowed signals.

He heard Angel call out to him, "You're such a goof, Jeb Nubey!" Then the screen door slammed behind her.

10

Here you are settling into this place when you should at least try to find your sister Claudia. Look at you with your schoolbooks in hand, ribbon in your hair. It's a fine kettle we got us, that's what!" Jeb held a letter in his hand, the envelope addressed to Church in the Dell, the contents from Reverend Philemon Gracie. According to what Angel read, the minister had extended his stay in Tennessee.

"That's not bad news. It's good, Jeb." Angel checked the green pleated dress in front of the mirror. "That Mrs. Bernard has a very good hand at sewing. You'd never know this once fit Mellie Fogarty's big niece Hester."

"Extended means nothing but that—that the preacher is going to come sooner or later. We're living in a fool's paradise, Baby, and it goes downhill from here on out." Jeb tucked the letter inside his shirt, drew it out, and then searched the parlor for a hiding place. But every nook and cranny looked to be obvious and a place that might tell tales.

"I like it here, Jeb. Don't you?" Angel asked. She never took her eyes off the mirror, but smoothed her dress with her right hand. Her books, given to her by Fern, she cradled in her other arm.

"Sure, I like lying to everyone I meet, knowing any minute I'm going to blurt out my own name and then go to jail for it.

I especially like waking up in the middle of the night in a cold sweat because in my dreams I see the barrel of a rifle aimed at my head. This is a fine life we have us!" Jeb paced, an angry strut, his hands behind him. "We all just chums, ain't we? Happy people hanging off the side of a cliff by our fangernails."

Angel retrieved the letter. She read it once more and said, "The preacher is in Tennessee, the ever-loving Appalachian Mountains, for Pete's sake! No way is he about to just tool on into town. You know where the Appalachian Mountains are, don't you?"

Jeb said, "I have heard of the place."

"Clear up in Canada, Jeb!" She tugged her ear. "It could be a year before he makes it this far. This feller, he is preaching his way all the way down the whole map of America." The ribbon tied around Angel's head slipped. She laid her books on the floor and readjusted it to make a headband. "Willie, if you don't come right this minute, you can walk to school alone!"

Ida May came in through the kitchen, crying.

"Now what's wrong?" Angel pinned the green ribbon behind her ears with hairpins.

"I tried to go pee-pee without you. But I can't," said Ida May. "You'll be gone all day and then what?"

Explode, Jeb thought.

Angel told her, "Ida May, you won't go when I'm with you, let alone when I'm not. Go and try again. I promise I won't leave for school until you do."

Ida May shuffled back through the kitchen. Her fingers clenched a doll by a few black wisps of hair.

Jeb took the letter from Angel. It occurred to him that she could tell him anything her lying lips wished to convey. He pointed to the first letter of the salutation. "What's that letter there?"

"D."

"And that one?"

"E, for heavens' sake!"

"That one, and that one?"

"A, R. Read it, Jeb."

"Dee. Are. That don't make sense."

"*Dear*, Jeb. It's how a person starts a letter. This is to Mr. Honeysack, the head deacon. *Dear Brother Honeysack.* I already read this to you. We have to leave for school."

"Wonder why Gracie didn't just mail this to Honeysack himself? That don't make sense, does it?"

"Maybe because it says 'Dear Brother Honeysack and the Congregation of Church in the Dell.' The letter's to everyone in the whole church, so he mailed it to the church."

"You realize how close we come to getting found out? Honeysack collects the mail for everyone in town and gives it to them when they come in to his store. He could have opened this, but instead he handed it to me himself. Wonder why he didn't open it?"

Angel looked at the envelope again. "It just says Church in the Dell. That means all church mail goes to you, Reverend Gracie."

Jeb tapped the table near the mirror. "This is what I mean. Every day I come within inches of calamity. Nipping at my heels, breathing down my neck."

"Willie, we're about to be late," said Angel.

Willie hefted a load of books to the door. "I hate this. Now Miss Coulter knows I can't read—well, compared to Jeb, I can read—but she's been after me ever since. A woman like her can make my life a livin' hell."

"No more skating through school, Willie," said Angel.

"Ida May's not back from the outhouse," said Jeb.

"If we don't leave now, we'll not make the bell. Willie, let's go." Angel handed a book to Jeb. "This is Ida May's ABC's. Study it, if you want."

Angel and Willie arrived just as the school bell rang.

The lone school building housed all of the educational rooms for every child in the hamlet of Nazareth. Fourth grade up to eighth grade studied in the same hall, while the younger children applied their attention to the basics of learning in a rear quadrant. High school students studied together in a drafty hall of a room, a few intent on college entrance exams, while the rest dreamed up ways to check out of school, never to return. The entire schoolhouse possessed the similarly boxed shape of the row houses that dotted the path into the schoolyard, bearing a hipped roof and windows so small the school appeared to squint in the sunlight.

Angel told Willie to count his pencils. As he did so, she checked his mustard-and-salt-pork sandwich, rolled it back up in tinfoil, and handed it to him. "Watch your things. I can't look over my shoulder all the time to see you haven't forgotten anything."

"I feel like a fool going in that younger class," said Willie.

"Miss Coulter says you'll get caught up if you'll work at it. Then you can move into my class. Act like the preacher's son and they'll treat you with respect." Angel enjoyed the new identity to a certain extent, the gifts given to them, however used they might be, and the occasional free pullet for the cook's pot. While she cried herself to sleep at night languishing for her mother, she hoped for the best of both worlds—her mother here in Nazareth with the trappings of being a Gracie. The simplified solution kept throwing itself upon the rocks of reality. "We have to make ourselves better people, Willie, while the gettin's good."

"We ain't better. We're just liars," said Willie.

"You got it all wrong. God put us in this place so we can climb out of the mud, away from Nubeys and no-account uncles."

"Maybe we're no-account, Angel."

"I woke myself up the morning Daddy came in and said he was sending us off to Claudia's. I knew right then that God had a special plan for my life, just like Granny always told me." Angel had never shared that with anyone.

"You're bananas."

"Listen, we know we can't stay here forever unless God wills it. That letter from Philemon Gracie, it said he was delayed. What if God did that to give us extra time? Next few weeks we get another letter. He's had another delay, maybe a year. Maybe more. That gives us time to make ourselves better. Like people who grow up and go off to college."

"You give me salt pork in a biscuit again. I am turning into a salt lick," said Willie.

"At the lunch bell, you meet me out on the school grounds with your books. We're going to get you caught up. This whole idea of being a Gracie, it's for a reason."

"I know. You lied."

"Meet me at lunch." Angel found her classroom, a room full of hand-nailed desks with mismatched shaky-legged chairs scooted up beneath them. Miss Coulter called the class to order and took roll. When she said, "Angel Gracie," Angel's hand flew up. "That's me. I'm her!" It felt odd to be so familiar already with the teacher.

Fern introduced her to the class, although she had met most of the students at church. "Students, we have a new family in Nazareth. Please say hello to Reverend Gracie's daughter, Angel."

Angel heard her name as a chorus.

❊

"Ida May, don't you think it's about time you come out of the outhouse?" Jeb still had the alphabet book in his hands. "Come out and read a little bit to me."

The outhouse door opened with a long rusted-hinge squeal. "Why, Dud? You can't read back to me."

"You finish your business or not?" Jeb asked, although he did not look her in the eye.

"All by myself."

"That's good. You did good. Let's sit under this tree and you tell me the letters, how about?"

"I don't have to go to school yet," said Ida May.

"If you go and you're the only one that don't know her ABC's, how will that feel?"

She didn't answer.

"Get your hind-end over here."

Her pace, languidly slow, finally brought her under the tree next to him.

He opened the picture book. "This here letter is A. Is that right?"

Ida May nodded and said, "It makes either ah sound or ay."

"No kidding? How you figger out the difference?"

Ida May shrugged.

"Well, then, we have us a dilemma. I see all these words beginning with A. How we going to know how to say them?" He hoped her shrug was only a sign of shyness and not ignorance of the letter A.

Ida May ran her finger over the first word. "Apple. That word is 'apple.'"

"I'll bet you're right," said Jeb. "It looks like it would be apple. But you reckon it's because they put a picture of a big red apple on the page that you figured that one out?"

Ida May laughed through her nose.

"Try the next one."

Her chest lifted. She sounded the vowels and consonants as a whisper.

"I can't hear you, Littlest," he said.

"An . . . duh. 'And.'"

"Kind of like, me *and* you are sitting here reading."

Her head joggled up and down.

"Let's try B."

"Ba . . . 'ball.'"

"So if we wanted to read about balls and apples, we could do that?"

She shrugged and gave a sort of nod with her shoulders up to her ears.

He tossed the book into her lap. "How they think we going to communicate on two words?"

"I don't know."

"Senseless, lengthy process, that's what I say." Jeb left Ida May to figure out the simple words. "When you get to something interesting like 'woman' or 'fried chicken,' you give me a holler."

While Willie recited multiplication tables, Angel wrote a letter to Claudia. She began three times, at each sitting tearing the paper in two and wadding it up to toss away. "If she writes back to me and Will Honeysack sees it, he'll see my name is Welby."

"First you got to know where Claudia went. So far no one here has ever heard of her. I think she never lived here, that's what."

"It doesn't make sense, Willie. We found an empty house right where her letter said she lived. How else would she know about that place if she didn't live there?"

"I think we'd find Momma before we'd find Claudia. At least we know she's in Little Rock," said Willie.

Angel told him, "You know we can't believe Lana nor nothing," she said. "But you think if we sent Momma a letter to the sanatorium, she'd get it? I'll bet not. She's at Aunt Katy's just like Daddy said."

"Daddy didn't give us no address. I don't think he counted on letter writing at all. You got to help me finish these arithmetic tables before lunch is over."

"He didn't give us Momma's address because he expected us to be at Claudia's. But I can't see her in no sanatorium. She always wanted to be a nurse, not crazy."

"I met a new boy from Louisiana. He's my age but put back, too, like me."

"If there is a sanatorium in Little Rock, maybe the man who puts up the mail for Honeysack has heard of it. Or maybe he's heard of Claudia Drake. I can make up a whole new story about trying to find a sick relative."

"Might as well add it to the other stories you tell. This boy is real nice. He's over there doing his tables, too. If we get finished, we're going to have us a game of stick ball."

"I know what I'll do. I'll write this letter to Claudia and tell her to send it to her old address, that we're staying there with someone named . . . Hildy Gardner and that she should address her letters that way. Then I'll tell this feller at Honeysack's about an old woman I visit on the outskirts of town named Hildy. He'll let me pick up her mail if I tell him it's for a old sick woman."

"I can't finish this table if you don't stop gabbing, Angel."

Angel pulled out a fresh sheet of paper. Then she pulled out another. "One for Momma and one for Claudia. They'll both be glad to hear we're doing so well."

11

M en go after women they don't deserve. I don't know why it is, but it is the gospel truth. Ever since evil came into the human heart, women have had their hearts crushed by scoundrels who coveted the white flower of their youth and would not rest until they had plucked what did not belong to them.

Jeb sat up in bed. The morning sun pierced his right eye, a stabbing fork that poked him awake. "Angel, you leave that radio on?"

"I turned it on to listen to Sister Myra, the Salt of the Earth, sponsored by Spear's Best Flour."

But I'm here, Sisters of Broken Hearts, to tell you today that if your heart has been crushed by a savage usurper, Sister Myra has the cure for you. For the cost of a Coke and a hamburger, I can send you a prayer cloth, anointed by my own hand—

"Turn that mess off!" Jeb sat up on the side of the bed, his head cupped in his hands.

"You look awful," said Angel. "I heard you out on the porch last night, rocking."

"That's all I was doing." He had not been able to find a drop of gin anywhere.

"Ida May is still in bed. Willie is still not ready for school. A real daddy would get the kids up, help them with their breakfast—"

"Could you shut that door?" Jeb asked.

Angel shut his bedroom door.

"No, I mean stand on the other side of it."

"You're the kind of mean man Sister Myra warns young virgins about." She stomped out.

"Watch your mouth!" Jeb imagined five cigarettes in his mouth, with Myrna Hoop kneeling at his feet lighting each one. He made a sucking gesture with two fingers at his lips and then blew out. The night before, he'd gone into Honeysack's store intent on pilfering another pack or a little something for his stomach. First, he'd told the clerk, Val Rodwyn, that he needed something strong for Ida May's cold. "Something for a toddy," he told him. But Val had told him that Nazareth was in a dry county and the strongest thing he had on the shelf was paregoric syrup. "I don't recommend that for the cold," he said. "Perhaps I could interest you in Dr. Gumpher's Expectorant."

The cigarette papers and Prince Albert cans had stared from a shelf behind Val. Jeb bought the expectorant and left. It tasted like extract of rye grass.

His head felt loaded onto his neck, a boulder tipping right and left until his forehead fell into his hands. Ida May and Angel fought in the hallway. Ida May's scream pierced through the door, punching holes into the silent asylum of his room. The birds outside on the windowsill elevated the noise until he felt his brain tattering in every direction. He knew what Fern, who heard melody where he only perceived clamor, would say. She would smile, disappear into the scene through a window, and find the happy nest cozied up where he saw a roosting mess.

Fern had that smell of white cotton and linen that followed her into a room. Except for some of her cooking, she was a whiz of a girl. She did not recognize her own purity, no more than she knew that she possessed a plumbing wisdom. He figured that was how such things came to dwell inside of her.

Jeb cleaned himself up, laced up his boots, and followed Angel and Ida May out onto the porch. "I'm taking you and Willie to school. Give me a minute to hitch up that mule."

"I'm not riding to school in that old wagon," said Angel.

"You will if I say! Willie, help me hitch up."

Angel made a sound like blustering disgust. Then her lips squeezed together to bar any conversation. When Jeb climbed up, whip in his hand, he scratched his jaw, the whisker nubs erupting, and said, "Now where is this school?"

By the time the mule pulled into the schoolyard, the wagon had filled with every child who normally walked to school. Arnell and Roe Ketcherside, the Lundy twins, Melody Bottoms, whose mother ran the Clip and Curl on Front Street, and four of the six Wolvertons. The Wolvertons said it was better than a hayride. Both Wolverton boys had been shorn like sheep, making them look like little old men. Jeb insisted that two of the boys sit in the floor to allow all of the girls a decent place to sit.

Two youths swerved around the wagon in a two-door Ford sedan, powdering the wagonload of students in road silt. The girls coughed and shielded their faces with arms and sweaters.

"They're Horace Mills's sons," said Angel, "Ernest and Frank. They think they got one up on everyone else 'cause their banker daddy bought them a Ford."

"Somebody needs to give them a ride from the seat of their britches," said Jeb.

Melody Bottoms looked at Angel and said, "I never heard a preacher talk like your daddy. He talks like my daddy talked before he left us."

Jeb felt part of his whitewash flaking away. Preachers had too many social graces to juggle.

"I didn't know your daddy left," Angel said. She stopped herself before her lips formed the words, "My mother and daddy did, too."

"I'm sorry you lost your daddy, Melody," said Jeb.

"Momma says it was this Depression that did it. Folks have trouble keeping they wits about them, my momma says, when they can't feed they own kids." Melody jumped out of the wagon before the Wolverton boys could raise another dust cloud.

Angel paused behind Melody when Jeb alighted, too. "You're not coming with us?"

"Mind your own business. I'm being neighborly."

He stationed himself in a convenient vantage point just outside the window near Fern's desk. He could see the crown of her head bowed over her work as she graded student papers. Her hair was the color of dawn. The side of her face was pale except for the pink of her cheeks.

Then an ugly visage appeared, red eyed, with a shadow beneath the eyes that stared back at him. Jeb recognized his own face in the window glass. But before he could pull away and hide the unwholesome pallor that reflected his midnight binges, Fern glanced up and waved him inside.

"Morning, Reverend. Come in, if you will." The window was cracked open.

The functional hallway, half-timbered, that fed into the four large classrooms was wide and, by Jeb's estimation, wasted space. The massive exterior deceived the eye—the interior looked patched and plastered together, a community project most likely driven by necessity but lagging in ambition.

Fern started to rise.

"No need to get up. The day drew me out and I thought I'd give the kids a ride to school. Save them the walk."

"You're a considerate father."

Her simple compliment made him stumble over his words. "N-not me. N-not I. That is, it was nothing."

"Willie's teacher tells me he is showing marked improvement."

Jeb tried to muster a look of concern or maybe pleasure and concern, chin up, lips parted in an expression he hoped looked like he gave a care.

"Before he left for home yesterday, I suggested that he show his work to you. Allow his father to interject some thought into his papers." She hesitated as though waiting for his response. "Did he?"

"Did he what?"

"Show you his papers?"

Jeb shook his head.

"Some of the fathers in our community can't read. It's a lucky boy in these parts who can go home to such a scholarly father."

The voices of two youths echoed from the canyon of hallway until quieted by some other teacher.

"Willie has a good mind. He just has to be drawn out of the fog. I don't know what it is that clouds a student's mind to learning sometimes. I guess if I ever figure that out, they'll make me president."

"A woman president. That's funny!"

Her luster dimmed.

Outside, a lucky chosen boy rang the bell. The gambol of heels in the hallway became the pounding of feet against weathered wood.

"I hope you have a good day, Reverend." She dismissed him and it was so sudden, he backed away, surprised by the change.

Several students entered, along with Angel.

"Good morning—*dearest*," said Jeb. The role of minister weighed on him, a tire around his neck that left him stumbling for words.

Angel sat next to Melody without responding at all.

Jeb could not think of a proper way to dismiss himself, so he walked out of the room and mounted the wagon to head for home.

It had been easy to talk to Myrna Hoop, say cozy words that opened the bloom of her heart. But talking to a gal like Fern Coulter was more like crossing a river during a flash flood.

Downtown, a man with holes in the knees of his britches sold apples out on Front Street. Faith Bottoms swept her sidewalk in the brightening daylight. Jeb purchased a Milky Way bar and a Coke, along with an extra sack of feed for Bell.

Ida May slept out on the floor of the wagon on a blanket.

He stared out the window at the sleeping girl and wondered how things would turn out for her. Back in Texas, his people so seldom took stock in girls and how they turned out; he'd never given much thought to women and what they might become. It came to him that maybe what he had said to Fern about a lady president could have turned her from him. "Jeb, you're an idiot."

Val's head popped up. Val Rodwyn was Honeysack's clerk. He had squeezed on a pair of drugstore eyeglasses and stared out from the fishbowl lenses. "Were you addressing me, Reverend?"

"Talkin' to myself, Val."

Guys like Val surprised Jeb, nervous twerps that could read anything but could never rise above the slave's role to which they seem so accustomed. Jeb took his candy bar and Coke past the display of canned peaches and through the doorway. First he peeked again into the wagon to be certain nothing had roused Littlest. No need to share a candy bar made for one. At that point, he might have kept moving on through the doorway had it not been for the drawing of his face fastened to the glass on the door. It was the same poster that deputy had waved around just outside of town. He got a better look at it. Some Texarkana local had sketched a pathetic likeness. The artist had taken creative license and drawn him with a sharper ridge of bone above his brows—ape looking. The rendering revealed narrowed eyes, he thought. The steel wool of a beard was nothing like his old one—he remembered a more rounded shape, and well-trimmed, too, for the ladies. He read the wanted poster, the part that said "attempted murder." The fate of Hank Hampton bobbed up before him. The criminal charges could be raised or lowered depending upon Hank's pathetic condition.

Val noticed his hiatus at the door. "They been looking for him for a year," said Val. "I'd say he's up in Canada by now."

Jeb hesitated. "A year?"

"Seems like it's been that long," said Val. "Yep. A year. I hear he's a real degenerate, a hotshot like Derringer. Beat his victim with the butt of a pistol, I hear tell."

Jeb enjoyed another bite of Milky Way, refusing to be drawn into the conversation. On the road home, he would stop by Marvelous Crossing to see if a few of the pluckier gals from Ezekial Hipps's poultry farm had dropped by for a swim.

Today he felt as lucky as any fool with an unidentifiable mug.

Tonight, using Ida May's ABC picture book, he'd pen Charlie a little letter. Good fortune was best appreciated when shared.

*

The dinner invitation from Fern left Jeb as stunned as when he had told her the prospects for her winning the presidency were slim to none.

Instead of allowing Angel and Willie to walk home, she drove them but made it clear that she could not make it a habit as all of the students might expect a lift from a teacher.

While Willie and Angel ran in doffing everything from socks to belts and any item that encumbered a spirited run in the woods, Fern did not follow. She situated herself at the door.

Jeb would not miss his cue this time. "Please come in, Fern." He plumped a pillow for her even though he could distantly hear Charlie call him a pansy for it. "May I fix you something for . . . refreshment?" He fancied he sounded like a radio advertisement for a Coca-Cola. "Or tea, perhaps?" He opened the door, took one step back, and then lowered his eyes.

She now studied him like she was trying to taste a cake batter and figure out all of the ingredients.

Jeb ignored her look and patted the sofa. "I'll take a Coke. I can fix it myself, though," she said.

"I'll fetch your Coke." He made small talk while she sunk into the old sofa. Between sentences, he peered back into the parlor from the kitchen, wanting to be certain that she did not evaporate. "We still have some of Josie Hipps's lemon cookies."

"That would be nice. You sure keep your house nice. I mean, for a man. That is, for anyone, it's nice."

"Florence Bernard swoops through on her broom—*with* her broom twice a week." Jeb felt it was to inspect, make sure the preacher never stowed smokes or alcohol in hiding places. But he accepted her help.

Jeb delivered the Coke to Fern on a tray. Instead of sitting next to her, he chose the gentleman's distance and took a chair. The distance between Fern and him equaled a long rock's skip across Marvelous Crossing.

Fern leaned forward to speak. But Jeb could scarcely hear her.

"I'm sorry. Could you repeat that?" He relocated to the farthest end of the sofa.

"I wanted to ask you to dinner. You may bring your children, of course." Fern set down the Coke.

Jeb was amazed.

"If tonight is good," she said.

Visions of suffering trophy trout swimming in vats of sizzling lard and molasses-laced pie disintegrating on the plate came to him. But when he read the first significant hint of insecurity in her eyes he blurted, "What time?"

Early September resembled summer in the day, but the evenings brought out a cool stirring breeze and a full moon, near autumnal. Jeb saw the sun descend and the moon appear on the way to Fern's house behind Long's Pond. In the distance, he could see her through her kitchen window working above her sink. She saw them too and waved.

Before he pulled into the lane that wound around the pond, Angel said, "Jeb, you do not sound like a preacher man. All that talk you talk, like you just came in from the field."

Angel had taken to correcting him so much on first one thing and then another, he ignored her.

"You have to learn to say your words right, you know, pick words that make people think you have some education about you." Angel's poise lightened as though she suddenly had gotten a better education herself. She sounded like a girl who cups her saucer in lace.

"Listen to the princess." Willie laughed. "Like you know about higher learnin'."

"For instance, I notice when Miss Coulter speaks, she don't use so many country words. Like she talks about our *fa-thers* and *mo-thers* instead of *daddy* and *momma.* You try that Jeb—*fa-ther.*"

"Won't work. It ain't natural."

"You can't say 'ain't' neither." Angel, her thin fingers clasped in her lap, practiced words like *fa-ther, mo-ther, mi-stress,* and *cle-ver.*

Jeb knew that Angel tussled with words to hide her Arkansas vernacular.

"I can't be nothing more than what I am." He wanted a cigarette again. "The way I see it, I'll lay low in this juke joint of a town for another week, two at the most. Build me up a little bankroll and then it's off for parts unknown. Places to go, people who don't care diddly about if I say *fa-ther.*"

"For somebody on his way out, you sure take a keen interest in this skinny old schoolteacher."

"I wouldn't say skinny."

"She can't even cook," Angel whispered. "Here you are crawling up to her door like a dog without a bone."

"More like slender," Jeb said. "Her feet ain't the littlest I've seen, but that makes her fast on her feet. Athletic."

"Maybe so she can run away from you."

The light on Fern's porch was palely yellow from a lantern hooked just outside the door. Several baskets of marigolds dangled along the porch, pungent and gold like the moon.

"This should be good. Miss Coulter's cooking is the best," said Willie.

Jeb thought that someday someone should introduce Willie to the finer side of life, widen his horizons on matters of taste, so to speak. Maybe take him to Tulsa.

Ida May, instead of following Willie pell-mell onto the porch, hesitated in the wagon, her arms still hugging the half-bald doll. "Are we lars? Willie says we are."

After struggling to form an answer that could be repeated and not be misunderstood, Jeb sighed and finally aimed her toward the porch steps. He said, "We are like the hands of God." He wanted her to practice saying it.

"Ida May, come see," said Angel. She held out her hand to her sister, drew her next to her side.

Fern had made biscuits, the first encouraging sign of an evening on par at least with the Biscuit and Bean in Texarkana, to the best of Jeb's recollection. Her breakfast biscuits, big as cat heads, had initially deceived him into thinking that she could cook. So it pleased him to see a repeat appearance of her better craft. She pulled a bowl of potato salad out of the icebox and set it on the checkered tablecloth. A yellow mum soaked in a Mason jar, the table's centerpiece. "I hope you all don't mind fried chicken. I don't know too many recipes."

Jeb looked around for the best place to toss his new hat.

She had changed out of her teacher's frock and into a pleasant navy skirt that swished around her thighs when she transferred dishes from the stove to the table.

A console-type table crafted with curved and fancy legs that some women tended to like, displayed a dozen framed photographs of what looked to be Fern's family. "Is this your da—*fa-ther*?" Jeb unbuttoned the collar at his throat.

"My father looks so young in that picture," Fern answered.

When Jeb sat, Angel sat next to him, and turned her face so that she could prompt him without Fern's knowledge. He folded his hands in his lap, then removed his hat, folded his hands again, straightened his back and said, "Lovely weather we're having."

Fern observed them both on the sofa. "You want some lemonade?"

"Have you some tea?" asked Angel.

Fern now narrowed her eyes as though she studied a bug in a jar. "Both of you want tea?"

"Please." Jeb counted tea among the drinks pushed by women on men as though it would satisfy their taste for liquor. "That is, I don't believe I will. Thank you."

"You all can sit yourself down for supper." She invited each one to take a particular seat and finally placed Jeb at the head of the table. "Reverend Gracie, you may ask grace."

Jeb bowed his head. "Thank you, God, for this, for thy food given to us for which we say grace. Amen." When Jeb opened his eyes, Fern stared at him for a long moment and then moved to serve. He let out a long, low breath of relief.

Fern served everything from bowls or platters right on the kitchen table. "Potato salad, Willie?"

"He hates onions," said Angel.

"Let your brother answer for himself," said Jeb.

"Reverend, while we fill our plates, maybe you would like to tell us about your family. The children have shared bits and pieces, but I think I might have some confusion about where you grew up." Fern passed the biscuits.

Jeb could not recall exactly what he had told her in the past, but it seemed fitting to at least use a place familiar to him. "I grew up in Texas in different towns as my daddy found work. Texas."

He could not tell if she were catching him in a lie or not. "Once, we didn't live far from a Cherokee family." Jeb remembered a boy named Iron Joe whose son, John, drank with him every Saturday night by the railroad station. Age of twelve on up. "They're a fine lot of families, those folks." John had gotten drunk and fallen into a barrel of kerosene one night and burned down the first filling station to come to town. Jeb had helped John home before he got his britches afire.

"Fine education to be gotten in Texas."

"What were your parents' names?" Fern never let the conversation stray from the subject of Jeb's family.

"Charles and Geneva . . . Gracie," said Jeb.

"You said you had a brother? So it was just the two of you. You came from a small family?"

Fern's query took on an uncommon weight.

"My mother died young. We were very poor, Fern."

Fern digested his history and then said, "You must have had to work very hard to make it through school."

"Oh, sure, sure. Work and study. Study and work. I believe I'll have another piece of that chicken. Say, this is really good." It was.

Fern passed the platter to him. "So what kind of college did you attend to become a minister? Did you take Latin?"

Jeb cut a meaty piece from the chicken leg and chewed it for a moment. The Latin question baffled him. He remembered a small college in Texas that attracted men of the cloth. What country spoke Latin, he could not remember. He felt it was something akin to Spanish, but to be safe, he contrived to make the girl feel as though she did not allow him to enjoy his supper. Halting his knife midway through the cut, he hesitated.

"You finish your meal," she said.

Jeb fixed his sights on the plate and decided he would use the children's schoolwork as a reason to leave, even though it was Friday. "You ever been to Texas?" he asked.

"Oklahoma is where I grew up. I went down to Louisiana once, and then, of course, here, Arkansas. That's the extent of my world travels."

"You've never heard of Texas Preacher's College, then?" He could not recall the name of any of the colleges back home.

"Never heard of any college by that name."

"That's where I went to school."

The answer satisfied her, he thought. All the talk of family had made him think of his daddy, Charlie senior. He had always favored his oldest boy and namesake over Jeb. Drunk once, he had said to Jeb while stupefied by his liquor, "You are destined for the rock piles at Benson Prison and I can't wring no better future out of your life than that. You was born under evil"—the fact that his hated brother Festus had shown up asking for money the night of Jeb's birth—"and evil will follow you for all your days."

"You must have been close to your father if your mother died young," said Fern.

"Close. Yes, we were tight. A tight family."

"And godly, too," said Fern.

Jeb sopped up the juice from his beans with a pinch of biscuit. "Yes'm. Godly. Especially that."

12

"M ake the top of the letter look like the roof of a house." Angel could not reach her back buttons of the church dress and had Ida May try. But her small fingers faltered at the task until Angel demeaned herself and let her brother finish the job.

"Like an A?" asked Jeb. He had made her stand and watch him scrawl out the alphabet.

"Now make two of them. You made an M."

"See if you can read this letter. Charlie is a good reader, always was good in his books. He'll know if this is done wrong." Jeb slid the letter across the table.

Angel read it aloud. *"Dear Charlie, I got me a gud job in a plas where the fud is gud and the likker is plenty*—you spelled *good, liquor, place, food* wrong and the last part isn't true anyway."

"Keep reading." Jeb retied his necktie.

"Dont you mary off befor we can get together agin and ti won on." Angel pushed the letter away. "Nobody could read this. I'll have to rewrite it. What did you do here at the bottom of the page? That's nothing but a big, fat X where your name goes?"

"It's a code between me and my brother in case someone else gets a-hold of it. I didn't ask for a sermonette, Sister Myra. I can tell that you can read my writing. Maybe Charlie will just have to figure it out, too. I don't have no more time for this. I'll have this whole business figured out real soon and won't have to put up with your mouth every time I need a little help." He folded the letter and tucked it inside his coat pocket. She liked the control and held it over his head. "Fact is, it wouldn't hurt you none to give a man a little help without landing all over his business with your nasty little opinions."

"You think Miss Coulter is on to you?" Angel asked.

"I do not." He really could not tell either way

"She's been acting funny. I can't really say how, though."

"You never liked her because she has her life all orderly and happens to be quite pretty to boot. Fact is, women are always jealous of a lady who is both beautiful and smart." Jeb practiced his text again, two Scriptures from John.

"I say you're blind to Miss Coulter. Maybe she knows something. You notice how she never said a word again about our other school grades and such?"

"I told her I made a call and found out your grades were destroyed by a fire," Jeb told her.

"You're nothing but a big nut if you think she'd believe that." Angel lurched away from Willie, who had skipped a button and fastened her dress together until one buttonhole stood out, undone.

"Fern Coulter is a decent woman, fair minded. And unsuspecting." That fact left Jeb carrying a melancholy empathy for Fern. "You think she really likes it here in Nazareth?"

"How should I know?" Angel modeled in front of the mirror. One of the local women had loaned her a hat created for a woman of twenty.

"She talks about cities a lot, it seems. How things are better in city schools, how she came here to try and help out. Something tells me she'd leave here in a heartbeat if the right offer came along." Jeb turned Angel around and refastened her buttons.

"You think you're the right offer, Jeb Nubey, you wrong as wrong can be," said Angel.

"Maybe I'm just what she's been waiting for. Willie, grab my Bible. I got to get this show moving before I up and forget everything altogether." He took the Bible, opened it to the marked page and studied the underlined Scripture. He recognized an *A*, an *M*, and a smallcase *e*. It would not be long until he could fly with the big boys, score with a woman of superior intelligence.

Angel seated herself back upon the farthest pew in the church, having found Fern Coulter entangled in too many threads of her life. She tucked herself one pew behind the thin-haired heads of the Wolvertons, although to mix with them, she said, was like social suicide.

Women with babies on the breast sat in the rear while the men sat politely three rows ahead. Doris Jolly played a gentle, sleepy hymn that sounded like the sun going down. Jeb asked if she could pick up the pace with an anthem but she could not readily recall one.

Evelene Whittington called from the second row for *A Mighty Fortress Is Our God.*

Doris covered her mouth as if to say, "Where is my mind today?" She chorded the chorus while the pews' empty spaces filled with the stragglers.

"You think maybe we're having revival, like we hear about in other places?" Doris asked Jeb. But he was busy troubling over the name Nicodemus. He concluded that if he gave the man a nickname some might consider it a sacrilege. A word he learned meant wrong in the Big Man Upstairs's eyes. Nick, Nicko. Doris stared at him, expectant. "I'm sorry, Doris. Did you say something?"

Doris hadn't removed her bright, Blue Jay hat. "I asked if you thought revival was coming. Or have you not noticed how the pews are filling up with more folk every week?"

He had not noticed. Way back in the clouds of his memories he thought his momma might have said it a time or two—revival.

Doris lifted her right arm and sang the words to the sacred hymn. The congregation followed her lead and sang, although most of the men moved their lips as though they might suffer a whipping if they didn't. So they sang with a faint undercurrent of melody, faintly sweet like old cedar.

Jeb remained seated on the platform as had been his custom for the last few weeks. Doris did a fine job without him and it gave him a moment to massage away the headache that lodged itself above his right eye. Besides, he still had not learned the lyrics. And Doris's tendency to change up the song list every week only drove home the fact the minister did not know his hymns. So Jeb stared hard into the open Bible on his lap, giving the impression that he ascended to the pearly gates themselves.

Ezekial Hipps, who wore a plaid shirt with his overalls, and then a corresponding necktie, opened the rear door and offered the incoming deputy sheriff a funeral parlor fan. The sheriff refused the fan and fixed his eyes on the front of the church, his eyes like shooting gallery ducks, until he fastened a bead on Jeb. It was the same officer who had waited for Jeb at the parsonage the day he stopped at Marvelous Crossing. He ignored Ezekial's friendly graces and declined the only empty seat on the back row. Instead, he stationed himself next to the back door, a sentry.

Fern, although she had made it her objective every Sunday to see that Ida May and Willie made it to the front row fifteen minutes before Doris struck the first chord, ears washed and socks turned down, was nearly invisible. Five rows to the left, her small yellow hat nodded slightly in time to the music. Willie sat with Ida May alone on the front row.

Jeb knew Doris had softened the music to allow him the timing to take his place behind the lectern. But many thoughts came to him, of Fern filling in too many puzzle pieces, contacting the sheriff. He would not give Angel the satisfaction of saying she might be right about Fern. But what if she had only invited him to her home to question him? Fern was a garden spider and he the insignificant little fly. Doris hit the last key. Someone punctuated it with a hallelujah. Jeb could not recall the text from John. He said the first thought that came to him, "I think revival is coming."

Doris sat back down on the organ seat. She hit a few well-laid chords.

He said it again.

Something stirred through the rows of faces; mothers lifted their heads from nursing infants. Jeb saw how the word stimulated and impassioned the church people. "Revival!" he said and his voice tremored.

"I think I feel something," said an old man who barely stood and then fell back in his seat.

"But before revival, you have to be born again." He hoped the name would spill out of him, so he began the sentence, "A man came to Jesus asking about being born again. That man—"

Florence Bernard clasped her hands together, ecstasy filling her senses and said, "Nicodemus "Nicodemus!" Jeb repeated happily. It seemed God played pinch-hitter with his morning message. "Before revival you must be born again. It is in this Book and no other."

The deputy sheriff had steady, watchful eyes, as though waiting for a prod in the chest to bring him out like a snake from his hole.

Fern's face lifted through the parting of many heads, an emerging snow lily. Her eyes were comfortably blue in the natural chapel light. She turned and gave a slight three-fingered wave to the cop. Jeb pieced one and one together and figured out the lay of things—Fern had found him out and told that deputy. Jeb wanted to slap her for her expression of pure innocence instead of that of a traitor.

"Born again, from treachery," he said, staring right at her. "Born again, from deceit."

Florence's expression faded, like her thoughts had turned inward, found a target, and fired.

Jeb wondered if Mr. Bernard had awakened some place from his Saturday night binge and right then felt a poke from hell.

Fern rolled a stick of gum into a snail and popped it into her mouth. Flippant, Jeb thought. Right there in my face and flippant. He could grab her by those luscious curls and give her a shake. The cottage on the lake, it could have been his and theirs together. Reverend and Mrs.

He found his original thought, the idea that he had drummed up about how to conclude the query from Nicodemus to Christ. But a new idea congealed, a quick getaway through the door just beyond the American flag. He had never roused the church to a fever-pitch, but it seemed he could.

The deputy sheriff checked his watch.

"Brothers and sisters, I charge you on this day to choose who you will follow. If it be Christ, then come to your feet!"

Florence Bernard was the first lone apostle. But two more women joined her. The men were nudged by righteous females in churchy hats. Finally, he had his gauntlet.

"Now all across this room, join hands in an affirmation of faith. That's right, stretch out across that aisle and join hands with the person next to you." Jeb came out from behind the lectern. The deputy sheriff had disappeared, but just through the partially open door Jeb saw a ring of smoke float by.

"Pray like you've never prayed. Like if you were Nicodemus and Christ was before you."

A young mother broke through, her skinny toddler clinging to her dress. "Pray for me, Preacher!" She stretched her hand out to him.

Jeb glanced at the platform exit. "I will, Sister." He took her hand, bowed his head, and mumbled a few words. Her hand inside of his pricked his heart. A trusting hand clasping a snake. He should slither away. Not utter prayers. The young mother opened her eyes. "Touch her, oh, LORD and revive her—"

"Forgive me, LORD!" she said.

It seemed he could not breathe.

Jeb felt a jerk on his coattail. Angel had somehow pushed her way to the front. "What do you want?" He turned his back to the congregation.

"That deputy sheriff has come around again asking for you," she said.

"I know. I have eyes."

"Something about your truck. I think maybe he found it for you. Just thought I'd better tell you," said Angel.

Jeb threw back his arms and raised his hands. "Praise be, praise be, we can all rejoice! We are redeemed."

Fern had a look of sincerity about her.

✳

The deputy sheriff, the same deputy pasting wanted posters around the county with Jeb's mug, stared at him. Not six inches from Jeb's face. "We might be on to something. Your truck have a dent in the right-hand fender beneath the head-lamps?"

Jeb considered how he might stomp the man that had put a dent in his brother Charlie's truck. "Not originally."

"How about a black covering across the back, like a lot of things is underneath?"

Jeb nodded. "Sounds more like it. I hate they dented my fender. Where is it?"

"We think two young crooks may have heisted it from you to use as a getaway truck. They up and robbed an old man's general store up near Pope County." The officer read the details off of a telegram. "Knocked him out and left him for dead. But when they pulled a gun on him, the old man's wife hid out in a side room and watched them pull away. She gave a pretty good description of both of them and what sounds to be your truck."

"Knocked out an old man. Couple-a cowards is all they are," said Jeb. "So they still have my truck is what you're saying." He thought the deputy looked as though he still believed him.

The deputy's shoulders lowered. "I'm afraid so. But every cop from here to Missouri is on the lookout. If they don't wreck it getting away, we'll try our best to recover your truck."

Most of the church people milled in small groups around the automobiles parked along the church lawn. Fern held the back of the arm Jeb recognized as the tailor's wife, Hazel Plummer. Her gout caused her to have to sit with her foot propped up behind the counter of Plummer's shop. On this day she'd wanted terribly to come and hear the new preacher so

Fern had driven her to the church and sat with her several rows back.

Jeb felt her distance could not have been for any other reason, not deceit nor any other pretense. She relaxed completely when she spoke to him, "Look who I brought!"

The Wolvertons paraded to the old T-model held together by wire and hay bale rope. They always had a pilgrim look about them, traveling but seldom settling. The children from ages sixteen down to three wore shoes scarcely soled.

Jeb thumped Horace Mills upon the shoulder of his serge jacket. "Those Wolvertons need help in the worst way, don't they?"

"It's a sad thing to see. You go inside their house and it has not a stick of furniture. Mr. Wolverton has knocked on every door in Nazareth looking for work." Mills pulled a gold watch out of his trouser pocket. "Mrs. Mills doesn't like it when I keep her waiting. Sunday dinner to finish up when she gets home. I'll see you next Sunday, Reverend. Good message. Fiery. Keeps them happy, their troubles off themselves."

Jeb grabbed his Bible and the plate of cash collected during the offering. Before he handed the offering to Will Honeysack, he watched the Wolvertons leave. The same sick feeling that had come up like acid when he prayed for that young mother now gave him a different kind of ill feeling. He didn't know what to call it. Some strange or guilty religious melancholy. But he wasn't comfortable with it.

"Up by five dollars," said Will. "I'll make the deposit in the morning and drop by your pay tomorrow, Reverend."

"Brother Honeysack, I think maybe we should give a few dollars to the Wolvertons for shoes or a little food or I don't know." Jeb watched the Wolvertons disappear into the dust. He'd said the first right thing he'd said all day.

"Every family is on hard times. If we give it all back, we

won't have the money to pay the church expenses." Will flicked the ends of the money to assess the amount. "It's a shame everyone is having it so hard. We have an election coming up, though. Maybe things will change after November. Folks is worn out with Hoover's happy-chats."

Jeb had seen his share of packed Hoovervilles, people living like rats in scrap-lumber lean-tos.

"I heard that a hundred men lined up along the streets of New York and Chicago selling apples. Too ashamed to outright beg. Then I look up and what did I see Saturday morning right on Front Street in our own town?"

"Mr. Wolverton selling apples." Jeb had seen it, too. "I bought some from him."

"Pitiful sight. Better go. The missus is fixing a roast. The A&P had a sale on them." Mills loosened his tie with the same hand that had just checked the offering plate.

"This brook is where I came and talked to God when I first moved to Nazareth. I didn't know a soul here," said Fern. She balanced on a rock midstream, her arms taking flight and then resting at her sides. Her hat and sweater dangled on a tree branch. "Church in the Dell was still without a shepherd, so I drove back here often what with it being so quiet. It is the best place in town for solitude."

Jeb mulled over the fact that he could reach out and assist her, but her surety did not call for a rescue and certainly not in a two-feet-deep stream. It just left him pleased as punch to hear her yammering about anything but "the children, this" or "the children, that."

"I'll bet you get your best sermons out here. I would if I were you," she said.

Jeb might have figured a streambed the most unlikely place for a sermon. But coming out of her mouth, it sounded believable. "Most of the time I can't recall ten minutes later exactly what I said from the pulpit."

"Everything you preach makes good sense. This morning's message, it was a real dandy." One hand went out and he took it to help her keep her balance.

"I never saw you get so wound up like that. I could tell you really meant it." Fern bent over the water as though she had just spotted her own face.

"You could tell I meant it?" The only thing showing in her eyes was sincerity—she had complimented him. But then there was that thought of the Almighty at work, right in the middle of his sermon. It had come to him once before. "You like it here in Nazareth, Fern?"

"I do. Don't you?" she asked.

"No place like Nazareth. But you ever think about moving away?"

A smile made her entire face lift. Fern clearly read him through ways that weren't in no book. "Never crosses my mind."

He shook his head, of course, and agreed with her like he'd found a little piece of Eden in Nazareth. Why wouldn't he? It was his turn to say so. But the dogged niggling bothered him again, like he'd never told a lie ever. In Texas he would have been moving in, figuring out the next best move. But here in Nazareth as Reverend Gracie, the entire notion of giving this schoolteacher the very best part of his lips left him dumber than a hammer. All he could think to say was, "Roots is the best thing for growing children. Let those little feet sprout and take roots. Nazareth is the place to be."

13

O utside Honeysack's Grocery, the Catholics from Hot Springs were collecting money for a church bell, a year-long project that every Saturday brought tables of lemon cakes and pumpkin bread and platters of watermelon slices arranged like Oriental fans on newspaper table coverings. The Catholics, like the Protestants, usually kept to their own kind. But for the collections they gathered from as far away as Hot Springs and rallied on Front Street with cauldrons and ringing bells, little bespectacled girls in blue sweaters singing songs for a penny.

The sky blued magnificently, a cathedral ceiling for the gathering of downtowners on Sunday's eve. The front page of the *Nazareth Gazette* headlined Japan's forceful occupation of South Manchuria, a likely blunder on their part, next to a photograph of the prize sow at the county fair.

Greta Patton counted six spools of thread—three white, two black, and bell-pepper green—onto the counter in front of Freda Honeysack. "My grandson says that not a one of the Wolvertons came to school this week and you know what that means."

"Careful. Someone might hear," said Freda.

"Shoeless and skipping school. That's what I say." Greta pulled a paper of needles from the turnstile and added it to the purchase while a display of Country Club chili tempted her noose-tight budget.

Freda, whose long mustine face was framed by a fountain-pen display, a tower of Coty face powder, and a running list of meat deliveries, dropped the spools and needles into a brown bag, *ba-dop, ba-dop.* "Will says he has not seen the Wolvertons all week. Could be they're away."

"Or holed up like mice. This Depression is eating families alive. What do my eyes see?" Greta pointed at the display of candies. "Half a pound of those horehounds for my grandson, since you have some spanking new."

"Hoover ought to do more." Freda rang up Greta's purchase. "Thirty-one cents. I hope someone up in the White House remembers it's an election year. We don't give a flitter about politicians and emergency committees if they leave the rest of the country to fend for itself."

"Or let children run truant due to shoelessness. Someone ought to write Hoover a letter," said Greta.

"You think he'd read it? I'll bet not," Freda told her in a way that needled Greta into position.

"Wouldn't that be the gab around this place? A letter from the president himself!" Greta mulled it around.

"You'd make us all jealous, Greta."

"Oh, doodle! I'm writing a letter to the president and I don't care what anyone says!" She minced around Jeb, who was collecting two cans of Del Monte beans from the center aisle. "Reverend, I guess you should know I'm writing a letter to the president."

Jeb noticed the grocery list bent over her wrist with the several items unchecked. "Don't forget to stock the grape juice for communion, Greta."

"I'll have to do it later. Communion isn't for two more

weeks. Busy, busy." She halted fully in the doorway. "I'll mention to Hoover that my husband fished last summer with the man who once cut his wife's roses."

"That'll show him," said Jeb.

"Do remember to speak of the Wolvertons," said Freda.

"Presidents lead hectic lives, Freda. And it is an election year," Greta said, and continued down Front Street, a bit of the temperance march in her step.

"After the Mississippi Flood, Greta sent letters to the governor. She means what she says," said Freda.

"Maybe Hoover will read it and stop the Depression altogether," said Jeb. He wanted sweet banana pudding but did not want to ask Freda for the ingredients when everything was clearly spelled out on the package. A sign hand-lettered by Hank Honeysack extended beyond a sugar display that advertised Jell-O, three for twenty cents. He knew his numbers good and the Jell-O picture helped.

Angel padded in behind him, one hand scooting Ida May through the door and the other looking at her own face in a hand mirror. The dress she wore had a wide yoke—too wide for a girl her size—that stayed in place like a box even if she moved her shoulders. She kept tucking her hand into the basket pocket, creating a posed expression, Jeb thought, like the movie star Loretta Young.

"What could I do for the Gracie family?" asked Freda.

"I need to post a letter." Jeb handed her the sealed letter, Charlie's letter, and the one that would surprise him since Jeb penned it himself, even if he was a bad speller. It had taken a week and several wadded up and tossed away sheets before he got it close to right, according to Angel, who had insulted him all the way.

"Texarkana." Freda examined the address.

"Cousin of mine, on my mother's side," said Jeb.

"None of my business. But you should put your return address on here. If they don't get it delivered, they'll need to know how to mail it back to you."

"I'm sure they'll deliver it."

"Never know. I'll scribble down your address on the envelope," said Freda.

"Then it won't be a surprise."

"Suit yourself." She dropped Charlie's letter into the out mailbox.

"So the Wolvertons are without shoes," said Jeb, getting better at the nice tactful touch, a pastorly concern that softened his phrases.

"I didn't say that."

"Greta said it, I know. But I overheard."

"But she doesn't know herself. It's all speculation."

Jeb sent Angel off with the shopping list. "Perhaps I should drop by, pay them a visit."

"Just don't mention my name. I know nothing about the Wolvertons' affairs. Nice family. Shame to see them fall into the pit of this Depression," she told him. "But everyone is hit by hard times. I just hope that Mr. Wolverton doesn't turn to crime. So many do, nowadays. Dillinger, George Nelson, Bonnie and that what's-his-face."

Every time someone dropped a nickel into the Catholic cauldron out front, the sisters rang their bells. Front Street sounded like St. Mary's Cathedral in intermittent jangling intervals, a lively fête that broke through the quiet Saturday spell that settled over downtown when the Grande Theater opened up for the matinee showing of *Dr. Jekyll and Mr. Hyde*. *Tarzan* in a serialized showing preceded the moving picture.

Jeb had never paid an official visit to the Wolvertons,

having made as few stops as possible around town, just enough to convince the locals that the Gracie train had landed. Another interval of chiming bells caused him to stiffen with his own thought. "Maybe we ought to have our own kind of charity bell ringing. *Shoes for the Wolvertons.*" He laughed about it, then got all of a sudden serious.

Angel announced, "We have everything on the list. Can I go watch the nuns now?"

"You all sell bells, by the way?" Jeb asked Freda.

"Cowbells, maybe. Nothing like the Catholics."

"Add up my bill, will you? And sell me one of them i ow hello." Jeb walked across the wooden floor to get a better look at the nuns. Their thin faces were wedged between the folds of fabric that shrouded their heads. They looked jittery, like Mexican dogs. Even the virtuous suffered skimpy meals during the autumnal grinding of days leading toward the November election. There was always the coming victory of voting out the old to usher in the new, but it didn't fill empty bellies.

Jeb figured by Christmas this Depression would be rolled under the White House rug, a ploy that could be laid aside or shoved in a drawer after the vote count. Maybe he would be in Canada by then. He envisioned Fern dressed in a seal coat, her legs lifting out of the snow, her Ardmore feet strapped in wooden skis. But a picture of a long habit raided his image of her platinum locks and snapped the lust out of the whole picture.

"Is this bell what you wanted, Reverend?" Freda rang it until he took it out of her hand.

"I'll take it just like that. No need to wrap it for me. Ever get in a supply of skis, Sister Honeysack?"

❅

Jeb made Willie count the pennies he had collected outside the Grande. "You need the practice," he told him.

While Willie painstakingly counted every penny aloud, Ida May sang, "Won't you try Wheaties? For wheat is the best food of man."

"This man and his wife walked nine hundred miles through Texas to look for work in the Rio Grande." Angel read the newspaper to Jeb.

He sat feet crossed on a bench sipping a Coke and watching the cinemagoers milling out and back to Beulah's Café and Fidel's Drugstore on the corner. Stiffness crept into his right hand from the bell ringing.

"Four hundred seventy-two cents," said Willie. "A fortune."

"We're in the money now." Angel folded up the *Gazette* and laid it over Jeb's lap like a Hoover blanket.

"We can buy shoes, I'll bet." Jeb raked the coins into a paper sack and plopped it into the sack of canned goods from Honeysack's.

"You ain't buying shoes for the Wolvertons, no way," said Angel. "This is another scam. I can read it on you like milk on a baby."

"Of course, I don't know the shoe sizes."

"I knew it. You'll find a way to keep the money," said Angel. "The day you go soft is the day I grow wings."

"If I give this money to Mr. Wolverton, reckon he'll use it for shoes? If I say it's a gift from the church and tell him, 'Go buy your children shoes'—can preachers tell people things like that?" If someone had said that to his daddy, he might have taken offense. An invasion like that could knock the wind out of a poor man's sails.

Angel told him, "Let's take the biggest four on a trip into town. Their momma knows we give them rides sometimes. The oldest ones can pick out their own shoes. Then we'll let them pick out the two littlest ones' shoes and take them home."

"Charity is a shameful thing to a man," said Jeb.

"Pocket the money like you planned to do all along, then." Angel held up her hand, bracing Ida May as she clambered into the wagon. She collected the cowbell and removed the sign Jeb had asked her to make. The penciled writing read, "Help buy shoes for poor children."

"They call me Clovis and the wife is Alma. You met the youngens." Mr. Wolverton's slight build gave him the look of a twig trapped between two opposing poles, a bowed appearance as though his back would snap under the weight of the next landslide. Even inside his own house, he wore an old felt-brimmed hat that added years to the windswept face. The hat and the habit of pacing made him look like a man who waited his turn for one big break. "My apologies to you for alla-us missin' yer church service, Reverend. We had to attend to other matters."

Someone had placed a small Bakelite radio on the floor with the electrical cord rolled up and tied with twine.

All six Wolverton children collected inside the one room shanty as though the electricity had come back into the house during the *Amos 'n' Andy* sketch.

"I'll try to get your names right," said Jeb. The oldest boy, he remembered. "Dillon, right?"

Dillon nodded with a weak smile. The school children laughed at his blackened teeth Willie had mentioned over supper.

Angel named the others.

None of them wore shoes and the oldest boys wore pants too short and so tight around their thin stomachs their hip bones squeezed against the seams. The girls' clothes had an oversized slouch, their dresses drop-offs left on their porch in the night, according to Angel, but that was gossip. The oldest girl, Wanda, confided such things to her.

"Angel and Willie had an idea, Clovis. We'd like to take your oldest ones for a wagon ride. They seem to like it," said Jeb.

"Ride to where?" asked Clovis.

Alma slunk into a chrome chair like one of the children and hid her face behind the youngest girl, who squirmed to leap from her knobby lap.

"No where in particular," Jeb told him.

Dillon's younger brother said, "I'd like a ride in Reverend's wagon."

Dillon batted the boy and then whispered a secret that his brother appeared to already know. He pushed Dillon away.

"Did someone send you by, Reverend?" Clovis asked.

"Nobody sent us," Angel answered for Jeb.

Jeb let out a breath. "The fact is, I ought to tell you, there was a—"

"A raffle," said Angel.

"A raffle is right," said Jeb. "And you all won."

The Wolverton children shouted support for the timely raffle.

"Best of my knowledge, we didn't enter no raffle. Alma, you enter something I don't know about?" Clovis asked her.

She shook her head and gave off a funny laugh that caused all of the children to laugh, too.

"A raffle for new shoes. For all the children." Jeb could tell that Clovis did not buy the raffle story. So it just laid there, a lie in the mouth of the town preacher.

"Someone's sent you," said Clovis.

"I can promise you not." Jeb picked up the youngest girl. "If you can give me the shoe sizes of your littlest two, Mrs. Wolverton, I'll bring them back to you. Then we'll just take the four oldest ones for a fitting at Whittington's Woolworth's. Why, Evelene Whittington, she's just silly about children. I'll bet she'll have some good shoes that are to your liking. If that would help you all out." Jeb had noticed the old Wolverton truck parked a mile away from the shack, as though it had blown that far on fumes and then expired.

"We don't need no charity," said Clovis.

Alma tried to speak but Clovis glared her into silent obedience.

Jeb pulled the old movie stub out of his pocket from when he and the Welbys had seen *The Miracle Woman*. He handed it to Alma. "If you change your mind, Mrs. Wolverton, here's the winning raffle ticket."

Alma turned it over. Her mouth widened. "We're the winning ticket, Clovis. I didn't sit out on that porch praying to God for nothing. You kids behave yourselves and go with this nice preacher."

"You'll not defy me, Alma," said Clovis.

"Just this once, Clovis. Sunday I'll atone," she said.

The Wolverton children goaded Jeb through the doorway.

They entered the downtown square with a whole Wolverton parade, four pairs of dirty bare feet gadding about the Woolworth's, dozens of hungry fingers touching luxury as though a pack of terrycloth towels belonged in a bank vault. In most cases of late, that was every bit the truth. Evelene met him at the counter. He said to her, "We are here for six pairs of shoes, the good ones, and a pair of socks each."

While Evelene turned to go for the shoes, Jeb had a brief mirage where he felt his body rise to a dizzying height. He did not hear a crack of thunder or stand fixed on the pyre of a burning bush. But a soaring sensation entered through his nostrils, filling him up. It took over his mouth and he heard himself say to Angel, "Oh, and don't tell Fern."

Angel led the oldest Wolverton girl into the shoe aisle, but she kept looking back at Jeb like he'd lost his mind.

14

I heard a haint in the wood last night, fierce like a bear and telling the summer to go away. It made me cry," said Willie.

"Hugh, and don't tell Ida May your bad dreams or you'll give them to her." Angel had grown good at stirring up biscuit batter. She cut the bread with a snuff glass just in time for Fern to show up any minute and give a dozen the final shove into the cook stove.

"It didn't seem like a dream," said Willie.

"Quiet. I'm listening to Joan and Kermit on the radio," Angel shot back.

Sunday came into the house, sunlight melting into the windows, sunbeam butter on the griddle of the house, quiet, and simmering golden and yellow while the tinny, muted voices spilled out of the new Woolworth's radio. Floyd Whittington had paid his church tithes with an RCA Radiola calling the last week the worst week of the whole entire year.

"Let's wait out on the porch for Miss Coulter." Ida May said her name now as though she breathed the sacred name of "Mother."

"I think you need to be careful about who you make friends with, Ida May. A teacher is the best friend to those that pay them; but children, we are a nuisance to them. Miss Coulter doesn't love us. Not like you think."

Ida May crept in sock feet out to the porch. Her dress ties trailed behind on the porch, waiting a proper tying at the hands of Miss Coulter. "I'm not listening to Angel, Dud."

"*It is a good thing I do.* I said that right, didn't I?" When Jeb spit out his first full sentence, he could have raised the dead with his whoop—E*eyah!* He'd read a sentence from Ida May's *Big Little Book*, a merciful story of a farmer.

"What would happen if someone called off church? Would God get mad?" Wearing her feed-sack slip, Angel finished dressing right on the front porch. She pulled on a blouse, white and crisp with sizing.

Jeb flew through the first word of the next sentence, onto a simple verb and a five-lettered word that sounded like the blade of a fan turning. "Wh-ere." He butchered the sentence and then stammered through the next. He held the book out in the sun and read sentence after sentence, his arms spread in a ritual between his mind and nature. "*It is a good thing I do. It is a good thing I do. Where no man gives mercy, I give it to you.*"

The girls rocked together, Ida May on top of Angel, their arms rising and falling like centipede legs. Ida May's skin had bronzed over the summer and the freckles on her face had darkened until her skin burst with the color of a pinto bean.

"He memorized it. That's not the same thing as reading," said Angel, speaking about Jeb as though he had gone inside.

"I really didn't," said Jeb. "Willie Boy, go fetch that Bible. Things is coming to me now, like a lightbulb coming on in this old boy's attic."

Willie brought Evelene Whittington's Bible to him and swapped it for the reader. Jeb opened to the book of Psalms. "Here goes nothing. 'I will . . . sing . . . of the mer-cies of the Lord for ever: with my mou-th will I make known thy faith-ful-ness to all german—'"

"Generations," Angel said in a monotone. "I don't believe you. Read one more."

He read the next verse of the Psalm and made "establish" sound like a vegetable, but the rest he figured out right nice. "Today, I preach straight out of the Good Book, on my very own."

Angel measured out her words slowly, dropping each like a fly before a fish. "Go-od. You'll so-und like Ida May when she re-ads."

Fern's Chevy Coup generated a red puff of dust at the end of the parsonage drive.

"Don't guess you'll be wanting to brag to her," said Angel.

"I don't brag to Fern," Jeb read another passage to himself. "We share—accomplishments. Wonder how you spell *accomplishments?*"

Angel shrugged. "I'm going inside. If she cooks again, I'm going to fast."

"Going too fast for what?" asked Willie.

"If I can do this, Willie, so can you," said Jeb. He practice-read the Scripture he had stuck together for the Sunday morning message in the same manner Ida May tried to create puzzles from newspaper pages.

Fern opened the automobile door, one heel down, with her entire ankle aimed straight into the toe of the shoe. When she stood, the trendy Ghillie Ties tossed back and forth on the front of her ankle. She wore a felt hat, brandy colored with one brim turned up above her left brow and held in place with cut-felt pompons.

Ida May announced to Fern, "Dud can read!"

"Of course he can," said Fern.

"Ida May, go and let Angel fix your hair," said Willie, the tops of his ears like rubies in the pearled morning light.

"I'll fix Ida May's hair," said Fern. "I'm glad she is realizing you can read, Reverend. It helps their eagerness for reading if they feel they are emulating a parent."

Jeb held the open Bible against his torso until Fern hauled Ida May inside to finish the bread.

Florence Bernard's remark followed the closing prayer. However shortened with brevity, the comment worked into him like a splinter and ate at him until it broadened as wide as Ivey's barn. "I stunk today," he said to Fern.

Several men—Horace Mills, Luke Hipps, and Daniel Bottoms—stood and formed an arc around the small sign in front of the church. Mills had hired a painter to paint the name "Reverend Philemon Gracie" in graceful lettering beneath the name "Church in the Dell." Mills made everyone who passed by look at it.

"Reverend Gracie, your slang is comical, but don't let the others hear." Fern drew him outside, her hands laced with crocheted gloves that scalloped right above her palms.

"Florence Bernard told me I sounded off my feed. Nice way of saying I smelled up the joint," said Jeb.

Fern's faint hint of toilet water made her smell clean, crisp, with an aroma that reminded him of the flowering vines that coiled around his mother's porch rail. She greeted the Lundy sisters and guided Jeb away from the after-church millers as though she steered him in all of his blindness through a heckling mob of rebels.

"Everybody just stared like I needed a bath."

Fern shushed him lightly, her lips puckering slowly as if she did not know how to silence a minister without summoning up disrespect.

Jeb let out a breath, like he wanted to air out everything inside of him. Those church people had laughed at him behind their hands and funeral fans. He had a feeling about such things. Not a pew sitter in sight had affirmed him, especially Angel. *She's been looking at me like I don't have sense to pull off nothing,* he thought.

He would have liked to have taken off a shoe and thrown it at her. Fern might consider him out of line.

"Reverend, you had a good message. I got it and if I got it, everyone did," said Fern. She led him beneath the elm where they had lunched weeks ago over dried-out chow fly pie.

He inspected the circle of privacy. "This is as good a place as any. Away from anyone else who wants to take a stab at why my sermon ought to be cut up and fed to the fish." He preached it back at the Florence Bernards and every do-gooder who might rail against him for trying to give the religious a genuine taste of what they wanted.

"You are kind of hard on yourself, aren't you?"

"I think I need glasses."

"Not that I know anything about preaching, but on Saturday I could find some time and let you try it out on me. Kind of a practice preach." She must have read more into his expression than he intended. "It's a stupid idea."

"None of your ideas are stupid. Do you mean that I could read to you?" She could help him with some of the more lofty, nobler passages than Angel wanted to show him.

"Not that you aren't a good reader, Reverend. I remember your letters. You know some of the greatest minds write down their thoughts better than they say them. Moses, for one."

"I knew it. I stunk."

"Most of the men sitting out in those pews, they never opened a book in their whole life, surely never opened the

Bible. You think they know you missed a word or two? They don't."

"Florence knows." Worse than that, he thought, Fern knew.

In the quiet pause between them, Clovis Wolverton counted children to make sure all the chicks were in order. He turned and held up a plucked rooster. "I give the Lord the best I got, Reverend." Clovis bagged the bird and tossed it onto Jeb's wagon seat.

"Those Wolverton children told me what you did," Fern said. "If I had to choose between good preaching or a charitable heart, I'd take the latter."

"Now I know I smelled up the joint." It came to him that she never wore dresses made from feed sacks. "Fern, that hat of yours is the finest I've seen. Have I told you that?"

Fern poked a stray curl back under the flap, the wild piece of cowlick bangs she frequently swept off her face. "Most men don't notice ladies' hats. I've always said we women wear them for one another."

"I want to take you to a place you've never been." He could not say Canada. "Marvelous Crossing."

"Everybody's been there, Reverend."

"Not to this place. But when we get there, I want you to call me—"

She turned her face until the shine appeared from under the coating of powder on her nose. "Philemon?"

The name had escaped him. He might have said Jeb.

"I will. I like that name. You look like a Philemon and I never met anyone else who did." Fern pulled out her keys. "I'll drive if you want. You just tell me where we're going . . . Philemon."

Jeb asked Evelene Whittington to keep an eye on the children and she was more than happy to oblige. Probably thought

their new preacher was all tuckered out and needed some reju-
venation.

He repeated the name "Philemon" to make it sound right
in his mind. Only it sounded more foreign, a sham painted in
giant letters as big as the bank president's name on the plate-
glass window of Nazareth Bank and Trust; a lie springing off
the lips of a guileless teacher. He should have asked Mills to
paint Philemon across his forehead—like on the church sign—
to help him remember the con that seemed sweet until people
recognized him for something he was not. He knew better than
any that they only looked into the soul of the moon to see the
light that belonged to the sun.

The canoe bumped against the underpinnings of the bridge,
just where Jeb had tied it. He'd found it unmanned after a
storm one morning and paddled it a good distance from where
it had run aground. After he and Fern had taken their float
around the lake, he'd release it again so the owner could have a
chance of finding it.

Fern asked him to go ahead of her so that she could change
out of the floral dress into a pair of trousers more suitable for
leisure. No other woman in town wore them. Just Fern, and
even then only when confident of as little scrutiny as possible.
She undressed in the back seat while Jeb fetched the canoe. Her
wardrobe assortment reminded Jeb of the Gabby sisters—four
daughters of a Dallas lawyer who changed outfits according to
the time of day. Morning dresses, bridge frocks, afternoon
skirts, riding habits.

Jeb gazed only once toward the Coup, a pleasant instant as
Fern unceremoniously tossed her garter into the backseat,
rolled up, he imagined, to conceal the brown stockings. When

she stepped down the hill in rubber-soled shoes with laces, she emerged in the sunlight in brown trousers and another one of those helmet hats. This one he wanted her to lose.

"You're right. I've never seen Marvelous Crossing from a canoe," she said before she climbed into the boat and picked up a paddle.

Jeb thought of telling her she looked manly paddling. She seemed to like not being told she had to be like the other women. It didn't sound right when he ran it through his thoughts. Instead he picked up the other paddle and pushed away from the bank. "You ever go canoeing in Oklahoma?"

"With my brothers in Ardmore."

Of course she had. What were his chances of being the first with Fern at anything? "I think you told me you grew up with brothers. Maybe press your paddle to the right so we can turn." He thought she might like to see the flowers along the banks.

"I have three brothers. Two sisters. Mother called it quits after my youngest sister, Faye."

Jeb tried to picture Fern matching wits with three brothers. "What did you do for fun in Ardmore?"

"Sometimes I played golf with my father."

"Women play golf?"

"Daddy invested in Dornick Hills. Sometimes I joined a mixed foursome, sometimes I joined Daddy."

"You never told me what your father did. I thought you might come from a family of teachers." His insight at least made her smile.

"Mother taught until Daddy's practice took off. He's a doctor. Both of my sisters teach. Didn't you say you went to school in Texas?"

"Grammar school."

"Oh. I thought you attended college there. Look at this

place. I've never seen this part of the lake before." Fern laid her paddle across her lap.

"I'd say someone has a liking for—what do you call those flowers?"

"Lilies. I'll bet it took that lady years to plant them all."

Whole swathes of yellow and orange dyed the petal-strewn hillside, two happy acres behind a house cloaked by a century's growth of trees. Nothing showed of the house except the peeping roof. Below, dipping like clumsy maids, a cloud of Monarchs swarmed, attracted to clusters of purple. Their wings touched and opened like as many conversations at once, rippling in and out of the field.

The canoe came to rest beneath the shade of several oaks that soaked in the cool, lapping waters of Marvelous Crossing. The lake water smelled of leaves, brown and green, like the smell of fresh-turned soil. "Touch right there," said Fern.

Her sudden comment startled him. He saw how she pointed to the corner of her mouth, but he did not get up. Common sense told him he had conjured a daydream, that Fern would want him to touch her mouth.

"On the corner of your mouth. You have something stuck there," she said.

He brushed away whatever it was, a thread from the rope, or a piece of splintered nothing that had stuck to him. "You a pretty good golfer?"

"Not as good as my father." She leaned back, elbows resting on the old paint of the canoe. He wished he had stolen a shorter boat, something with closer seating.

"Maybe I'd like to try golf sometime."

"I wish you could know my father. He is the best golfer in Ardmore. I should take you there. But someone like you can never get away from Nazareth, not the Church in the Dell minister."

He would like to have said that he was not the minister. It would sound clean and right. But then she would ask him to take her back to the bank and as she slogged back up the hill in her flannel trousers, she would hate him every step of the way. The police would make their appearance shortly thereafter.

"You're right. I can never seem to find the time to get away." He asked her more about herself. The less he talked about himself, the more at ease he felt around her.

"Back in Ardmore, I was Dr. Coulter's daughter. Here in Nazareth, I'm just Fern, the schoolteacher. I like the plain sound of it."

"You like Oklahoma better than Nazareth?"

"In some ways. I mean, I guess it all depends upon where you live. Times are tough all over. People here seem so lost. I keep hoping I can help them pick up, start over. Daddy wants me to come home."

"Must be hard to leave a good home."

"Nazareth is needy, though. You know that already. That's why you came, I'll bet." She helped row the canoe again, enough to ease them back into the oak shade.

Jeb could not remember the place from which the Gracies had relocated.

"Take the Wolvertons. Everyone has known for some time that family needs help. But Clovis, he's got some pride. Maybe everyone thought if they helped, he'd be too ashamed to show his face. But here they all marched into church, spit-shined like the dew, new shoes to boot, and a chicken for the preacher."

Jeb felt a keening need to confess. "I want you to know I didn't pay for those shoes out of my own pocket."

"I heard. Ida May tells all. Funny girl, isn't she? You made her think you're learning to read right along with her. Not many fathers would sacrifice their image to encourage a child to read.

Most ministers I know are kind of hard, like they think they have to set an example. You're not like other clergymen, are you, Philemon?"

"Ida May's a pistol." It was true, he realized, the way she always shot off her mouth.

"I just wish I had half of your intelligence. Once you wrote a letter—I still have it. Somewhere. I made Will Honeysack give it to me. He couldn't have appreciated it, no offense to the man. But his idea of literature is the farmer's almanac."

"What letter, Fern?"

"The one you wrote about the Civil War and correlated it to climbing out of the dust of failure. You were trying to encourage our people. Everybody felt so downtrodden having gone for two years without a minister. If you had not agreed to come for such a low salary, we would still be without a preacher. Not many men will work for chickens, although I'll bet we'll see more of such things as this Depression winds on."

Jeb imagined Philemon Gracie, the admirable fool. "You want to return to Ardmore?"

"Some nights I sit out on the porch and I can smell my mother's spaghetti. She grew her own tomatoes and made the best sauce out of all the mothers where we lived. I miss that smell, the smell of her cooking. I don't miss Ardmore."

"You miss golf."

"That I miss."

"Don't have much golf around here."

She shook her head to agree with him.

Jeb's face lifted. "You taking a box lunch to the raffle on Wednesday?"

She answered him, "Why? You plan on bidding?"

"The holder of the box lunch gets to join the girl for a meal that made it. I'd hate to see you sitting all by your lonesome."

"Maybe you won't be the only man bidding, you ever think about that? Some people like my shoo-fly pie." She straightened and it made her look tall on the canoe seat.

"I got nothing against your shoo-fly pie. Much prefer your biscuits, though," he said.

"Church in the Dell's been holding box lunches for years. People come from all over just to meet new faces. You'd be surprised what those men will bid on." That made her laugh. Jeb pictured her sitting around a clubhouse laughing out loud with all the men.

"Maybe I should get a loan from Nazareth Bank and Trust," Jeb said.

"I'd do that if I were you."

"Naw, first I think I'll buy me one of those Packards. This year, a Packard. Box lunch maybe next year."

She wet the paddle, flipped it over, and turned the boat back toward the bridge. "We better get you back to the children. This is a nice place. I'm glad you showed it to me."

He tried to think of the best way to get her to stay.

"Something on your mind, Philemon?"

He ran some words through his mind again, trying them out.

"My oldest brother says that I intimidate some people. I don't think I intimidate you, though," she said.

He shook his head. "Fern, you got to understand, I have things I want to tell you. But it never comes out like I want."

She brought the paddle up and the boat slowed. "I think I understand."

"You really don't."

"It's your wife. You could never replace her. You think I got designs on you, but I really just enjoy talking to you."

"It's not that."

"It is. I'm not trying to take Mrs. Gracie's place. What was her name, anyway?"

Jeb said, "Verna." It sounded like a preacher's wife.

"I'll bet she was a lovely person."

"I didn't intend to take the conversation in this direction." He felt just as trapped as when Hank Hampton had found him locking lips with Myrna Hoop.

"Maybe it is the best starting place." She poised her face teacherly again. "Tell me where you met Verna."

He could pick any place he wanted, he realized. But it should be someplace besides Oklahoma. He'd grown up in the next state, one year not far from the Oklahoma border, never realizing those Okies let angels play in foursomes and girls dress in trousers. Their paths never could have crossed. If they had, at any rate, she would have tossed a coin into the tin cup of his station and joined the College Joes for tea. "We met in Tennessee." He knew he would never remember it again. "No, we met in Texas. Verna used to say I get my facts confused."

"Tell me what you remember about Verna and Texas, then. I really want to know," she said.

He wet his paddle too, needing to deliver her back to the bridge before his story liquefied into the lake. In that case he could just walk back on dry land the same way he walked into town, a bum and a liar.

15

Twenty thousand Americans committed suicide in 1931. Angel knew that and the thought of her mother's mind drying up and blowing away with the rest of the country troubled her. She had convinced Val Rodwyn at Honeysack's that an infirm woman by the name of Hildy Gardner lived on the edge of town, reliant on the goodness of neighbors to bring her mail. Finally, the day before the New York Yankees played the Chicago Cubs in the third game of the World Series, Angel got a letter from Aunt Kate, her mother's sister in Little Rock. Kate had addressed the envelope to Mrs. Hildy Gardner just as Angel had instructed. "My daddy will see this gets to Mrs. Gardner, Mr. Rodwyn," she told him. She tugged her ear and left the store. She read Kate's letter out on the sidewalk, three blocks away from Honeysack's Store.

Dear Angel,

I was surprised to hear you are living with a stranger, but glad she is taking care of you all until you can get kot up with Claudia. We have not heard from Claudia since she had that baby girl, we thot, down where you are. I believe it was a little girl. Your mother is still not well. I know she wants to be her very best when she sees you all again. We do

not have much here, so if you could get that daddy of yours
to telegram mony, your mother and I could use the hep.
How is it this Mrs. Gardner came to hep you all out? They
is still Christian peple in the world and it makes me glad to
know that.

Much love, Aunt Kate

Willie read over her shoulder. "You didn't tell her about
Daddy. Why didn't you?"

"I didn't want to worry Momma. Sounds like they don't
have nothing to live on."

"She doesn't say anything at all about Momma, like is she
living with her or is she in the hospital?"

"All she says is that Momma is not well. What am I sup-
posed to make of it? Is she in the sanatorium like Lana said?"
Angel stuffed the letter into her bag and waved down Mellie
Fogarty to ask for a ride home. "Get your books and things,
Willie. Jeb will be wondering why we're so late coming home
from school."

"Maybe we should go find Momma on our own. We made
it this far, Angel." Willie strapped his books into the belt and
carted it over his shoulder. He had gained an inch on his sister
and now met her eye level.

"Little Rock, Willie? Why don't we just go to the moon?"
Angel leaned into the passenger side of Mrs. Fogarty's automobile to ask her husband for a ride. Mrs. Fogarty touched her cheek
and smiled. Angel told Willie, "Get in. They'll give us a ride."

It seemed right to Angel that as the lambs of the minister,
they had a roof over their heads and a ready, free ride over long,
dusty roads any time they wanted. The name Gracie had done
her more good than Welby. But if she could just rest her head

in her mother's lap again, in the starchy cotton folds that smelled of safety, that might seem right, too.

The Fogartys motored them back to the parsonage. Nothing seemed right or wrong. Just filled or hungry. Angel preferred filled if she could not have her mother.

Horace Mills set up a battery-operated Philco radio on the lawn of the church even though Florence thought it might be sacrilegious. But the fact that a gospel singing came across the air waves once a week on Sunday night appeased her and she said she would not be offended.

Babe Ruth played outfield for the Yankees. Yankees fans collected around the Philco, each man taking turns with turning the radio off and on during the advertisements to save battery power since the replacement batteries cost four dollars at the Woolworth's.

Jeb had been asked to auction off the box lunches as had been the custom in previous years. But between boxes, he leaned toward the radio with the rest of the men to listen for the scores.

Single girls and young men from Hope, Camden, and even as far away as Hot Springs, parked all over the church lawn. Some drove their father's automobiles; a few looking too young to do so. Young swells in college sweaters tossed a football into a group of girls just to hear the squeals. Boxes tied with crepe paper in various sizes had been stacked on a table normally used for communion. When the tabletop was jam-packed, the remaining box lunches were stacked underneath on the grass.

Jeb picked up a bulky box tied with pink crepe paper. "Smells wonderful, fellers. Says it was home cooked by Betty LaFevre." He stared over the heads until he saw a hand, nails chewed to the quick, waving at him. "Here's Betty and she's glad to raise money for the church."

The young woman, small as a child, leaned cross-legged against an automobile bumper, her plaid flannel skirt spread out like a flag. She appeared to know some of the college men.

Several university boys bid on the box until it sold for seventy-five cents.

Jeb auctioned off six more boxes, the sixth of which was cooked by Angel. It sold to a fourteen-year-old boy who promptly asked Angel to join him. She declined and walked to the church steps to sit alone.

"Boys, we have a fine box of fried chicken here. It is cooked by . . . Miss Fern Coulter."

The local boys laughed and made comments about the minister running away with the Coulter dinner. The flirtation had spread around town.

But a man from out of town stepped up and bid a dollar.

Everyone fell silent.

Fern came up on her toes to get a look at him.

He had a slender look about him, with long arms and worsted sweater sleeves pushed up, making rolls around his elbows.

"We have a bid from an out-of-towner," said Jeb. "Want to give us your name, young feller?"

"Oz Mills."

Horace Mills did not look up from the radio, not with the Yankees at bat. But his other two sons stood behind their older cousin, Oz, and appeared to watch for a reaction from Jeb.

"Horace Mills's nephew." Someone told Jeb quietly. He said, "Home from college, I gather."

"No, my father's bank in Hope," said Oz. "I'm in the banking business same as my Uncle Horace."

That would explain his high bid of a dollar, Jeb figured. "Come on, boys. You going to let a Hope feller take this one away from you?"

"You bid, Reverend!" said a Wolverton boy.

"All right. Dollar and a nickel," said Jeb. "Just to make it interesting."

A little distress made creases around Fern's eyes. Jeb got the idea that she wanted to stop him, but then figured she was having fun with him.

"Dollar and one dime," said Oz. He jangled the coins in his right pocket.

"Dollar and a quarter." Jeb wondered why Horace had never mentioned his banker nephew. He bragged about everything else in his life.

Fern excused her way through the crowd. She whispered something to Oz. He responded by touching the tip of her nose.

Oz shot back, "Dollar fifty, then. Fern Coulter's worth every penny."

"So she is," said Jeb. "Sold to Mr. Oz Mills for one dollar and fifty cents." Fern was worth a week's wages, but something existed between the teacher and this banker that had obviously escaped his attention. Oz took Fern's box lunch and led her by the arm to a blanket on the lawn. Jeb watched as they exchanged words, pleasant eye contact, and appeared to catch up on old times.

Back on the lake in the canoe, Fern had goaded Jeb with the intimation that more than one bull occupied the paddock. He wrote it off as a woman's bluff. Fool that he was.

Jeb auctioned off the remaining boxes and then helped Will Honeysack take the money inside and count it. He left the money to be deposited with Will and joined the married men around the Philco. He listened to the roar of the crowd whenever the Babe's name was mentioned. He joined the overall-wearing bunch in baseball blather, drivel regarding the cost of a bale of cotton, and the national concern about the sad fate of the Lindbergh baby.

Fern opened two Coca-Colas; one for herself and the other that she had surely intended for him.

It was hard to tell.

Jeb ate his evening meal out on the porch. Angel took the Monday beans, stirred tomatoes into them, and served them with spaghetti noodles and cornbread. He had just put the coffee to his lips when Oz Mills pulled up. He jumped out of a Packard and helped Fern out, complimenting her on her helmet hat.

Jeb drew in a mouthful of coffee, slightly sugared, but too hot to drink. It scalded his tongue. He sat up, spilled a black, hot droplet onto his lap and had to keep from swearing. When they made it to the porch, he stood, both hands full. "Evenin'," he said, although he knew it lacked luster.

Fern sounded formal again. "Reverend Gracie, I want you to meet Oz Mills. I mean, I know you met today. You haven't been formally introduced."

"Oz." Jeb set aside the plate and cup and extended his hand.

"Reverend, I'm glad to meet you." Oz had a polished drawl, as though he had spent time in Atlanta. "No hard feelings about the box dinner, I hope. Fern chastens me for competing over every little thing."

"No hard feelings. The box lunch is all in fun for you youngsters. It's fun for the rest of us to watch." Jeb squeezed Oz's hand harder than a normal handshake.

"Oh, Oz, we've interrupted the reverend's meal," said Fern.

"Nothing to it," said Jeb. "Just a little something Angel whipped up."

"I don't think she wanted that boy from town to buy her box dinner." She filled Oz in on the conversation. "Angel is the reverend's daughter. He has done well with her since her mother's death. Especially hard on girls."

"I don't know if it's any easier for a boy. When I lost my mother, I don't think I ever got over it," said Jeb.

"My mother passed on when I was only sixteen," Oz put in. "My stepmother has done as best as she knows how with my little brothers. Do you have sons?"

Jeb realized he was addressing him again. "One boy."

"You might think all he needs is you. But losing his mother while young, well, it's something he needs to talk about. Get things out in the open with him. You'll be glad you did." Oz never looked at Jeb, but seemed to make the speech to impress Fern.

"I see what you mean, Oz. Willie is such a quiet boy in school, too easy to overlook." Fern's sympathy clearly remained on Oz's side of the paddock.

"Can I offer you all something to eat? Coffee?" Jeb addressed Fern only.

Oz cut to the chase. "Fern said that you own a canoe. I was hoping we could borrow it. She said the view from Marvelous Crossing is amazing."

"That wasn't my canoe, I'm afraid. Matter of fact, it floated under the bridge one day and I sort of borrowed it myself," said Jeb.

"What happened to it?" asked Fern.

"After I took you out in it, I just released it. I was hoping the owner would find it floating around and claim it. Not mine to give." Jeb hoped Oz would not spot it tied to the rotted oak just beyond Marvelous Crossing Bridge and the lily banks.

"I guess we'll just have to skip the canoe ride, then," Fern said to Oz.

"You're more than welcome to borrow my fishing pole," Jeb offered, "if you're wanting to wet a line. Right back here in the stream, we got good-sized trout." He and Oz exchanged awkward gazes.

"I didn't quite have fishing in mind, Reverend." Oz brought his hand under Fern's elbow. "Fidel's Drugstore then, Fern. I'll split a malted with you."

"Sure, why not?" Fern's arms swung back as though she planned her exit.

"How did you two meet?" Jeb asked Oz.

"My aunt had a summer party once and invited my family and a few people from around town. Fern and I met at my aunt's party. About two summers ago. We're both so busy with our lives, it's been difficult to get together."

"I'm sorry you have to go back home to Hope. Daddy Mills needs you, I guess."

Fern's eyes narrowed.

"Tomorrow I'll travel back to Hope. Tonight, dinner with my aunt and uncle. Fern, you'll join us won't you?" Oz faced Fern and when he did, it was as though Jeb faded completely from the porch.

"Your mother has already invited me, don't you know? Tempted me with her pork roast. She does with oranges and pork what my mother does with pasta." Fern touched Jeb's arm. "I'll see you Saturday for . . . you know what."

Jeb, although he would not have wanted Oz to know he was getting help in sermonizing by a grammar schoolteacher, enjoyed the moment of secrecy between Fern and him.

"Saturday it is, Fern. And stop calling me Reverend. You know we don't do that anymore." He returned the touch on her arm.

Oz made several cagey glances back at him as he escorted Fern across the yard and to the pale-yellow Packard.

"Ida May sends her love." Jeb waved good-bye to Fern only. The beans and spaghetti had grown cold.

Jeb went to bed while the sad state of affairs stung his insides like acid. Wherever he had lived, his plans always blew up in his face, like the time he and Charlie found dynamite down by the old railway, south of town in Temple. Charlie wanted to see how high a milk pail would fly if they set a stick off under it. But the wick, too short and dangerously dry, had fizzled—Jeb thought. So when he returned to relight it, the explosion caught him in the face. His mother had shrieked and said he would be a monstrous sight, unable to go out in public. But the healing came and left him with a faint curving scar to the right of his left eye, a crooked finger pointing at his eye to tell first this one and that one the folly of his boyhood. He was not left a monstrosity but he had yet to find a place where he could settle down without feeling the breath of failure steaming straight down his collar. He'd left Texas under the cloak of night with Charlie when a cornfield burned one afternoon and the two of them were blamed for it. They knew who did it—Uncle Festus got drunk and lay smoking in the middle of the field. Gave them each a cigarette, but they did not start the fire. They left town and found work in Texarkana.

Myrna was really Charlie's problem but somehow she'd become Jeb's trouble.

Jeb connected stars through the window and thought of the fresh clean feeling of coming in new to a town. People greeted you kindly, tipped their hat. Ladies smiled at the new blood in town. Merchants lighted up at the sight of a new customer. The new boss had no prior notions about you, no biases. It was like being born again. Like going to sleep with the law on your back but waking up in a church and being handed keys, a chicken for your pot, and a warm place to sleep. Respect, admiration, pretty girls stopping you on the sidewalk to have you comment about a new dress.

Jeb's mother, Geneva, had told him once, "I agree with yore daddy about one thang. You don't know how to go about your business without falling into the fire, Jeb Nubey. Some people like to live in peace among their fellow human beings, but you like to take your hullabaloo stick and stir up trouble. If there is a fight to be had, you land the first blow and bring all the tumult down around your own ears."

He listened to Geneva complain about him and to him while he watched the stars. Neither she nor Charlie senior had ever made sense to him. But now, in the quiet of the church parsonage, he wanted to hear her out. The burned cornfield came to him and he tried to imagine ways out of the situation. He could have confessed, told the deputy Uncle Festus started the blaze. Be the family snitch. Charlie could have taken the blow for dating Myrna Hoop, and Jeb's kiss a mere brotherly gesture. Everybody could have taken their own medicine. He relived his past a lot to set straight the things that had gotten away from him.

But what to tell Fern eluded him. He wanted to sit down with her and explain how the situation had gotten away from him. Out of all of the bad men in the world, he was the least among them. He said it out loud. Didn't have much of a ring to it. He played out the scene in several different situations. Fern would help him prepare a sermon but he would flip-flop to something else entirely; he would preach the truth to her, sit her down, and ask her to stay and hear him out. He practiced several confessions. But every declaration of guilt sent her packing; her look of disappointment deflated his entire scheme.

In his mind, Charlie senior scolded another of his bad ideas. *I don't know how I raised a boy with no character. I don't know how you got so seared in your thinking.* Much different was when he sat at his momma's knee as a young feller and she told him he had the sign of an apostle on him. She'd only said that once. It had come to her in a dream. In any case, after the fire, his daddy had said, "*It scares me to death to think you'll end up on a rock pile someday.*" Scared young Jeb to death, too, like fate hovered over his life sucking him up into its cyclone. Jeb saw the whole picture through his daddy's eyes, as though he looked straight into the theater of his mind—him chained to six other men while an oversized guard poked him in the shoulder blades with a rifle muzzle. Ol' Charlie's words always had the intended effect—the very word *jail* scared the wits out of him. Even worse, the threat of being locked up seemed to follow him around as though he had been fatally picked to spend his life pounding rocks, just as Charlie would spend his days married to Selma from Oklahoma.

Often when they visited a dry goods store in Dallas, Charlie senior had pointed to every law officer that passed in front of the plate glass window. "They will haul you off if ever you steal what don't belong to you."

One lazy Saturday he had examined a rubber ball from a whole bin of them, a red bouncing ball just right for stick ball or hurling at Charlie to inflict mortal wounds upon his freck-led skin. Without thinking, or maybe seized by the forces of nature, he'd walked past the clerk and out into the sunlight imagining how high into the sky the ball would fly if popped in the sweet center by his hard pine beauty. He'd tipped his hat at the town deputy, Wesley Bishop, given the ball a good bounce and then felt his knees buckle when he realized he had walked out of the store without paying for the ball. Daddy had known he had the thief inside of him. At that moment guilt had swept over him. He'd stumbled back inside with the ball tucked underneath his shirt, past the clerk, and down the aisle to the rubber ball bin. When the clerk had glanced up at him a third time, his eyes, he felt certain, had rolled back in his head. He had dropped the ball at his feet and left it spiraling on the floor. Without stopping, he ran two miles to escape his destiny.

Every time the deputy came sniffing around Nazareth, Jeb thought it a matter of days, maybe just hours, until Charlie's prophecy found fulfillment. He had dreamed of good and evil, men in chains, and stars colliding. He wanted to believe Momma. And believe that divination might have been her lot as much as an early death. But Charlie senior never left his head. Never stopped telling him his fate.

A cloud came across the moon, dappling the white face that lit the edges of trees and the hills of Nazareth with unearthly silvering. Jeb rolled onto his face. It came to him that he could not remember the past he had invented for Fern's sake.

He pulled pen and paper from the crate beside the bed and wrote down every pertinent fact he thought he had given to Fern. Making the letters lean, he wrote faster than he had the week before. But even Will Honeysack's handwriting had a shaky line. He had noticed that when he wrote down the offering funds. The lantern flickered and he raised the wick to read what he had written down already. His script read well enough. But compared to Fern's liquid penmanship, his was doddery, like the handwriting belonging to a feeble man. *Wife, Verna. Born in Texas.* He had said Texas, hadn't he? *Moved here from—*

Tennessee. Or was it Atlanta? *Brother, Charlie.* He might have mentioned Charlie to her but even if he had not, he was certain to do so. Stories of Charlie and him could fill volumes as well as interjecting homey repartee into the quiet moments of a Sunday afternoon.

Repartee. He'd read that word from a poem and had decided to try it out on Fern this Saturday. *Repartee.* It looked false coming from his Woolworth's pen.

He swapped the pen and paper for a book left tucked into a basket of Fern's bread. She had called it the writings of Pascal and seemed surprised when he did not respond with a comment. Out loud, he practice-read until the rims of his eyes stung as though filled with rubbing alcohol. He practiced sounding fluid. The moon disappeared entirely. The last thing he remembered was laying Pascal across his chest.

When he awoke, the children had gotten themselves off to school. Ida May rocked on the porch alone. Best of all, he was not in jail.

16

*T*he Yankees win had lifted morale as though every out-of-work Joe had hit the home runs themselves. Majesty ebbed and flowed into every nook and cranny of the country, spilling down into the mousiest holes. Even into Nazareth. Saturday, everyone flooded downtown, anxious to share the united good spirits, and that is how Fern happened to pick up the letter from Charlie.

Jeb did not know if she had read the sender's name on the smudged corner of the envelope but suspected she had. Informing her that he had a brother Charlie without explaining the difference in last names complicated the plan, so he took the letter from her hand and dropped the idea entirely. He only addressed the matter by thanking her for dropping by the mail, and left it at that. Charlie had scrawled his alias on the front—Philemon Gracie.

Fern sounded short on breath but euphoric when she showed up on the parsonage porch, Charlie's letter in her hand. "I've never seen so many people out and about town. You'd think a holiday had come the way folks are out milling through all of the stores. Woolworth's is full to capacity. I'll bet Floyd Whittington has to squeeze customers in with a shoehorn. The Honeysacks are sitting in chairs in front of their store with a fruit stand right out on the walk. It's kind of like those outdoor markets in Europe I've heard about."

He didn't ask her about Europe. "October brings out the best in people, even when they're dickering over a nickel's worth of beans to save a penny. Maybe the cooler weather does it, or maybe it's just a *collective* mood." Jeb did not know if he had used "collective" in the manner he should, but it sounded clever and Fern agreed so quickly he felt all right about it.

She dug through the beaded handbag until she found a band for her hair. She pulled her hair back away from her face. "I hope you aren't apprehensive about today," she said.

"No reason to be, is there?"

"I keep thinking maybe I'm not the one who should be helping you." Fern had a stack of books, including one of the oldest dictionaries Jeb had ever seen.

He liked the thought of it, a woman listening while he talked. She sank back against the sofa and closed her eyes as he read something to her from *Pensees*. It did not sound as profound as it had the night before. So he pulled out his notes, although he did not want her to look at them. "Nice fellow, Oz. That must stand for Oswald or something."

"Oswald Thurman Mills, after his great-grandfather on his daddy's side. Are your children awake? It's so quiet." She slipped out of her shoes and pushed them next to the sofa.

"Down by the stream. Catching crawdads or tadpoles. You're right. For once it is quiet." He liked the way she casually deposited her shoes onto his rug, as though she had just gotten home. Her toes were long, especially the chief toes, which appeared able enough to pick up a pencil.

"I think we should do this out on the front porch. Sunny but cool. Persimmon in the air." She left him in the living room as though she fully expected him to follow her.

Jeb left the copy of *Pensees* on the sofa arm. He followed her all the way out.

She must have noticed how he faltered when he picked up the Bible. "How about if I stare down at the porch and you just act as though you're preaching to the woods." She looked intently at the porch until she realized he had offered no sort of response.

Jeb asked the first thing that came to him. "Are you and Oz Mills seeing each other?"

"Not often."

"Often as once a year?"

"Things like that matter to you?" she asked.

"Of course they don't."

"What is your subject matter for tomorrow, if I may ask?"

"But some things matter, because I don't know this Oz very well. He rolls into town and just expects you to drop everything. I think that seems like a peculiar dating ritual." Now he felt more clumsy than before, when he wanted to say more. He didn't.

"That's your subject?"

"Paul on the isle of Patmos."

"So my dating rituals interest you?"

"I imagine he was lonely."

"Paul or Oz?"

"Oz. That is, Paul. I'd like to get back to the preaching materials," said Jeb. He had not intended to bring up Oz at all. It was one of those subjects that had buzzed around his thoughts for a few days until it spilled out, as though he had just asked her what she thought about Babe Ruth, but instead asked her, "Is this a serious thing between you and Oz?"

"I don't know," she said. "We've never discussed it."

Women knew more than they confessed, he felt. But he left

the subject alone. "I think there's something to be said about Paul and how God left him to write letters on the isle of Patmos."

"What do you want to say about it?" she asked. A bit of something that stirred inside of her sparked when she spoke, shelling him like little bullets. But she stayed to task.

"If he hadn't been cut off from the rest of the church folks, we would not have his letters or this part of the Bible." Jeb had not fully developed that thought, but was hoping she would.

Instead she sat down in the rocker and stared into the trees. "Why don't you just preach? I'm not in the mood to talk, anyway, if you don't mind."

Jeb opened the Bible to gather the first thought of the lecture.

Fern crossed one leg and tapped her foot in the air. The mulish way that she refused to look at him thickened the air so that even the crickets' pipes were muted.

Since the last few minutes had plodded ahead unrewardingly, like a badminton contest with no drops, he found her silence agreeable. With at least the quiet in his favor, he read from his notes until a certain comment about Paul caught her attention. "Do you agree with that?" he asked.

She nodded. "Maybe say that Paul's persecution wound up being enlightenment for the whole world."

He cottoned to the word *enlightenment*. But he would not stoop to ask her to spell it. After he had continued for what felt like another ten minutes, Fern said, "You know, Paul had it in his mind that he would go and preach to certain places. But instead, he spent his last days writing letters. Maybe he didn't even have the assurance that anyone would ever read them. I wonder if he felt like he had failed God?"

Jeb wished he had said that, or even thought it. But then all of a sudden, he just knew it. He didn't know what to make of it, as though a con like him could get inside the head of Saint Paul or would even want to. Jeb had always run around the tree of his problems and just kept running until he ran out of rope. But he expected that of himself. It came to him that Paul had felt the same way. He wrote down her comment and decided to study on it.

They continued. When Fern would fall silent for a while he would prompt her until she would pick up where she left off. What she said had plainness but stirred things up inside of him. It felt as though he was eating her little truisms, He finally got up off his rocker and sat down in front of her. "I like listening to you talk."

"That's a kind thing to say," she said.

"I'm not trying to be kind. Oz, I'll bet he knows all of the kind and right things to say to you. But I could just lay on a bank, listening to the river, your voice, and nothing else."

"Could you tell me why you have such an interest in Oz Mills?" she asked.

"He appeared out of nowhere."

"We've known each other for a couple of years."

"That's a long time. Seems like he would do something about now, find ways to see you more often." Jeb leaned against the porch railing. His feet were inches from Fern's elongated toes.

"You think I should see him more often? Try and deepen things between us?" Fern never lost momentum when Jeb questioned her, a practice that kept knocking him off the fence post.

"That's not for me to say. Just seems like if he's going to try and keep a girl on a leash—"

"I'm not on Oz Mills's leash!"

"So what you're trying to say is that Oz and you are just friends?"

She pulled her bare feet up under the cotton skirt. The fabric enveloped her like a mushroom. "Something like that. You and I, we're friends, aren't we?"

He did not know how to answer her.

Angel ran through the house, as though she had come up the back steps, and bolted for the front porch. "Jeb, Jeb!"

Jeb stood and met her at the door. Her voice sounded like an alarm.

"What name did she call you?" Fern asked.

Angel saw Fern and pulled her hands up to her mouth. "*Daddy*, we saw the deputy coming through the woods, down the road to our place. See, he's coming."

Jeb's lips came together, not a smile nor a grimace, just the steady pretense of a man in hiding. "Nothing wrong with that, Angel. You go back inside and check on your brother and sister. Maybe the deputy has news about the truck."

Fern's feet dropped onto the porch. She went back inside to look for her shoes.

Jeb met the officer out on the lawn with a smile as wooden as an Indian nickel. "Afternoon, Deputy. What can I do for you?"

The deputy did not offer a friendly greeting this time. "I need to discuss something with you, Reverend. Maybe you want to step away from the house, so the kids don't hear."

Jeb craned his head to the flank and saw Fern and all three kids staring at them. "You coming to the potluck social, Deputy Maynard?" Jeb asked. "Last chance for potato salad until the spring, I hear."

"It's about your truck and a bit of trouble down in Texarkana," said the deputy.

Jeb hid his hands in his pockets. His fingers came around a bit of old cork from a bottle of Texarkana home brew. "I don't know anything about Texarkana."

"Seems your vehicle was the getaway for a man who bludgeoned a landowner's son to death. You ever heard of a Mr. Leon Hampton, owns a cotton plantation down near the Arkansas-Texas border?"

"This Hank Hampton, he died?"

"I thought I said Leon. Appears so. This Jeb Nubey, he's the man they been looking for all these months." The deputy held up the wanted poster.

Maynard studied his face. Jeb didn't dare look at Fern, who might have heard Angel call him Jeb. He walked a few paces out and Maynard followed.

"But you say your truck was stolen outside our town. Not in Texarkana? Do I have your story right, Reverend?"

"Seems there was a little business one night about my truck." Jeb steadied his voice. "It was down around Texarkana. Remember when we were slowed up coming here? My truck turned up missing, but I got it back. I thought some boys went joy riding." His throat felt like something had been tied around it and yanked by the worst knot yet.

"That is such a relief to hear, Reverend. I'll write this up and get it down to the sheriff in Texarkana."

He did not feel relieved but sick to death. "No need to report it. Not any harm done that I can see."

"Best to report these details. Keeps us all straight with one another across county lines. I don't see how this has anything to do with the boys on this robbing spree, the ones who done stole your truck. Appears to be a different matter entirely." He started to turn away, but then threw in, "Many times as you get robbed, I'd say you're too trusting, Parson. Me, I got to figger out some missing pieces. Somehow, I'll study on it. Something will come to me. Always does. I cracked a case two years ago that had those Washington swells completely bumfuzzled. I got the nose for these things. My wife tells me that all the time."

"Glad to hear that," said Jeb.

"Best I can figger, this two-man crime spree across upper Arkansas has me thinking we're closing in on finding your truck. I will let you know as soon as we get these boys nailed. See you in church, maybe. Wife's been after me to go. Food's always a good bait."

Jeb watched him go. His chest felt as though an anvil had dropped on him. Hank Hampton was a fool, but Jeb did not want him dead. The sun of noonday drenched him, poured over him through the baring oaks, but he felt a chill. He had to choke back an anxious moan and the urge to run at the same time. He was convinced that all of the sky light over Nazareth pointed into his dirty past. Maynard had braked at the end of the lane when the urge to run after the deputy overtook Jeb. In the dust of the police automobile he imagined running behind the deputy waving his arms, keen on confessing his crime. Angel ran into the dream behind him shrieking and begging him to stop. Then Fern called out his stolen name and it all disappeared. He felt guilty and safe all at once.

"You scared me today. I never saw you like that before. You came back with trouble all over your face." Fern had her hand behind her holding open the screen door. "This Hampton must have been a close friend of yours."

"He shouldn't have died. I just don't understand why. He was young, kind of stupid, but didn't deserve death," said Jeb.

Every wood and town between Texarkana and Little Rock swarmed with cops. But all Jeb could see in his mind's eye was Hank Hampton laying in repose with a lily in his hands. Fern's face blurred and he saw Hank's momma. He covered his face with his hands. "This is a nightmare, that's what!"

Angel stayed near Jeb, her hand cupped right behind his elbow as though she no longer trusted him to say the right things. "Good night, Miss Coulter. He'll be fine in the morning."

Jeb wanted to explain his pain to Fern, but two things barred confession: nothing he could say would be the truth and he could not bear another lie. So he pleaded in his mind, something that sounded like a prayer. A bit of relief. Something along the lines of "Don't strike me down before I make things right."

"Walk me out, Reverend?" she asked

Jeb told Angel, "Go on and wash up for bed."

"I can walk Miss Coulter out," she said. She squeezed his hand as though she was trying to speak to him in secret codes, and that surprised him. When he looked into her face, she did not look hard or sarcastic but like a teenaged girl groping to find her way. Scared for the first time, it seemed. His past had not threatened her security too much until now.

"Angel, just go. We'll talk in the morning." Jeb opened the door for Fern.

From the front yard, Angel's head could be seen through a window like she had grown a halo. Then the living room went dark.

Fern had to pull on her sweater. The night air had a hint of cooling. Winter was not far off. Jeb helped her pull the wrap around her shoulders so she could slip her arms into the sleeves. "You're sure you're all right, Reverend?"

The way she kept patting his arm and telling him how sorry she was that his friend had died comforted him, even though he did not deserve it. "Go get some rest and don't worry about me, Fern. I shouldn't have gotten so torn up like that."

"You're up to preaching tomorrow?"

He had forgotten entirely. Sunday was only a few hours away. Then after that, everything she knew about him could dissolve right in plain sight of her. Maynard's report would be sent out on Monday to the Texarkana law enforcement officials. He thought of that one thing and of Hank Hampton lying in his grave. He lied to Fern once more and told himself it would be the last lie, one more invention. Even in his tone, without any trace of boasting, he said, "You'll like tomorrow's message. Paul on the isle of Patmos. Paul and me, we got things together." He hoped to make it the last lie.

He felt her hand brush against his shirt. When he looked down, he saw her hand resting against his chest. "Fern?"

She lifted her face to him.

"I need you." It slipped out. He kissed her but even that felt like a lie. Common sense told him to walk away, slink into the night, be gone by morning. Then out came more confessions to entangle him further. The kind of words a bona fide man of worth should say. But not him. "If you don't need me, I'll settle for this." He kissed her again and when he did it seemed she needed him back.

Her touch took him to a place far from deputy warrants and dark Mondays. For an instant, he could see the two of them on a blanket sipping lemonade at Marvelous Crossing. Four children played around them on the grass making dandelion crowns and soiling the blanket with bare muddy feet.

Other pleasant things crowded out worry like a happy dose of life with a nice kick to it. October had come with more good than bad and wasn't that something to consider? This time and place he had found on the way to no place in particular had somehow made him better. Maybe he just wanted to be better. He was a literate man, for one. In his arms this night was some lovely thing that smelled like the heavenly hosts and all things honorable. Monday could not send him running away, tail tucked, to a new town to start again. He wouldn't allow it to unravel right in front of him. But guilt got the better of him. Fern should know him and know about him.

Then she kissed his neck and he died again.

Tell me, God, this ain't the beginning and dead end of all things good. He could not believe that destined-for-jail Jeb Nubey had come to like the taste of good people and their simple life spread out like a banquet. To see it end made him feel like the kid shown a peek into a kaleidoscope only to have it taken away for good. It should not be so. He pushed Monday away. Something within reach had to make it all true for him—Fern, Church in the Dell, and this man whose shoes he had put on. Hang tomorrow or Monday! Sunday would row pleasant things onto Jeb Nubey's muddy shores—a little sacred music, some community admiration, and the girl. Tomorrow would be his final gift. He thanked God for it.

"I love Sundays, don't you, Fern?"

"Philemon, you have to kiss me like that again. It felt like the power of God between us," she said.

17

Jeb slept only until just before dawn. Too soon to know if a miracle would show, but he had asked God for it more than once in the night. *God.* He had used the name for cheating and getting by. He'd made a money-spinning livelihood of the backstabbing of Christ. Now with nothing to look at but the night, he sidled up to Him like a mad dog begging to be shot.

He pulled out Charlie's letter to read again. Near dawn, he read the letter stamped with a Texarkana postmark in the paleness of daybreak, no pigment yet of true daylight.

> *Dear Jeb or Philemon (haha! how did you come up with that name anyway?) Your first letter, and me the first to know about it! I always said you was a capable man, even when Daddy doubted it. This cover of yours sounds like a good one, so I'd keep doing what you're doing and lay low. You did not say how you are making it, but I guess you always manage to make a living for yourself—must be good money in religion. Bad news, brother. Hank is dead. But you don't need to hear all this. You sound like you got things going your way now and . . .*

Jeb tucked the letter into his britches' pocket, pulled it out again, slipped it under the mattress, and then pulled it back out to rip Charlie's woefully regretful mail into a dozen strips for the garbage pail. It had not brought him a speck of comfort. He could not bear Charlie's bragging on him for scamming a whole town—not this town. Somehow, he had lost a taste for it. He picked up Evelene's Bible, opened it, then just held it next to him.

"Comfort me, God, will you?" He whispered it like he was ashamed to ask out loud. His hands shook like rattlers. All sense drained from him. *Run, Job! Like you always do.* It was time to fly the coop, wasn't it? But too many things anchored his feet in this lush place called Nazareth. As of last night, Ruth was his for the asking. His old white shirt still held enough of the faint scent of her perfume to prove it. The feeling of his hands and arms wrapped around her gave him a taste of what time spent with her would do for a man—like a miserly taste of chocolate on the tongue.

In any case, there were other things that tied him up in ropes and left him ready for the block. People treated him like he was respectable and that had never come up before. A small girl's cough in the next room cracked open his heart. He liked the sound of "Daddy." Angel, Willie, and Ida May had shown him what it felt like to be needed. Made him soft as butter. He could hear Charlie laugh at that. Turning soft had ruined him and in a queer way gave him a life.

Somehow the lie had become his life. Or his life was just a lie. Everything clouded again and he rubbed the wet from his eyes.

The edge of another peaceful hitch was once again at hand as it always had been in the past, coming round like the moon's orbit. His life had known so many beginnings and endings and he hated it. Hated who he really was. Ruination slipped over him. It was the only stinking blanket he really owned and the way he carried it with him everywhere he went like a railroad tramp only proved his vagrant blood.

He pressed his face into the pillow, half-hoping for suffocation, and rolled over on his side. Sleep escaped him, but he thought he must have drifted enough to enter that place of half-sleep, somewhere between the world of mind and spirit, because he lost a whole half hour he could not account for. He blinked, but dread haunted him like a handful of loaded shot made ready for his coming execution. A wind like the voice of Hank propelled a chill through the window screen and seeped through every drafty crevice in the house. A flash of white moved, ghostly and mixed with shadows, underneath his door. The sun had not lifted even a nub of rays, but the sky had lightened, indicating Sunday hummed just down the hill. It seemed to sing his dirge.

The doorknob turned. Jeb closed his eyes, ready to swallow punishment, even if Hank's ghost delivered it himself.

"I couldn't sleep," said Angel.

"Don't ever bust through the door like that!"

"Somebody woke up Crabby." She set a lantern on the floor beside her.

Jeb rolled onto his back with the pillow still covering his face. "It's too early to deal with kids."

"There's something I need to know."

"After my first cup of coffee." Jeb tried to dismiss her, and waited to hear her pad back into the room next door.

"You're already awake, so what's the deal anyway?"

Jeb sat up, hugging the pillow like it was the only thing holding him up, and dangled his feet off the bed. The clothes he had slept in were rumpled. All the fight was gone out of him. He said with a peppering of kindness, "Best to get on with it, Angel. You'll not let me go back to sleep until I do."

She looked past him, sort of through him, like her eyes were fixed on something beyond him. "You're leaving, aren't you?"

He hadn't come up with a reasonable solution yet that sounded humanly decent, so he didn't know what to tell her.

"If you want to run, I'll go to the church and tell everyone the truth about us." She still had not looked him square in the eye.

It took a con to know one. But something about her, the soft pitch in her voice or the innocence of her eyes before daylight made him listen

"It's four hours until you got to get up and preach. I figure you can go down by the highway we came in on and catch a ride out of town."

"So you're going to tell the truth—to everyone, school buddies and all—and I walk away scot-free."

"By the time the church people know about us, you could be in Texas or anywhere but here."

"There you go again, just like always." Before she could jump in with another argument, he said, "You think you can get up and plan my morning, just like that?" Still thinking she might be running a con, he knew what he had to do anyway regardless of her motive. "I'm not running, Angel, but nice try. If I'm a murderer I don't want nobody adding coward to the mix. That Deputy Maynard, if he's not on to me now, will be by tomorrow." It wouldn't surprise Jeb at all if Maynard didn't already have it in his mind to keep an eye on his goings-on anyway.

"I'm fresh out of ideas then."

"This has to end. I'm the one ending it. Make you happy?"

"That's the problem with me, Jeb. Part of me doesn't want it to end, like I could lie forever just so's everyone would think I'm somebody. That makes me a big fat hypocrite, don't it?"

"Angel, we both found something we liked here. Maybe something we needed. At least, I did." He touched the side of her arm and she didn't pull away.

For the first time, a tear tumbled out of her like it had escaped. And then another followed. "I don't have no place to go, Jeb. I want my momma so bad it hurts, but I can't have her. But the thought of Willie and Ida May being treated like orphans makes me sick." She cried. "But here's the whole deal—that preacher man, I know he's coming soon and the gig'll be up anyway. All I been doing is stretching things out, like one morning I'd wake up and all my dreams'd be real. It's time I grow up."

"Here's the deal as I see it. For once, I'm the grown-up. I am going to go into that church and preach the best little sermon these folks has ever heard. Maybe time is more on my side than you think. Fern has got to know about us. But I want her to know too that what she saw in you kids was real. I'm the phony."

"Tell her when?"

"Maybe this afternoon, if she'll listen. I don't know. But one thing I won't do is run. Not until I've said what should be said. Maybe we have a few days to think on it."

"Maybe we don't. You're doing this for her, aren't you? This is about Fern."

"Fern, you, Willie, Ida May."

"You can't love her, Jeb! Or us! You have to get out of here, put her out of your thoughts. Time is up in this place!"

"I can't leave. Not yet." The fantasy came back to him, the blanket and lemonade scene at Marvelous Crossing.

"But you're not that man, the one she thinks you are. That's not Jeb Nubey at all!"

"You're a kid, Angel. Act like one. Go and get a little more sleep. Don't worry for me." He had found his taste of Eden in the form of a day in the life of a good man. For one day, of all days, Sunday, he would be that good man, the man his daddy thought did not exist. "I'll wake you in time for church. Rest until sunup."

"I should have shown you this already. Maybe I thought it would all go away." She pulled a letter out from under her arm. She had hidden it there the whole time they spoke. "I heard what that deputy said to you, Jeb. They'll hang you for killing that man. Even if you didn't mean to do it. You have to run now, while you can."

Jeb had never heard Angel let slip a shred of concern for him. "You care about me, don't you Biggen?"

"I think you should read this." Angel gave him the letter.

"Who wrote this?"

"The man you wish you was." She left the room.

Jeb turned the letter over and read the signature: *In Christ's abounding grace, Reverend Philemon Gracie. p.s. Expect my arrival within the week.*

The letter was dated September 15, 1932.

For the Lord's Day, Deputy George Maynard exchanged his rural police uniform for a dark sport jacket that matched exactly his plaid worsted trousers, stretched tight around his porking stomach. It was every wrong sort of combination that fought his wife's floral dress.

The Whittingtons kindly invited the Maynards to sit next to them, three rows behind Fern, Angel (who kept clinching her stomach and running outside), Willie, and Ida May with her recent infection of poison ivy.

Fern approached Jeb twice from the onlooker's galley—the

first time to tell him that she needed help with her kitchen plumbing and would he mind taking a look, and the second time to tell him her mother and father would be in town the next Sunday for a visit and would he please join them for Sunday dinner. Both jaunts to the platform resulted in Fern stroking his hand with a bit of feeling, as near a massage as she could muster without drawing attention. "I especially want you to meet my father, Francis."

Jeb's head lifted to affirm the invitation, although he knew by then he would be in jail in Texarkana or shot dead on the side of the road. He grabbed her hand the second time, and she looked back, surprise in his eyes.

"Fern, you and me . . . I need . . . You see . . ."

She laughed out loud. "See you after church." When she walked away, he thought she whispered, "Philemon."

He dodged another urge to purge himself, realizing all eyes were on him. At any rate, the imagining of it all—a life minus Fern—got the best of him and he felt dizzy. Him as the privileged guest of Francis Coulter III at the Dornick Hills Golf and Country Club was nothing more than an outlandish thought that came out of his life as liar and could not be indulged. Golfing with the swells—that was a laugh.

Fern kept track of his every move. That one thing he knew to be a fact. But instead of melding happily with the rest of his imaginings, he felt her eyes ever on him. He approached the lectern with the worst case of smallness he ever remembered having. Out of habit every head bowed. Even Fern, who closed her eyes but then stole another glimpse at him and bowed again, respectfully. Jeb read her signal and it felt like charges had been dropped into the depths of his pathetic soul.

He imagined how a confession would spill from him, tumbling from his tongue in silver magic that caused the listeners to rise in union and applaud him for his honor and upright ways. That wouldn't work. Then he fantasized that Fern would fall into his arms and love him for being Jeb Nubey. No more would he hear the name Philemon come from her throaty voice. *Jeb.* It sounded sweet, like sap from a maple trunk. And untrue.

Jeb opened his eyes. A few restless toes shuffled in the sawdust, uneasy at his hesitation to attack the platform with spiritual genius. The awkward silence confronted his daydream; he had drifted while the faithful awaited direction. "Let us pray." He coughed.

Onward and upward, he told himself. The writings of Paul spilled as freely from him as if he had sat watching over the apostle's shoulder as he wrote. He used Fern's suggestions and whenever he did, it had the effect of caressing her. She smiled at him, an intense bit of light coming from her, more forceful even than the smile she had given to Oz Mills. But he reshaped her wise little nuggets and deepened each teacherly thought and it was truth, even if missing from his black heart.

At one point, he felt as if he had stepped aside to let the God of Evelene's Bible probe places he had never visited. He was the undone man. God seeped inside of him. Finally. The message he spoke into the rafters grew bigger than Jeb Nubey and he felt split in two. The one part lay collapsed on the floor as though killed, while the other soared to leave behind the lies of the past. Truth took on life. The Christ of Christendom had reached inside Jeb's puny clichés, and resurrected the truth—not Jeb's truth, but Christ truth. What he said surfaced from his wreckage as something more than a con job. The fact that such a wretched guy could crawl to Christ and find approval bewildered him. In front of the whole church he had to wipe his eyes. Surrendering to God was not like surrendering to the cops. Instead of jail, he got freedom. Finally.

"This I know, good people! This I know—I believe, I believe, I believe, I believe!" Jeb felt himself step aside and watch in terror as the robe of his charlatan-self fell into a fire not of his own making. He knelt, arms outstretched to the rafters, face turned upward. "I believe," he whispered. Then jubilation rose from the ashes of sheer terror.

Florence Bernard rose to her feet and wept.

Fern handed a handkerchief to Angel, who put her face in her hands.

George Maynard stiffened, grabbed by the throat of invisible hands. Horace Mills's shoulders sagged and he breathed in and out in shallow pants. A few cried, "Hallelujah" and "Yes, Lord!"

Doris Jolly, who had in the past taken her cue to run to the organ, instead turned around in the pew and, knees covered in sawdust, prayed.

Even Ida May halted her relentless scratching and grew still.

"I think we sometimes think we can play at church," Jeb said as he rose to his feet. But he preached to his own self. "You're looking at the kingpin of that little game. Religion was my game of the week. Babe Ruth one day, God on Sunday."

The men chuckled, a quiet rolling back and forth of something they felt only males could understand.

Jeb knew remorse and all at once believed his own words. "In this regard I stand before you the biggest fraud of all. I thought for much of my life religion was a refuge for women to run to and a haven where children could find comfort. Faith is those things—a refuge and a comfort—I'll agree, yet so much more. God, for this man, was a high and distant thunder, not something I could grasp. Religion, I thought, was for the weak, the feeble, or a game that little girls played." He looked at

Angel. "But I read of gentle Timothy who faced rock throwers, of Paul who faced both the religious and the big-time thinkers of his day. For his bravery, men tossed Paul into a lonely place, isolated from everyone he loved. It comes to me that a quiet little band-a God-lovers went before us, beat up for the words they spoke. Now, good folk, somethin' springs from inside of me, a cry, like the voice of many waters. It says that for some, faith is no mere amusement. Nor do we set it on a museum shelf, once a thing to be admired and oohed at, but now covered in dust."

Most had bowed their heads. Florence sat back in her seat, but nodded as Jeb preached. If she had had doubts about him before, she bought his goods now.

"Prayer is something we do on the way to somewhere else. A task, a chore given by God to man as an interlude in man's ever-important day."

The stillness that had settled across the congregation did not sway Jeb, but pushed him to continue. The words welled up inside of him, like a spring crossing its banks. Something, Someone was at work in him, and he couldn't have stopped if he tried.

Jeb quietly said, "When every apostle gave up their life just as their Savior, Christ, had said would happen, did it ever come into their thoughts that what they died for would become the passive food of the church today? Did they know that their words would pass through the lips of lesser men like me? Yet these words should ring like a bell inside us. For me. For you. Whether or not I say these things or you hear them from some truly great preacher, truth can't be changed. We wish by heaven that we could make God in our own image and that our reputation would pass onto the next generation to give us what we think we deserve. It is just like a human to want our names remembered—increase, Self. Lessen, God. And then we take our last breath and our words haven't changed a thing. While our lies lay in ashes, a bright and shining sword slices through the mess we make for ourselves. Our Christ is who he says he is, in spite of us, in spite of our schemes or the things we think we got to get. If you don't want to hear it from a fraud," he said, pointing to his chest, then holding up the Bible, "you can hear it straight from God himself."

He finished something he had never intended to say, nor could he have said it on his own. The closing prayer brought most of the members to the front of the church to pray.

Florence Bernard's skeletal fingers gripped Jeb's clasped hands. She murmured just so he could hear, "I am a fraud, too, Reverend. We all are."

Fern walked beside Jeb outside her house with a list for which she directed all of her attentions while he waited for the instant he needed, the moment when he would confess the remainder of his crimes to her. Under the guise of helping her plan for her folks' arrival, he had followed her home. Angel took the other two to the parsonage to decide what to pack and what to leave.

"I'll need some extra blankets for the sofa. I'll give my parents the bed. It's gotten so cold at night. Do you suppose Daddy will want to go fishing? You should take him." She hesitated and lifted her face to see into Jeb's. "If you want, I mean. Maybe the two of you should have some time to talk. Guy talk or whatever it is you men do off in a fishing boat."

"Fishing sounds like a good way to spend the day." He answered her like his mind had taken off to go fishing.

"The next order of business is dinner. I'll bet you could eat a horse after the message you knocked off. Truth be told, you made me cry. Are you listening, Philemon?"

Jeb listened to try and decide at what point in the conversation to tell her everything. When she looked at him, he knew she was looking at the man she thought she knew. Waiting longer did not increase his chances for having a chance with her. But he grieved over the life that might have been.

"Have you ever imagined yourself with someone of a lesser mind?" he asked.

"I can't imagine it," she said.

Everything would change. Oz Mills would show up to console Fern and tell her how lucky she was to know the truth about him. "If your father asked you to return to Oklahoma, would you go?" If she did, it would take her from the reaches of a man like Oz, at the least. Not that it would ever be any of his business.

"Your questions mystify me," she said.

He knew inside that the very reason he asked anything at all had to do with the fact that he still hoped coming clean would not wreck things between them. Even now, he still fell back on scheming.

She tucked the list into her handbag. "I don't want to go back to Oklahoma. I like Nazareth." She smiled all of a sudden. "You're afraid of my leaving, aren't you?"

Any answer he gave her would tell her more than she wanted to hear. He decided right then, that now was the time. "Fern—"

She studied him in puzzlement. "You are afraid I'm leaving. I don't know how you got it in your head that I want to leave this place. I couldn't leave now, Philemon."

There was that name again. He had to tell her now, if for no other reason than to hear her say his name, even if spoken as a cuss.

"Daddy says that I seem to talk about nothing but 'that Nazareth preacher.' What does that tell you?"

He held the confession for a moment. "What did you say about me?"

"That you're intelligent, educated, and a funny guy. I didn't say mysterious, but you're kind of that, too."

"You said I'm funny?"

"And that you are good to your children. Best of all, you love God."

Lightning struck. "I do love God, Fern. That is why I have to talk to you. It's about that fraud thing I talked about this morning."

"Pure genius, but more than that, humility. Philemon, I want you to help me find it for myself. I want your kind of humility. I'm afraid I've been coasting along in my faith myself. I covet your fire." She placed a kiss right at the corner of his mouth.

"Likewise," he said. Then he blurted, "I'm not the one to help you, Fern. I am a fake." He finally said it.

"That does it. I'm cooking you a whole platter of pork chops and a chocolate cake," she said.

"All right. But after dinner, we have got to talk," he said.

After dinner, the sun went down and Jeb had no way of knowing that Fern had decided that they should make out. She walked him down the back way from the parsonage to the stream where he remembered his first recollection of lust for her—the first morning she had stepped out of the clouds. He could have simply walked her out the front way like a decent individual, said his peace, and slipped out of town. On foot, of course. There were many deterrents.

"Philemon, you have to know that I am in trouble when it comes to you. Tomorrow, I'm going to ask Josie to be sure that she is with me from now on when you are around. I'll tell her everything. That I cannot be alone with you. But for tonight, I have to tell you that I want you. Alone. If that makes sense. I know you think I'm an awful person."

Jeb watched her as she knelt at the water's edge and looked at her own face. Her shoulders had slackened and she no longer looked like the woman who could swing from a tree and pound a ruler while whipping up a pan of biscuits. Fern looked lost to him. Kneeling beside her, he brought her to her feet. He had to hold her, for her sake. Her mouth met his.

"If it makes you feel any better," Jeb decided he needed to interject an appropriate comment into the throes of passion, "I love you."

"I knew it. Somehow, I—I needed to tell my mother that I thought you might be serious. Then I worried I had spoken out of turn."

"I'd rather not talk about it anymore," said Jeb. He kissed Fern and it came to him that he might be willing to go to jail for such a kiss. "I'm never leaving Nazareth," he told her. "You have to understand that now. I can't."

"I know. Neither can I," she said.

"We'll just both have to stay here then." He could not let go of Fern, not even if he had to go to jail for it. She possessed him as surely as Christ himself.

Now he just had to come clean about all the rest. Tomorrow perhaps.

18

Jeb dreamed of lying inside a bird's nest, naked. He felt sick inside and out. Sick of being himself. No means to lift him from his naked state, to cover him. No way of getting off the rocky crag where eagles belonged. Not Jeb Nubey.

Then he woke up.

He wiped wetness from his eyes. The mist on his lashes had formed in the night, the dew of frustration.

It came to him in the darkness that the option of climbing out altogether, out of the land of vultures and cliffs, and finding a peaceable dwelling place had come from the loins of another man's desire. He had only smelled that dream while peering over the shoulders of all those worldmakers. What jolted him awake in the night was a whisper that trickled into his soul—the understanding that he had hit the black bottom of the world.

Fern still did not know the truth.

He got up to read the newspaper. Parts of it lay scattered on the sofa, the other pages sloppily mislaid. The urge to run for a fresh newspaper made him restless. He possessed no fast escape into town. With restless bullets zinging up his spine, he walked outside and slammed open the screen door to sit on the porch. But instead of sitting, he walked down the steps, his bare

feet scarcely touching the October cold grass—islands of weed
in the dirt. His eyes searched out everything in the night: the
dead-end motionlessness of the church yard, the invisibility of
the croaking toads, and a glisten, a silver twinkle, of chrome
that flickered from the road.

Then he heard the engine idling. Before he could approach
it, a figure appeared. Deputy George Maynard waved him onto
the road.

"Evening, Deputy. You're out late," said Jeb.

"Sorry for creeping around, Reverend. I didn't want to
alarm your children so I parked up on the road. I was hoping to
find you up and here you are. I've been fishing up around
Marvelous Crossing. You'll never guess what I just found." He
continued to lead Jeb to the ancient truck he drove for unoffi-
cial business.

Jeb followed, puzzled and still not convinced that he was
awake.

"May be your truck parked right down in the woody part
just behind the lake. I need you to come and ID the thing. Will
your youngens be all right?"

Jeb nodded and climbed into his cab.

Maynard pulled down onto the dirt road that surrounded
Marvelous Crossing with his lights off. The two of them
walked with nothing but the moon for a light. Maynard put his
finger to his lips then led Jeb into the thicket and crouched
while he pointed. Someone had parked an automobile, near to
undetectable, behind a copse of cedar. A ray of moon refracted
light off the fender. Jeb stepped into the darkest shade of the
trees and, still as a fox, waited for the sound of an idling engine
or a closing door.

The wood sat undisturbed, so Jeb and Maynard moved like
cats through the quiet of the brush hidden behind the tree

trunks until they could see the vehicle up close. Jeb could hear his own breath and a noise as gentle as a cooling motor. A popping sound. He held his breath and saw a thing almost beatific beneath the awning of stars. The Model T truck had returned to him—Charlie's truck with all of his own goods duly consumed. The two thieves slept, one man curled up on the front seat and the other, the tall shaven-head blond youth, asleep in the truck bed. Both his feet stuck out the back with the butt of Jeb's rifle protruding beside his bone-thin legs.

"I've never seen two such fools," said Maynard. "All but laid theyselves down at our feet."

Wisdom told Jeb not to react when he saw the busted front grill. Instead of mauling the nearest thief, he held his breath and got himself a better look at the situation. Maynard followed right behind him. His heart the loudest thing about him, he crossed the road behind the truck. He slid the rifle up and away from the youth in the empty truck bed, felt a bit of resistance, and then jerked until the youth babbled and then fell back to sleep. Jeb opened the door and the driver fell out onto the road. Jeb aimed the rifle into the thief's sleepy eyes and said, "I'm the only one between you and God. It's a tight spot for you. You need to consider the outcome to the best of your ability." It sounded good for a man who couldn't kill . . . again. "Get your buddy up. This deputy here wants to talk to you. So do I."

Nebula Maynard turned up the lantern wick for her husband. George examined the ropes tied around the ankles and wrists of Jeb's prisoners. "For a preacher, you got a talent for rope tying, Reverend Gracie. Truth be told, I never seen such tying. Not in my lifetime."

Jeb had aided George in dragging both men from the truck bed. Nebula poured him a second cup of coffee, occasionally pulling the scarf forward over the rollers in her hair, a self-conscious gesture brought on by the unexpected appearance of early-morning company. Every time she touched the hairpins, she said, "I know I look a mess."

"You don't act like no preacher," said the man who had fallen out of the truck.

"This'n is Carl Beaumont," said George. He read the boys' statistics off the FBI file. "He's the tall one with the scar." He toed Carl Beaumont. "That'd be you.

"They know your name, Carl," said the bony, shaven youth. "What we going to do?"

"Shut up, Rabbit!" Carl would have belted the boy if he had not had both hands tied at his back.

"This younger feller is Duke 'Rabbit' Johnson, wanted for three counts of automobile theft. Both wanted for armed robbery and murder. Cold-blooded."

Nebula made a sound like good plumbing awaiting the first flush of water.

George backed away. "Either one of you give me a bit of trouble and I'll blow your heads plumb off."

"No trouble from me, Deputy," said Carl.

"What made you two fools stop dead in the same town as the man you stole it from?" asked George.

"It was that church spire, distant-like it was," said Rabbit. "It shined like a beacon in the sundown and I told Carl it was a sign."

"I said shut up and I mean right this instant!" Carl bellowed.

Rabbit jerked like Carl had slapped him too much but he could not stop jabbering. "So we stopped, tuckered and feeling all peaceful for once, parked on yonder lake." He batted his eyes and flinched. "You know it's true, Carl."

"I guess you can take your truck, Reverend. Take yourself home if you want. I'll call the state police out here first thing. They'll have a few questions, but minor things. If you don't mind."

"Not at all," said Jeb. He left the Maynards to keep vigil over Carl and Rabbit. By the time he made it back to the truck, the set of keys felt hot against his palm. The inside of the truck smelled rank, worse than when the migrant boys had piled in one night for a jaunt to the Biscuit and Bean. When the engine started, the gasoline meter read close to empty, the real reason the two robber boys had stopped so suddenly, perhaps, with the need to ration fuel an immediate concern.

Jeb drove past the road that wound round Ivey Long's pond and ended at Fern's porch. Tomorrow he might drive up and see if she would like a malted at Fidel's. He made the left turn that would take him straight through town. If Val Rodwyn came early to open Honeysack's, he would buy a paper off him just for the sake of feeling a part of humanity again. As he neared downtown Nazareth it came to him bright as the bulbs strung along Faith Bottoms' Beauty Shop awning that he could leave town right this instant. George Maynard had no inkling of his real identity. No one else even knew of his waking up to find the truck parked so near to home. He could just tool away. Some fuel stolen from that gas can Honeysack kept on the rear steps of the store might get him to the next city. A day's work might get him to the next place and so on and so forth until he crossed Canada's border.

Or he could buy a paper off Val Rodwyn and take Fern tomorrow night for a malted.

Climbing naked from the nest out into the open world had

its down side. He stopped just two blocks from Honeysack's store to weigh the matter. The engine rattled, jingled, and then coughed to a stop. He waited with the window down, listening to the quiet streets before dawn. Faith Bottoms might appear soon and put up a new sign advertising a sale on permanent waves. Floyd Whittington would pull Flying Racer wagons out onto the front walk so that boys would beg their daddies for the red, steeled beauties.

Another truck stopped short of Beulah's Café, one block away from Fidel's Drugstore. The headlights dimmed. The driver opened the truck door and stepped out. It was not his slightly bowed and thin frame but the furtive creep of his step that caught Jeb's attention. The man pulled the brim of his hat down across his brow. Jeb recognized the tattered felt hat. The weighty rock that Clovis Wolverton snugged against his skeletal ribs with his right hand made him lean to the right.

Jeb lifted his door latch just as he had done to cause Carl Beaumont to tumble onto the street. He slipped out of the truck and remained in the dark protection of the Main Street elms.

Clovis ran and stood in the shadow of awning over Fidel's doorway. He drew back to hurl the rock through the glass.

"Clovis, wait," said Jeb.

Jeb startled Clovis and threw him off balance. He dropped the rock and turned to run.

"It's me, Clovis. Reverend Gracie." He kept his eyes on the man. It worked to keep him in place. In a kind of hush, he said, "You can't do that and get away with it."

Clovis's eyes had the kind of kicked dog look Jeb had seen in the faces of the men forced to live off along the railroad tracks. "Reverend! I guess you think I'm shameful," he said.

"I think you almost were. Beulah will be opening the café

soon. Let me buy you the first cup of her coffee. It will do us both some good." Jeb extended his hand to see if Clovis might take it.

Clovis brought his arm to his face and cried.

"It's all right, Clovis. We all hatch plans in our minds that we shouldn't do." He let out a sigh, like his own confession had been too long in the brine. "But when we don't go through with bad schemes, that's when manhood starts to grow on us." Jeb put his arm around the father of the six youngens who lay in bed with empty stomachs. "You ought to let others help you out. Better than jail."

"I never met no preacher like you, Reverend," said Clovis between sobs.

"I'll grant you that's true. Look, the light just came on in the café. We're in luck," said Jeb. He beckoned Beulah until she came to the door and let them inside.

"Coffee, gentlemen?" she said.

"Coffee, breakfast. Give this man anything he wants." Jeb invited Clovis to enter ahead of him.

Jeb felt the slipping-away sensation leave him due to the fact that he had lost the momentum to imagine himself on the run by daylight.

The sun rose like a golden mum pinned to the pocket of the Ouachita Mountains.

Fern had driven into town to pick up a few things from the grocers'. She couldn't hide her elation. "You're up early, Philemon."

"Just doing a little shopping while the children sleep. I got my truck back."

"Congratulations."

Her smile had a powerful warming effect on Jeb. "I'll see you later on. Best I finish this shopping—it's for Clovis." He touched her hand and pointed to Clovis, who sat inside the café nursing another cup of coffee.

Fern held his arm like she didn't want to let him go. Then she excused herself for the sake of Jeb's worthy cause.

As Clovis returned home with a bottle of aspirin for his youngest girl's fever and a sack of food from Honeysack's, all of it care of Jeb's pocket change plus a whispered request to Freda Honeysack, Jeb returned home. He gathered the children for a house cleaning, delegating the task of porch sweeping to Ida May. Willie washed windows while Angel complained when asked to scrub the kitchen floor and wipe down the corroding appliances so early and before the start of school. She threw a scrub brush, a cake of Palmolive, and two ragged hand towels into a pail. "If I scrub any harder, there'll be no stove left to clean."

Jeb pulled the sofa out away from the wall and swept webs and spider egg sacs away from the baseboards. He gathered laundry into a heap for the wash. The wringer washer shook and vibrated while he pulled out a sopping wet shirt from Woolworth's and fed the tail of it to the wringer. Water poured back into the machine as the flattened shirt landed in Jeb's hands, stiff and ready to be shook and hung out to dry.

"You never got us up so early before, not to clean and do up the clothes," said Angel. "You must've told her."

Jeb looked at Ida May, who took an interest in the talk. "If you're finished with your chores, then please go and dress, Ida May." Jeb popped the shirt into the air to tease her with it as she left.

"You're going to leave surely, Jeb. The truck's back. Nothing's making you stay now."

"I ironed you a dress for school and not a bad job if I say

so. But take care to wear stockings. It's a cold morning." Jeb kept his back to Angel and looked through the window out toward the stream. The leaves had mostly fallen away, making way for a clear view of the water and the rocky slope beyond the banks. Soon the cold would complete the undressing of the summer thickets and leave the hills grayed over, exposed.

"Not that I give a care what she thinks, but how did Miss Coulter take the news?" Angel pulled a pair of white stockings out of the basket of dry clothes.

"Go dress yourself."

The fact that he answered quietly made her turn and stare at him. "At least tell me if you'll be home when we get back from school today." She waited.

Jeb fished out a soaked pair of trousers.

Angel padded out of the kitchen, across the floor she had mopped, and disappeared into her room to dress for the day.

"I have good news." Angel sat upon her bed, already made and fixed up with a doll and pillow.

Ida May dropped the broom onto the floor and climbed back underneath her quilt.

"What good news?" asked Willie.

"We'll be going to live with Claudia soon. I know for a fact she lives in Fort Smith now and I wrote a letter just last week. Any day, she'll write back with the money to send for us," Angel said. Her stockings pulled tight at the knee, a hint they would soon be too short.

"If you knew all this last week, why are you just now telling us?" Willie, still wrapped in a sheet, allowed his jaw to drop and his mouth to hang open. He did not believe her.

Angel answered, "I shouldn't be telling you yet anyway. But

it's such good news, I figured why wait. May as well tell you now. That's why Jeb's doing up the clothes and wants us to leave the house all spiffed up."

"Jeb knows?" asked Ida May.

Angel let out a sigh. She drew each stocking up to the thigh and then turned her back to Willie. "He knows."

"Is Jeb taking us to Claudia's?" Willie asked. He lay on his stomach and rolled his pencil between his hands as though he were trying to build a fire on the cover of his schoolbook.

"We're through with Jeb. He's moving on now. It's best we don't know where he goes. If he's got business with the police, why should we get in that kind of mess?"

"I don't want to leave, Angel." A pearl-sized tear slipped down Ida May's face. "Jeb takes care of us, and Fern, too. I'm telling Fern. She'll let us stay."

"No you won't tell Fern. You're staying right here until I get home from school today and if Fern shows up, well, you won't say a word. This is for big people to squabble over, Ida May. She's not our momma. We got a real family, like Claudia. You just can't remember her because you were so young when she ran off and married. After a week or two with your real sister, you won't remember Fern."

Ida May wailed.

"You think she'll be all right here with Jeb, Angel?" Willie asked.

"Why wouldn't she?" Angel tied her shoes in double bows to hold them on her feet.

"I mean, he wouldn't go off and leave her today, would he?" Willie ran his thumb through the hole in the toe of his sock.

"I used to worry he might, Willie. Lately it's hard to say. But he's different, that I know. Ida May, you just stick close and ask Jeb to read to you and stuff like that," said Angel.

"Jeb can read," said Ida May.

"Big words, too," said Willie. "I heard him reading to Fern out on the porch the other night. They sure been cozy lately. Reckon they'll run off and marry like Claudia?"

"Fern's not like Claudia, Willie. Ladies like her get their pictures in the paper when they get married, so they don't dare run off to do it. They don't marry men wanted by the police, neither." Angel gathered up her books.

Jeb opened the door. "Time for you all to go. Ida May, get your shoes on. I'm driving Willie and Angel to school. You may as well go, too."

Angel did not comment either way. She looked at Jeb as though she did not recognize him anymore.

19

The mountains and the foothills smelled of smoking timber, wood crackling in the stoves and smoke billowing from the chimneystacks of whoever had the wherewithal to own a good brick fireplace. Not many in Nazareth. The air that permeated the churchyard was stiff with smoke, a white aroma both fragrant and stifling to Jeb.

He loaded up the children and drove them down past the lane that led to the impoverished, junk-strewn Wolverton yard, past the neatly manicured entrance to the Mills estate, and on to the school.

Fern met Jeb out in front of the school. "Let me get a better look at the famous truck."

"Not too much to look at but it runs like a racehorse. I thought maybe tonight you'd like to go for a malted at Fidel's. Or, if you're too busy, some other time." Jeb said "some other time" as though he had another time to give her. He prayed for a long Monday.

"I should be finished with grading papers by six or so. Malteds will be too cold to get come November. Guess I had better seize the last one of the year." Fern looked at Jeb until it seemed inappropriate to look any longer. "I'll bet you children are happy to get a ride to school, what with the frost covering every blessed thing in sight." Fern addressed Angel and Willie. Ida May had taken a blanket and curled up on the front seat for a little more shut-eye.

"We just barely got here. Them robber boys left it near out of gas," said Willie.

"Lots of folks are out of gas these days, Willie," said Fern.

"I'm headed for town to get fuel," said Jeb. Will Honeysack had paid him sixteen dollars on Sunday, well near the salary paid to the Catholic priest between Nazareth and Hot Springs.

Fern waved the Wolvertons in. They all tramped out of the woods on foot, but it had become less shameful to be out of gas when everybody was in the same boat. The two youngest walked wrapped in a blanket, Siamese twins running for the heat of the schoolhouse as fast as blanket-trussed legs could carry them.

Fern, careful not to talk over the heads of her students, said, "Angel, I got your paper on President Lincoln graded. You got an A, girl. I think you ought to be really proud of yourself."

Angel walked away without comment and met the oldest Wolverton girl at the gate.

"Angel, you come back here and answer Miss Coulter, like a polite person ought to do!" said Jeb.

"It's all right," Fern told him. "Angel's been off in another world lately. At least, I've noticed that about her. I don't think she means anything by it when she doesn't answer, other than, 'I wish someone would ask me what's bothering me.' I don't suppose she's mentioned anything to you that's troubling her?"

Several things that might possibly trouble Angel came to Jeb. "No, nothing that I can think of."

"If you don't mind, I can take her aside this afternoon and see if she's up for a little girl talk," said Fern.

"Fact is——" The truth bubbled to the top like a well finally uncapped. Jeb blurted out, "Fern, I've had something on my mind and it has something to do with Angel, with all of us. Tonight I need to discuss it with you. I'll pick you up at six if it's all right with you." He could not sit on it anymore. By tonight, he would have his things packed. He would tell her the truth about him. If she cared about the children, he would ask her to care for them until they could be returned to their family. Then he would drive to Texarkana and turn himself in.

The sun came up fully now. Fern wore a white blouse and a russet skirt and had tied a sweater around her shoulders, a kitten-soft woolen dappled like a Pinto pony. It made her look fresh off the ranch, with a faint hint of Manhattan. "Sounds important, Philemon."

"It's important that we get together tonight and talk, yes."

"I look forward to it, then," she said.

"Until then." When he turned he felt Fern clasp his hand, a gentle fondling of fingers against his own.

"Malteds and something very important." Naturally she laughed. She did not know of Jeb's plans to ruin them.

Jeb dropped by Honeysack's and bought a few gallons of gas. Val Rodwyn handed him a big stack of mail. A faint smattering of hope made him dig through the stack in hopes of finding a letter from Gracie telling him that their plans had changed and that they could not come after all. But not one piece of mail was from the minister.

That was the icing on his flattened cake. It was better, he decided, to let the chips fall. Let everyone know that he was not the man he said he was after all, before Philemon Gracie pranced in and made the announcement for him.

Either way, he was a miserable man.

Jeb drove home with the stack of mail, a bundle tied neatly by Val and given to him. Every letter addressed by Angel to her sister Claudia now lay on the passenger seat with various messages scrawled through the addresses indicating that no such person lived at such-and-such address. Before he met with Fern, he would have to tell Angel that her search for Claudia had come to a disappointing end. She would have to find a way back to Snow Hill with her daddy or to Little Rock with her aunt and insane mother. But he could not take them along to his eventual arrest. To do so meant the Welbys would wind up in a state home. He would promise Angel that would never happen.

Jeb arrived early at the school. Ida May played hopscotch in the dirt. He waited by the gate in hopes of catching a glimpse of Fern. Angel appeared first. Finally Willie and another boy appeared. "We have to talk some things over, but not here."

Angel and Willie bid good-bye to their friends. Angel lingered a little longer, almost as though she could not expect to see them again.

Jeb took them home.

"You're awfully quiet," said Willie.

"And still here." Angel toted her books to the front porch and left them on the steps.

"I've got something to show you, Angel. All of you." Jeb led them inside. He gave her the stack of letters. "Claudia never got any of your mail. All of those places your aunt thought she might live are no good."

Angel went through the envelopes reading her own handwriting. "Claudia didn't get any of them. Daddy just sent us away without knowing anything. He's a liar!" she cried.

Willie stormed away. Ida May sat down on the floor like she needed someone to translate all that her sister had told her was not true.

"It doesn't do any good to blame your daddy. Maybe he truly thought he knew where Claudia lived," said Jeb.

"He didn't know. We were just too many mouths to feed so he sent us off. It don't matter to him where we are just so we're out of his hair." Angel dumped the letters into the garbage pail. She ran out of the kitchen, down the back steps, and away from the house.

Jeb followed her.

She ran through the small clearing toward the stream. Cattails bobbed in her wake. Bright yellow clusters of tickseed lay flattened next to the dead pods of bee balm and frost bitten chicory. She circled the shrubs where Jeb and Willie had set trotlines and cut across the stones until the frigid water stopped her midstream.

The lofty shadow of a sweet gum wrapped a cold blanket around Jeb.

"Ain't you got things to do, Jeb Nubey?" Her sobbing wrenched him in two. "Places to pack up and go to? Leave me alone and just go, will you? I'm not your problem anymore."

"You have every reason to be mad," he said.

"Go away." She wept. Her head came back, her slight frame twisted like an emerging larva, and she wailed. Both hands came to her mouth and the tough exterior fashioned from hunger and hopelessness crumbled into the creek.

Jeb slipped out of his weathered oxfords and with his bare feet waded into the cold water. The stream bit his legs like nails. He imagined her plummeting headlong down the same cliffs where he had lived for so long. Even if it took his own life, he had to pull her back. "Angel, you listen to me!" He plucked her off the rock and carried her back through the stream. She fought him the entire way. "Stop it, now!" He held her next to him and said as quietly as he could, "Listen, baby. You've got to listen."

She threw her arms around his neck and cried with her face against him. Jeb stood with one foot on dry land and one in the water and let her cry. He held her crumpled against him until the only sound was a faint sob and the gurgling babble of creek water. "I been your daddy now for these last few months and I want you to listen to what I have to say. No matter what happens, I'm getting you back to your family, Angel. This Depression is eating up everything in sight, but it ain't going to eat you."

"Jeb, you can't do nothing for us. You got to get out of here."

"In due time. Maybe I never should have left Texarkana in the first place. If I go back, maybe all the trouble I caused since then can be righted."

"They'll hang you, Jeb. Don't go back!"

"Maybe I got to do what's right, Angel. Sunday's coming." That is, if Gracie tarried. "I'm going to tell the truth and then get my troublesome self out of the way. I learned some things about God these past few months, even if I didn't mean to. Amazing what you can do with a little book learning. He don't like it when you get in the way of his work. I been in the way of God's business ever since I came to this place. When I leave, everyone here—Fern, the Honeysacks, even the Wolvertons—will all hate me. But they'll know it wasn't God that sent me here. I won't cast no more shadows on his work. I can live with that."

"Maybe God did send you here. What if he sent all of us here? It could be that he did and if so, I know why."

"I don't follow you, Angel."

"He knew me and Willie and Ida May needed you to help us out of a jam, Jeb. And we needed Fern. Do you have to make me say it, you jerk, you?"

"Say what?"

"I love you, Jeb!" She threw her arms around him and cried

over her adopted and condemned-to-die daddy. "Please don't leave me. I don't want you to go." She sobbed louder than when she stood holding the rejected mail from Claudia.

Jeb wiped his eyes and set her down easy in the grass. "I love you too, honey. But don't cry over me. I don't deserve anything good. You are full of goodness, heaven knows, you crazy girl. Everybody needs a girl like you around just for the gladness you bring, even when I'd like to pop you one sometimes. Always know that in case you ever question your worth."

It came to him why he had never known the life of a good man. He had not sought it. Not until it was too late.

Jeb left Angel with the other two, the three of them listening to *Amos 'n' Andy*, stomachs packed with salt pork, gravy, and biscuits. Through the truck windshield the moon was bright like the bowl of a silver spoon. A trace of film formed around the perimeters of the window, but nothing as cold as frost. By the time he pulled into Fern's drive he wanted the truck engine to have warmed the cab. The only flowers he could find for a nosegay were the tickseed, a yellow wildflower with the face of a daisy. Angel had tied the flowers with a hair ribbon. Jeb considered the sacrifice worth an inch of growth on her part.

He rehearsed the things that he should say until he saw his eyes in the rearview mirror, the ones that had looked back at him when he had memorized Bible text for lies. The image punched a hole in any resolve that he had mustered. If any one word that came out of his mouth was possessed of truth, it was equally laced with grief. No explaining would with ease fill in the gap between the falsehood he had invented and reality. It was time for him to spill it out. Only truthful words with mortal wounds.

He saw an oncoming vehicle. Jeb slowed on the narrow road and drove the right tire onto the slanting roadside. The vehicle slowed and the window came down rapidly. Deputy Maynard pulled chicken from a bone with his teeth. His lips were shiny in the dusk. "Reverend Gracie, I was on my way out to your place to see you."

Jeb remained calm, as calm as he had learned to be around the law in the last few months.

"Tomorrow a state policeman wants to drop by and ask you a few things. I sent a telegram to them Texarkana boys. Told them we had apprehended the crooks that have been on a spree from Texarkana up." He tossed the leg bone into the dirt. "Somehow I figure this will tie in these two fools down in the jailhouse to that Texarkana murder that never got resolved. State police says a reward may be on its way to you."

"George, forget the reward money."

"Forget it, nothing. You were right beside me in that capture." He patted the side of his A-Model. "Glad I caught you. Nebula's making cobbler. Come by and have some, why don't you?"

"I'm meeting Fern for a malted."

"Don't say? It's about time somebody wised up and married that little gal. Rich daddy and pretty to boot. You have yourself a fine evening, Reverend." He drove away.

Sparse green leaves and kudzu wound throughout the trees on Fern's lane around Long's Pond. The leaves not blackened by the cold were drawn and shuddering on the limbs. Vines rose from the earth and draped across the road, a net with a partial view of sky. How soon the feds or the Texarkana cops might want to question him for the sake of releasing the reward money could come within a few days. Jeb prayed for one last Sunday. He could make everything right if God obliged him.

Fern wore a new dress, or perhaps a dress new to the cooler season—a blue crepey knit. She waved from the window and then answered the door with her grading pencil still stuck behind her ear.

Jeb pulled it out and handed it to her. "Finish your school papers, schoolmarm?"

"Watch yourself, mister. I look harmless, but many's the poor bum who's fallen under the deadly spell of the schoolmarm. Your children all right?" One foot touched the top step as she peered toward the truck.

"Listening to *Amos 'n' Andy*. Maybe doing some school work. No, nix that last one. They don't seem to do much unless I'm standing right over them," he said.

"Come in, unless . . . If you want, I'll grab my jacket. We should go."

Jeb watched her run for the jacket. He took off his coat and stepped inside. She looked surprised when she saw him.

"Maybe it's too cold for a malted," he said.

"Philemon, it's all right by me. But I can talk as easily here as down at Fidel's if you prefer."

"Here is fine. We'll sit at this table looking outside. Nice and bright." He touched the tabletop, his shoulders widened as though he framed out the whole quaint scene. "I watched you through this winder from the road one night." Maybe more than one night, he thought. He pulled the chair out from the table. "I notice you sit right here in this big window and work every single night of your life except Sunday. One day, you reserve for God."

"Spying on me?"

"Admiring." He held out the chair for her.

"May as well sit yourself down. I've got to make coffee now," she said.

Jeb took her arm. "Coffee can wait. Fern—"

She did not resist him, but reached for a window pull and let down the shade.

The talk he had in mind did not coincide with Fern's interpretation of an evening designed for two. "You may want to pull the shade back up."

"I like it down."

"It's important that I tell you about me. You should know something."

"I keep hearing about this important talk, Reverend. But I want you to know something. Freda Honeysack told me what you did for Mr. Wolverton."

"Does it seem kind of warm in here?"

"Things like that get all over town. You really care about the people of this town. Everyone knows it."

"The thing is, we need to talk about some things. Get them out in the open," said Jeb.

"But as special as you are, the one thing you should know about *me* is I don't rush easily."

"I don't plan to rush you."

She kissed him. "This is crazy. I'm getting my jacket and we're going out. No more important talk, Philemon. It's just that all the world is in a hurry. My father was always in a hurry. Hurry and make the grades, Fern. Run ahead, lead the pack." She retrieved the jacket from the arm of the sofa. "I finally meet someone interesting and off you rush with the important talks. We're going for malteds. I'll sip mine slowly and you—any way you want." She slid away from him, out of the doorway.

Jeb turned the knob on Fern's electric lamp, the one with imported glass that lit the table where an underpaid rich deb graded schoolwork. He followed her out to the truck unsure of how she might look on a Saturday night inside the partially wrecked cab of a 1927 T-Model. In 1932.

The thing that Jeb realized about Fern was that she could talk the ears off Hoover. She spoke of nights sitting up with her sister making each other up with rouge and rolling each other's hair with old bed sheet strips when her father was just starting his practice. None of her family originated from Oklahoma but from California, transplants not far from a reservation. The force of the evening ebbed and flowed from Fern and her uncontrolled energy that brightened as the night slipped away from him.

"The closer my walk with God, the farther I needed to get from Oklahoma and from my father," she said.

Jeb observed her mannerisms, the way she opened her napkin as though she expected it to weigh nothing at all. "Your folks not church-goers, I guess?"

"Never missed a Sunday. But everything my family does is all part of the Coulter machine. The cogs that turn the wheels that supply the power for more. It is not as satisfying as you think to have no need of anything."

For a moment, he would just like to imagine the pain of it.

She removed her jacket. The small stove in the corner of the drugstore warmed the only two malted customers present. Jeb did not want to react in a way to stop up her philosophical well. But she made him want to delve. "The whole country is desperate to have what your folks have."

"I can't prove this, but I think that if you satisfy the nation's lack, she'll lose her soul."

"What do you need when you don't need anything? Is that what you mean?"

"The need to see. Affluence is a stumbling block."

She spoke in broad, sweeping strokes. He wanted her to refine her answers to the present company. "What does Fern need?"

"A greater mind, a deeper pool of spiritual understanding. Humility. Want the whole list?"

He waited until they had both taken a breath. "Seems to me your shopping list is filled."

She pushed aside her glass. "I wish that I could explain what you've done to me. In Oklahoma, I'm the girl no man could catch. Not that I'm any great prize. I know I'm not the queen of femininity. That is why I was wise to the designs of those types—snatch a girl and a piece of her dad's pie. But you don't care about those things, Philemon. I've never met a man with your spiritual leanings. See what you've done to me? I can't get enough of you." She lowered her voice in case Fidel's wife eavesdropped behind the soda fountain. "That is the reason I can't be alone with you, if you have to know." Her cheeks reddened.

Fern had bought into his pitch. He now felt less of himself than he had an hour before. If he told her the truth now, she would loathe him. "We should go now."

"Not until you say what you've come to say. You didn't invite me here just to hear me wax philosophical over a malted."

"Look who we have here," someone said from behind Jeb.

"Oz, what are you doing here?" Fern sat back and folded her hands in her lap.

"I thought I'd surprise you. Had a bankers' meeting with Uncle Horace and dear old Dad. Looked up and saw you through the window when we walked down the street for coffee." Oz wore a long woolen coat that gave his lean appearance a look of authority.

Jeb pushed away from the table and rose to face Oz. "I was about to see Fern home. Good evening to you."

"I wouldn't mind doing that for you, Reverend." Oz kept his eyes to Fern.

"It's all right, Oz. Philemon will see me home," said Fern.

"Philemon. So that's it. Maybe tomorrow morning, then? A cup of coffee before I leave town?"

"Not this time, Oz." Fern pulled on her coat.

"'Night, Oz." Jeb turned his back to Oz and assisted Fern with her coat. He walked her to the truck and felt Oz's eyes on him as he opened the rusted door.

"Never leave, Fern, with a man who can't pay for a box lunch," said Oz. He turned and followed his uncle and father into Beulah's. As Jeb drove away, he glared through the window.

"That was uncomfortable," she said as they motored toward Long's Pond. "Oz is a little low on manners."

"Don't apologize for him. Not your place." Jeb could not look at her. Oz was right. He couldn't afford a box lunch or a wife. The drive home tormented him; Oz's mocking grin toyed with his need to confess. When he finally brought her to her doorstep and left her with a faint, "Good night," he turned to meander back to the truck cab and realized that he had not kissed Fern good night.

He returned and rapped against the door with the brass knocker he imagined she had screwed on herself, as every old fixture had been replaced with something new. The door opened and she smiled. One arm of the jacket dangled down her back, only half peeled from where he had interrupted her ritual dressing down for the night.

"I was wondering about you, Philemon. It seems like I have to remind you about so many things." She remained one step higher and kissed him. Her fingers were long and reached up the sides of his face and around both his ears. Fern had controlled every part of the evening.

"You don't know me," he said. He pulled her off the porch and they kissed until the moon warmed, pale, delicious. Like good cheese in hard times.

20

Sunday morning, the cold weather and the national problem with cash flow filled up the remaining spaces on the pews of Church in the Dell. Florence Bernard arranged a vase of mums for the communion table, a mound of yellows, pale spidery petals, and potent foliage. She called it a communion Sunday bouquet and placed a crocheted doily beneath the vase.

Greta Patton stopped in the aisle, woefully sickened by her mistake. "Florence, I forgot to buy the communion juice. Reverend Gracie said he needed it ready first thing, only my grandchild was sick. It completely escaped me."

"Not to panic. Let's ask Freda to let us in the store. She won't mind," said Florence.

"Buy and sell on Sunday? It's a sacrilege." Greta paled.

"We'll pay her tomorrow then. Just pick it up today." Florence grabbed her handbag.

Greta followed her down the aisle.

Florence met Jeb at the door. "Reverend Gracie. We've a little problem. Would it be possible to serve communion at the end of the service? Just delay it a tad? Someone forgot to stop by Honeysack's and pick up the fruit of the vine."

Greta dabbed her mouth with a handkerchief, still a mite nervous. Jeb was feeling weak in his knees. Distracted by his own problems, the women's voices were nothing more than a distant humming, like mosquitoes. "Do whatever you have to do." He walked past them, tucking the indicting confession into the folds of his sermon notes.

Fern and Ida May conversed on the front pew. Ida May laid her head in Fern's lap. "I don't want to leave." She said it twice.

"Of course you're not leaving. Church hasn't even started," said Fern.

Jeb had rehearsed how to reveal to Fern the worst of his life in less than ten faltering seconds. Each time he'd ended up stretching it out into a hard-luck story that might at least draw sympathy. The fact that she did not look sympathetic at all this morning, but rather a little starchy, threw the whole speech off.

"Fern, whatever happens today, know that to me you are the fairest lily of all."

She laughed. "That is what makes me laugh. How you look so serious and then say sensitive things like that."

He didn't bat an eyelash.

"As long as you aren't embarrassed with that silly confession I made," said Fern. "There I was asking you not to rush things, then I haul off and spill out who-knows-what. It was just the power of the moon."

"I don't remember a confession," said Jeb.

She lifted so only he could hear. "The one about not being alone with you."

Jeb laughed nervously.

"Everyone is looking at us," she whispered.

He saw a corner of his confession sticking out, one corner curled up and pointing at him. Her throaty laugh and the way she brought her hand to her mouth demonstrated that she took him to be florid of speech when in fact he spoke out of desperation.

Florence and Greta hooked up with Freda Honeysack and left, Greta with a face full of guilt and Florence the problem-solver.

Every step Jeb took toward the lectern weighed heavier than the last. The organ keys jarred him. Doris played a lively tune, something like a barroom melody set to religious poetry. "Communion Sunday, Doris. A more somber hymn, perhaps?" he suggested.

Doris ran her fingers down the keyboard. A sacred melody, familiar and customary for such days, quietened the talkative. Her voice lifted across the hat adorned heads and everyone stood. *Oh sacred head now wounded* . . .

The bottoms of Jeb's feet prickled as though someone held him over the yawning mouth of a canyon. He went through a series of motions, first laying his notes on the lectern, then pulling out the confession, laying it on top. Finally, he decided it better to at least deliver the message and feed the Lord's flock before he landed the glancing blow.

Deputy Maynard and his wife, Nebula, slipped in and took a seat on the last pew. George looked a bit apologetic about his appearance. He still wore the official trappings of a town deputy, as though he had just come from the jailhouse.

Jeb's chest was a cage, iron clad and doorless, making it difficult to breathe. He wanted to beg forgiveness of every person who walked through the door. *Forgive me. I am a fraud—a big ol' phony. It is the fault of no one but myself.*

The singing lifted like cherubim, rising above the chapel joists, above even the country hills of Nazareth.

He moved off the platform while Doris led the music, but he did not remember leaving the lectern at all. For every stanza, he embraced a member, held on to them, and said, "God loves you." He felt as though he lifted out of a shell and watched his pathetic self try to squeeze approval out of the last unsuspecting dupe. Nothing good had come out of him.

A gentle hand movement made him look. Doris needed her cue to end the round of chorus. Her old fingers needed a rest.

Jeb glanced at her with a look of apology and returned to the lectern.

He heard the slamming of automobile doors. The ladies' communion rescue committee had returned. The opening prayer sounded hollow to him, as did the sanctuary when he spoke.

The church doors opened a hair but not fully.

"When we are sick and visit a doctor, we know that by seeking out the best doctor we have a better chance of getting well. We can look on that doctor's wall and see how he got his education. However, it is not only the paper on the wall that is important to us, but the knowledge the man has gained. His education is very important to our sense of well being." Jeb tucked his notes away, into the Bible. "It is not always so simple to know the difference between a real man of God or a fraud. Christ chose twelve disciples, yet the one who lacked sincerity was the very man that placed the Son of God in the hands of the enemy. Christ allowed it because when the wicked are brought out into the light, God's power is fully shown. But if we allow a big put-on to replace God's genu-ine instrument, the church flounders." Jeb thought of something that he had read. "A lack of sight without God's eyeglasses gives us a defective view. We see what we want to see instead of what is true. If it smells religious, we idly agree, and then invoke heaven's name."

Clovis Wolverton nodded. In his lap was a burlap sack, a fresh poultry offering for the preacher.

Fern's gaze had dropped as though she mused inwardly.

Angel was crying, until her bony shoulders shook, until an older woman behind her touched her lightly on the back to hand her a handkerchief.

"Christ told us not to worry about the bad seed sown among us. I want you to remember this today. God has his own way of separating the good from the imitation."

The doors came open. Autumn sunlight, so bright that the forms standing in the light appeared as radiant beings, blinded Jeb. He held his hand up to catch the glare.

"Fraud! Liar!"

"You'll hang for this!"

"Charlatan, that's what you are!"

Jeb recognized the voices. Florence, Greta, and Freda accused him.

A man plainly costumed in a modest dark coat and pants walked past Jeb's accusers. On his flanks were three children, two older girls and a young boy the spitting image of his daddy. The oldest girl wore copper spectacles and held a Bible at her chest. All three of the offspring followed their father in composed obedience, their heads poised and scarcely lifting, as though floating on his train. Every one of them looked as though they had been cut from a big-city newspaper—black garments, stiff white collars, and the snappy walk of young scholars. Four people chiseled from marble, a cultured bunch with refinement coached into the pores of their lily-white skin.

Jeb stepped away from the lectern. He knew who they were.

Angel buried her face against Fern. Fern shook her head, angry at the outbursts of the obviously insane. Jeb kept his eyes on the floor and said softly, "This is your pulpit, sir. It has missed you."

Philemon Gracie did not take the platform, but made a

half turn and addressed the congregation. "I've listened outside your portals to this man. You have listened to his words, no doubt." He addressed Jeb. "Wise words from a tongue so unpracticed."

Horace Mills rose, both hands lifted, staring accusingly at Jeb. "Wait one minute. If you are not who you've pretended to be these last few months, I demand you tell us today. God help your soul!"

"Jeb Nubey is my name."

Fern looked slapped.

Maynard sat back as though kicked in the head. Then he held onto the pew in front of him, squeezed his pear-shaped body past Nebula, and stepped out into the aisle. He yanked a set of handcuffs from his belt loop. "This is a bad dream."

Clovis Wolverton brought his bowed back erect. "Say it ain't so, Reverend." He addressed Jeb, looking through the real minister as though he had never walked down the aisle.

"Arrest him, Maynard!" Mills joined the deputy in the aisle.

"Going to be a lynching!" Floyd Whittington pushed out of his pew.

"No, you can't!" Alma Wolverton lifted, as if her meatless bones were pulled upward by a thin string. "He's a man of God. I can testify on that count! Tell 'em, Reverend!"

Philemon Gracie crossed his arms, long fingers pink against the thin white cotton cuffs. His middle daughter moved next to him and pulled her father's arm around her neck.

"Calm yourselves!" Jeb could not be heard above the shouting.

A faint rapping noise added to the clamor, persisted like a metronome until, in the stillness of an interlude, it was finally the only audible sound. The minister lifted his walking stick into the air and then brought it down once more to the floor in front of him. "Mr. Nubey has something to say. As your minister, as your new pastor, could I beg you for a crumb of mercy? Let's hear him out as civil people ought to do."

Unnoticed, Fern picked up her handbag, meandered through the men in the aisle, and left the building.

Jeb covered his eyes until his tongue had moistened enough to speak. "I wanted to tell you all today. I am the fake they say I am. I regret that I took more time than I should have to tell you."

Maynard dangled his cuffs from two fingers as though they were an exhibit. "You're wanted by the law, might I add. For murder."

"What Deputy Maynard says is true. Everything is explainable, but I don't want to explain it. Because to take on the life of another man is enough crime in God's eyes. I'm tired of defending my actions. I am a guilty man." He held out his wrists, fingers clenched. "The fact is, I lied. If I get off on one count, then by God's hand, I'm still justly hanged."

"What kind of shenanigans is this man trying to pull?" asked Mills.

"God is our ultimate judge, Mr. Nubey," said Gracie. "You have learned a lot in my pulpit. For we are all guilty of something."

Gracie turned and addressed the others. "It is the Lord's grace that allows us to slip around in the shadows undetected, kind of a blissful folly. But it is a higher mercy that stops us in our tracks and makes us accountable. Even if fallaciously accused of one thing, then justifiably we are punished for the transgressions of a lifetime."

"But he's a guilty man," said Maynard.

"That is what I'm trying to say," said Jeb. "Fern? Where is Fern? Will someone find her? I need Fern."

"What made you think you could make a laughingstock of the whole town?" asked Mills.

"He saved me from the rock piles!" Clovis wailed. "Glory hallelujah, from hell and despair!"

"God saved you, Clovis," said Jeb. "Not me."

Alma Wolverton dropped her face in her hands and wept.

"Christ is our redemption, don't you see, Clovis? Look at me, a fugitive with not a lick of sense. But you all, the life you bring to this little town, you made me want to be a better man. I used to spend my spare time thinking of ways to separate a man from his pocketbook so I could have a little gin and some smokes to roll on Saturday night." By now, Jeb stood in the center aisle, Evelene Whittington's Bible open-faced in his hands. He faced the banker, Mills. "But here I was in a place called Nazareth, staying up all night learning ABC's with Ida May and reading from this Good Book." He took a step toward Evelene and handed the Bible back to her. "I never thought I'd be much account, and to you all, I'm not. But I have been lifted up. I can see above my former self. You can hang me by the throat but I will go willingly if I know these things: 'But now in Christ Jesus ye who sometimes were far off are made nigh by the blood of Christ.' Clovis, that is good news for you and me. That means that once we were far away from God and now we have been brought near to him by that thing he did with nails and wood."

"I have been redeemed. Halleluyer, Reverend!" said Clovis.

Jeb extended his hands. "Maynard, do your worst. I am a ready prisoner."

Mills stepped aside to let the deputy cuff Jeb.

"Mr. Nubey, I will see you again. We've much to discuss," said Reverend Gracie.

Doris Jolly cried and followed behind Jeb all the way to the church door. "I'll pray for you, Reverend. Don't you give up now. God don't shine to no quitter."

"I'm not a reverend, Doris. Just a man who has to get back up."

Once out in the churchyard, Maynard pulled manacles and chains from the back of his automobile. Horace Mills assisted with shackling Jeb Nubey, the murderer.

The space normally filled by Fern's Chevy Coup was nothing but a tacky set of tire tracks on the grass.

Will Honeysack lingered three yards away in the shade of the tree where Jeb had shared pie with Fern. He turned his back when Jeb was driven from the church. He placed his head against the tree trunk, forehead against the back of his hand. Then the head deacon cried.

Carl and Rabbit called out to Jeb from the cell next to him. The sun descended and from the darkening cell they mimicked him. "Beloved children, come unto me and I will give you lies from the bottom of my dirty old heart," said Carl.

Rabbit laughed and cried out, "Amen, y'all!"

Carl pressed his face through the bars. "I believe it was you, Parson, who had it in mind to let a certain couple of honorable gentlemen take the rap for your little homicidal blunder up in yon Texarkana. Memory serves me correctly, that is."

"I confessed, boys. You want more than that, get a lawyer."

"Confessed after the gen-awin preacher come rollin' into town," said Carl.

"You better thank God you didn't get put in our cell, Nubey. Maybe you would-a woke up behind the pearlys you been preachin' about," said Rabbit. He slammed the ball of his hand against the bars.

"Mercy sakes, Brother Rabbit. Forgiveness is in order. After all, it was the good parson here who accommodated our modest venture with the use of his fine automobile."

Rabbit fell onto the cot and laughed.

Through the bars to the outside, Jeb watched headlights here and then gone move across the jailhouse wall as vehicles turned the corner on Front Street. Maynard clipped across the parking lot, the heels of his shoes popping. The jailhouse keys jangled from his belt.

"Deputy Maynard, please, you've got to help Angel and the other two find their daddy."

"Don't you have enough to worry with, Nubey?" The sun disappeared right behind the deputy's head.

"I'm not what's important, George."

"Look, Nubey. I had Evelene Whittington do what you asked. She tried to call some of the neighbors in Snow Hill. She finally got a fillin' station attendant to answer the phone. The only number she could dig up in Snow Hill."

"It's a small place. Filling station will do," said Jeb.

"Lemuel Welby, he packed up and left town months ago when the itinerants all headed west. Took his brother with him and never left trace of where they headed off to." Maynard checked his watch. "Ain't no place left for those three kids to go but to a home. I don't know much about them, but the sheriff up in Hope, he said he knows of a place."

"I promised the kids they wouldn't go to an orphanage, Maynard."

"A guarantee from a jail ain't no kind of assurance. Evelene Whittington took them in for the night. She'll see they get took care of until we find permanent quarters. Get some sleep. State police want to see you first thing in the morning." He left, his A-Model gone in a cloud of dust.

"Nice con, Nubey," said Carl. "Play up the waifs and strays. Make them believe you got heart."

Jeb bowed in front of the window. "Please, God, don't punish those kids on my account. Let me hang but find them a good daddy, a real accountable man like Preacher Gracie."

"Reverend, it's me, Clovis."

Jeb lifted his face to the window. "Clovis? I'm ashamed for you to see me here."

"Don't give that a thought. You just back away. Me and the boys are going to break you out of here." He pulled a rope through the bars and made a knot.

Jeb untied the rope. "Not a good idea."

"You kept me out of jail. My turn to help you."

"Clovis, I thought I taught you some things. Now here you go—back to the hog pen," said Jeb.

"They've no right to do this to you." Clovis slipped the rope back around the bars. His boys waved from the driver's seat and gunned the truck motor.

"I brought this on myself. Don't you see? That's what I have been trying to teach you, Clovis. Bad moves land you in the pokey. Ain't possible to climb out of this one. You bust me out of here and then I'll just turn myself in again. I have more peace in this little block room than I ever did out there."

"Bust you out?" Rabbit yelled. "Hey, buddy, we're his friends. Bring your little rope on over here."

"Reverend, let me help you," said Clovis.

"You can pray, Clovis, but not for my old dirty soul. Pray the Lord finds a good place for Angel, Willie, and Ida May."

"Me and Alma, we can take those kids in."

Jeb hung his head.

Rabbit yelled, "Take me in. I'm up for adoption!"

"Clovis, your quiver is full to running over. But you could do one thing for me."

"I'll do whatever you ask."

"Find out if Fern is doing all right. I'm worried about her."

Jeb held to the bars, his head still hung down between both arms.

"I think that Miss Coulter always does well for herself, but I'll ask around."

Jeb settled back onto the cot. "That I know. Fern always rises to meet the next summit." That was what he loved about Fern, but also what distressed him. That she could rise with or without him.

The sun was gone and with it, the sky and everything pleasant.

21

Time to wake up, Mr. Nubey."
Jeb had dreamed wild boars ate him alive, so when the voice came to him in the hushed prelight of Monday, he thought he had awakened in heaven. His stiff back and the flimsy wood frame of the cot boring into his shoulder roused him into reality. He sat up. His head dropped back and hit the hard stone jailhouse wall.

Philemon Gracie sat upon a bench. "I hope you don't mind. My family slept in the parsonage last night. The girls are being careful of you and your charges' things."

His obliging ways made Jeb feel more ashamed.

"I could not find your shaving soap. Mine lies packed in the back of our sedan."

"Welcome to anything I have. I get a shave down at the barber on Waddle." Jeb ran his fingers through his hair. It stood on end at the front of his scalp.

"Might I recommend my brand, Barclay Crocker? Softens the beard nicely and doesn't chafe." With the tips of his fingers the minister stroked his chin.

Jeb's eyes felt like circles of fire.

Gracie told him, "The good Mrs. Florence Bernard had a crisis of the conscience, it seems. She brought us by a tray of her baked goods. I told her we should offer them to you. If I were you, I'd indulge a little charity."

Jeb reached through the bars and accepted three slices of pumpkin bread. "Couldn't be Florence Bernard. She hates me."

"That genteel woman couldn't hate anyone, Mr. Nubey."

"Where are your children?" Jeb asked.

"Now there we have something again. It is those things you say—'Where are your children' or 'Handcuff me, Deputy Maynard'—that tell me something about you. You are not the same man who walked into this town with the Texarkana lawmen nipping at your heels, are you?"

"You joking me?" Jeb chewed the second piece of sweet bread.

"My daughter, Constance, is supervising her two siblings in their morning devotions. Thank you for asking. She tutors them. We have moved a great deal in the last year or two so her teaching skills are invaluable. As she is invaluable."

"Angel is a bright girl, too. I'd like to see her placed in a family like yours."

"You've relied so long on manipulation, you would try your skills on me?" asked Gracie, but he did laugh.

"Desperation, Reverend. It's my only motive."

Gracie breathed a shallow breath and gentled his eyes. "I know that. I'm not a well-equipped man, Mr. Nubey. My training in theology ill equipped me for life as a widower. Six children might push me completely over the edge. Since my dear Ellen left me, I have been only half a man. To bring on a bigger load would be the same as laying more on the shoulders of my fourteen-year-old daughter. If you wish, I'll do my best to try and inquire about town."

"The children have been labeled bad blood because they've been with me. You won't find a family here to take them in."

"Charity is not in such short supply, surely. Even in these hard times."

"Even shorter supply, I'm afraid."

"This Mrs. Wellington, she's a good woman?"

"Evelene *Whittington*. She and Floyd brag of six grandchildren scattered about town. They own the Woolworth's to boot. I'm fairly sure she hates me, too."

"For whatever your foibles, Mr. Nubey, don't think the families here are against you. Somehow, out of your ignorance came a heart. You touched at least a handful of souls."

Jeb finished the last piece of Florence Bernard's baked bread.

"Do you care about any of them?"

"It was coming to me that I did," said Jeb.

"Your words on legitimacy stirred me. You're sort of God's little paradox, aren't you; the illiterate man assimilating a premise on legitimacy? I stood outside the door and listened. You moved me."

"I'm well practiced. What you heard came from the mouth of a bona fide fraud. Can't get no more authentic than that, Reverend. Nothing like experience to put silver on a man's tongue."

Rabbit rolled onto his back, sucked in three nasal gasps, and then fell still again.

"So would you say that you know more about God than when you first began your brief career as minister of Church in the Dell?" Gracie helped himself to Florence's bread too.

"I would say yes to that."

A bit of dawn entered the eastern sky.

"Mr. Nubey, can you say you know him? You've moved beyond the formal overture. You find ways to converse with the One who bore your sin?"

Jeb pinched his bottom lip into a bow. "That would be a yes, too. I don't say it as good as you do, though."

Gracie brushed the moist crumbs from his lap. "Excellent."

❋

"You forgot something, Mr. Nubey. Reverend Gracie thought it would be appropriate if we brought it by." Evelene Whittington held the Bible she had once picked out of a stack on the Woolworth's sales floor out to him. "It certainly looks worn."

Jeb waited as though either one of them might break into a rage.

"Angel says you learned to read on it." Florence Bernard carried a plate of something covered with a napkin.

"Are the kids with you, Evelene?" Jeb asked.

"I can bring them by." Evelene's mouth kept twitching as though she wasn't sure what to say.

"Maybe it's better you don't. I don't want them to see me in here."

"I had more ham biscuits than I needed, what with living alone." She examined the bars between them. "I'll slide them through."

"Maynard says the state police are on the way. That isn't good, is it?" asked Evelene.

Jeb read the worry on her face. "Thank you for the Bible. I'd like to keep it."

She turned it sideways and handed it to him.

Rabbit and Carl moved to the front of the cell to watch and snoop.

"I don't know why they have to bring in the state policemen. Aren't they all just interfering in our town business, anyway?" Florence poked a ham biscuit through the bars like she was feeding rabbits.

"We ought to have a talk with Maynard. I practically give the man his shoelaces every few months." Evelene carried on the conversation with Florence as though Jeb were absent altogether.

"I don't suppose either of you ladies have seen Fern?" Jeb covered up the plate of mash that Maynard had given him with a napkin.

Evelene and Florence connected gazes. Then Evelene said, "You're not who you said you was, Mr. Nubey. Thing like that effects a girl."

"I wanted to tell her before everyone else, before the Sunday message." Before he had decided he liked who they had become too much to change things.

Florence poked the rest of the ham biscuits through the bars. "All of this explains why I kept noticing things about your messages."

"Now Florence, you never said such a thing," said Evelene. "I was deaf as Job's turkey myself, truth be told."

"The thing is, Reverend Gracie says we have to forgive you and he is right as rain, you know." Florence slid him the plate too.

"They can hang me three times, Florence, Evelene, but I have to know you both forgive me. That everyone here in Nazareth might some day forgive me."

Maynard opened the pale-green door. "Mr. Nubey has more visitors if you two ladies are finished."

Florence and Evelene touched Jeb's cold fingers and left.

"Hey, Nubey, you ain't going to keep them biscuits to yourself, are ya?" asked Carl.

The way that Maynard marched in, an official sort of stalk into the jail commons, Jeb expected to see the state badges or the feds. Instead, it was Charlie. His brother.

Jeb reached through the bars. "Charlie, Charlie! I never expected to see you."

Maynard opened Jeb's cell door. Charlie threw his arms around Jeb. "I bring good tidings, brother."

"You look fit, like they been feeding you. Does Daddy know? About me?" asked Jeb.

"I thought it best not to tell him. Daddy's had pneumonia. Don't worry, he's some better." Charlie held up his finger. A welded silver spoon handle formed a ring. "Me and Selma got married. That's why I'm starting to look so round. Little Oklahoma gals, they can cook, don't let nobody tell you no different."

Jeb could not stop patting his brother's back. He invited Charlie to take a bench. "I want you to know, brother, I got redemption."

"Do tell."

"I am not the same Jeb who left Texarkana."

"You can read. That I know."

"I'm redeemed, Charlie. Consecrated to the Lord is my old ragged soul."

"When I saw you, I said to myself, he's got hisself a glow about him." Charlie helped himself to a Bernard ham biscuit.

"Gin is not my friend anymore."

"Selma tries to get me to church," said Charlie.

"You ought to go."

"The thing is, I'm about to be a daddy. Selma's with child."

"Her daddy must have come after you for that one," said Jeb.

"I don't mean like that. You have been away a good while, brother. Of late, she's with child." Charlie turned his back to the two boys staring through the cell at them.

Jeb lifted the plate. He handed Carl and Rabbit each a biscuit.

"Here I've gone and forgot myself," said Charlie. He came to his feet. "I'll be right back." He rushed out into the commons.

A man with his hat in his hands waited in the doorway. When he stepped out, his head was lowered a bit, near to respectable.

Jeb said, "Leon Hampton?" He braced himself for the punch that Hank's daddy would give him. But Leon waited outside the jail cell. His eyes cast down, he said, "I'm here to make amends for my boy."

"Don't it beat anything, Jeb? Anything you've ever seen?" Charlie ushered Leon two steps closer to Jeb.

"Here I have prayed for the chance to tell you what I should have stayed to tell you," Jeb said, "and I'm just dumb-struck as an old mule." Jeb could not account for Hampton's modesty. "Mr. Hampton, if there is anyway you could forgive me . . . I am sorry as can be about Hank. I'd give my life for his right about now."

"I'm sorry, too. That's why I came to you. It were my idea. Charlie was good enough to bring me. I finally got the truth about Hank. He provoked you over that silly Myrna, like he cared two cents for the poor little gal."

"I shouldn't have hit him back," said Jeb.

Charlie told Leon, "Hank did land the first blow."

Leon nodded. "At least a dozen men saw it. Then when Hank got well, didn't he just turn around and pick a fight with my field boss, Lem?" He and Charlie exchanged facts about the matter.

"Hank got well? I don't believe I follow you." Jeb felt strength coming into his limbs and neck as though revived by Florence's cooking.

"Sure he got well. Then he hauled off and got drunk and plowed into my best field boss. Fell down a hill. Broke his neck."

"Funeral was filled with all those boys from the bunkhouse. Myrna was just sloppy sad," said Charlie. "You think she had any sincerity in her?" he asked Leon.

"I didn't kill Hank?" Jeb had trouble digesting the news. "Charlie?"

"When I finally got that letter and spilled it to Mr. Hampton, he made me swear not to tell you, Brother. He wanted to tell you hisself."

"Looks of things, I liked to have waited too long," said Hampton.

Maynard entered with a letter. I finally got through to them Texarkana cops, Mr. Hampton. Your letter is legitimate. Mr. Nubey, all murder charges have been dropped against you. Sorry about the mix-up." He opened the cell door, then turned to Leon Hampton. "You think your field man will get sentenced?"

"I got him a lawyer myself. Paid his bail. My word is good in that county. Lem's got a good chance of having the charges dropped." Leon Hampton sat on the bench as though the weight of the past week sat itself upon his chest. "I gave Hank everything." He put his face in his hands and sobbed.

Jeb walked out of the cell and knelt on one knee at Leon's feet. He held Hank's daddy while he cried.

Hampton took Jeb's extended hand. "You're a good man, Jeb Nubey."

Jeb liked the sound of that.

Will Honeysack sat on a stool in the corner of his store. Whoever tried to swap small talk with him received either no response or such a weak reply they turned and went back to their shopping.

"Will, you got to snap out of this fog. People are starting to talk," said Freda. She took off her apron and left it on the counter.

The bell rang. She glanced at the storefront. Then she turned around complete. "Deputy Maynard? Reverend—I mean, Mr. Nubey."

"I'm here on official business, Mrs. Honeysack. Is your husband about this afternoon?"

Will came off the bench "I don't have anything to say. Everything's been said that can be said."

Jeb politely nodded at Maynard and then stepped out front. "Will, the murder charges have been dropped against me. I wanted you to be one of the first to know. I'm not guilty."

"I knew you couldn't murder nobody. But you're not Philemon Gracie. That's a fact, is it not?" Will asked.

"Mr. Honeysack, you being the head deacon, Reverend Gracie asked me to drop by and ask if you'd consider dropping charges of fraud against Mr. Nubey. If not, I will take him right back to that cell."

Freda, with her back to Jeb, either mouthed something to Will, or he simply read her face after three decades of marriage. "I'd rather our new minister make that decision. I don't know why he sent you over here."

"Because I want to ask you myself to forgive me." Jeb reached out and touched Will on the arm. "I set out to see Fern, but what with you being right here across the street, I figured I owed it to you to drop by here first. If you don't want the charges dropped against me, Will, then I want to take my punishment. Whatever it takes to earn your forgiveness. I realize it's too late to earn your respect."

Freda cried. She walked around the counter to remove herself from wifely influence.

"When I saw them take you away in those handcuffs, it seemed like we were the wrongdoers. Something about it was just wrong." Will studied the matter, staring at his open palms as the weight and measure of the matter.

"The wrongdoing was mine, Will. If you forgive me, I will work here in Nazareth and earn back your friendship. If you want justice, I will try to earn your respect from behind bars. Either way, I have found something worth living for."

Will's face cleared. He stood tall. "Jeb Nubey, you are my friend, just the way you always were." Will extended his hand.

Jeb embraced the grocer and head deacon of Church in the Dell.

Freda cried some more and went for the phone. She muttered something about calling the Whittingtons and even Horace Mills.

Maynard held up his hands, open stars, and said, "I'll be back to my business, folks. Mr. Nubey, if there's anything I can do to help you settle in to Nazareth—or be on your way—let me know. Just keep it honest, this go-round."

"I've got to find Angel, Willie, and Ida May. If you can give me back my truck keys, Maynard, I'd like to ask that they be released into my care."

"Kind of unusual. But I'll talk to the social worker and see what can be worked out." Maynard turned to leave.

"Social worker?" asked Jeb.

Maynard told him, "The Nubey children are a government matter now. Whether or not they've been picked up from the Whittingtons' place, I couldn't tell you, Mr. Nubey."

Jeb took his truck keys from Maynard. "Will, Freda, I'll never forget what you've done for me." He shook Will's hand.

Freda rolled the top down on a sack of something. "Mr.

Nubey, here's some licorice whips for the children. It's their favorite." She had not stopped crying.

Jeb kissed Freda's cheek. "Looks like a little rain moving in. I'll run over to Woolworth's and see about the children."

Will saw him to the door. He followed Jeb out and, so the missus wouldn't hear, said, "I saw that social worker over there this morning. I hate to say it, but I think they've taken those kids away."

22

Maynard told us you'd likely drop by to see the children," said Evelene. Her eyes showed she was still peeved with him and her fingers kept twining as though she'd rather be in the back of the store unbundling socks than talking to him.

"If you all will consider having me, I'd like to stay on in Nazareth and find some work," said Jeb. The store looked pretty to him, all the bonnets and laces a mite more pleasing than staring through the bars at Rabbit and Carl.

"Not too many jobs in Nazareth." Evelene reorganized a rack of spools by color.

"I've asked Maynard to help me get custody of the Welby children. They don't have anyone and it may as well be me."

"You know the children are not here, don't you?" she asked.

"I was hoping I could still find them here."

"The social worker left with them not fifteen minutes ago. Am I telling it right, Floyd?" she asked her husband. "I was at the jailhouse when it all happened."

"That youngest has been upset ever since they took you from the church," said Floyd.

"Ida May is easy to cry." Jeb headed for the door. "If you could just tell me where they were headed, I'll catch up with them. I'm not letting them put the kids in a home."

"They aren't in a home, Mr. Nubey," said Evelene.

Jeb hesitated between the welcome rug and the outdoor mat.

"Fern Coulter asked for them. The government much prefers a teacher over an orphanage for homeless children." Evelene took the broom from Floyd.

"You telling me the kids are with Fern?"

"That's what I'm telling you," said Evelene. "Good-bye, Mr. Nubey."

Charlie met him out on the street. "Remember me?"

"Charlie, I need you to go with me. I've got some matters to settle. I'll explain on the way."

"There is a place for men who have no home, Charlie," Jeb said as they drove. "It is with their God and under the good graces of a woman. For God, a man can die. For a woman, he has reason to live."

"Fern's a good cook?" asked Charlie.

"That is a debatable matter. But nonetheless, she is Fern. When I say to you, Charlie, this angel has come down from the clouds and turned this old boy inside out, know that I am a man undone."

"Nobody back home would believe what I'm hearing." Charlie's gaze indicated he set eyes on Jeb as he would a stranger. "This Fern has you horn-swoggled. That is a dangerous place to be. Best you weigh the matter, Brother. Selma and I, we have us an understanding."

"Fern is not ordinary, Charlie. What we have is like twin hearts, two souls, interlocked," said Jeb.

Charlie rolled up his window to take the chill out of the cab. "I thought you said she hates you."

"I'm purty sure she does." Jeb parked the truck at the end of Long's Lane.

"This must be her place. Say, it has a fine pond. You catch some fish out of it, I guess."

Jeb pondered how he should pull into her drive. If he walked up the road, then he could come up on her porch quiet-like and give him time to figure out what he should say.

"Can't quite see her house from here. You going to drive on in or what?" asked Charlie.

"I'm thinking on it."

"Maybe I should stay here in the truck. Is she prone to ranting? I hate it when they do that." Charlie inspected the pond again.

"I'm driving in. She's seen me on foot too many times. Man's got to come up to a woman's doorstep with some dignity." The Model-T lurched and then died before completing the turn.

Charlie told him, "Maybe you ought to walk."

Up Long's Lane, the tree limbs were partially bare, gray bowed and reaching, scarcely possessing the languishing threads of summer garments before the first snow. No bouquet at his disposal, Jeb approached Fern's cottage with the same nothing he had carried on his back into Nazareth. Beyond the cottage stepping-stones, a single spire of color dipped in the breeze at the edge of the meadow. Jeb plucked it, a red flaming cardinal flower not bitten by frost. He carried that last flower of summer to Fern's doorstep. Inside, he heard Angel and Willie squabbling in a sibling battle.

He rapped the knocker against her door.

Angel saw him first. She stood in Fern's open doorway without a thing to say.

"I guess you're stunned to see me," said Jeb.

Angel threw herself against him. "Jeb! I knew you'd be back."

Jeb passed hugs around, but Angel never let go of his front coat pocket. He asked kind of low, "Is Fern about?"

"She don't want to see you," said Ida May.

He strained to see into the kitchen.

"I'll try to get her to come out." Angel left him outside on the porch. She yelled Fern's name twice before she got a reply.

Fern carried school papers across the room. "You all have to do homework first, then we'll see about playing outside." The papers were disorganized, so when she stopped cold, several papers fell to the parlor rug. She paused all of a sudden. "They let you out." The words came so slow he sounded like an idiot to himself. "I didn't kill Hank Hampton. I'm free."

"You just committed fraud, then. Lied. Well, that changes everything." She bent to pick up Willie and Ida May's scattered papers.

"All that Texarkana mess's been dropped against me, Fern. I was hoping we could sit down so you can finally know the truth."

"You kids take this stuff into the kitchen. I'll let you shell some pecans for a pie." She waited while Angel led the other two into the kitchen. "You're a free man. I'd think you'd be headed out of town then. Be about your business."

"I was hoping you might help me figure out my business," said Jeb.

"You're a grown man." Her gaze indicated that he should figure it out on his own. She had made her way to the worktable and stared at nothing through the picture window.

"I've been figuring some things out, Fern. Reverend Gracie and I had a talk, even though we haven't worked everything out. If he'll hear me out, I plan to ask him to let me apprentice."

"As what?"

"A minister. Legitimate and legal, of course."

She came aright. It was the first time that she seemed to care an ounce about what he said. "Takes a lot of study."

"I'll be needing a good library. You know anyone who might loan me some books?"

She now sat at the table with her back to him. Jeb knew better than to rush her. The pictures she'd had of him in her mental box of photos were nothing like him at all and to find that out meant she'd had to set fire to the whole lot. To Fern, he was a sad box of ash.

"You left your truck parked out in the road, I guess you know," she said.

"My brother, Charlie, is here. He's working on it for me. He got another set of wheels, him and his wife, so he give me this one." He couldn't remember if it was the first she had ever heard of Charlie.

"Before you make some overnight decision, being a minister takes commitment, Phil—Jeb—" When she stopped, she had a look that said she did not know how much to say or what name to use when she said it.

"All this is coming at you kind of fast." He decided he should have started with something smaller. If all she'd allow was his driving past at night to watch her through the window, he should've settled for that. "I don't want you to hate me, Fern."

She chose to watch Charlie drive the truck up the lane toward the cottage, as though she was waiting for any reason to end their talk. "I guess he's got your truck running. Lucky you."

"I don't know much about luck. Meeting you was luck. Meeting you as—as somebody else, that wasn't lucky. Nobody is more sorry than me for lying to you. But if it took that to get to know you, I'm not sorry about that."

Fern leaned as if she had to check on the pecan shellers one more time.

"You ought not to let me off the hook, I know better. But I'd like to pass you on the street and know you thought you could tip one of those hats of yours to me. Far as you're concerned, I guess you'd just like for me to disappear. But there's things that need tending to. I'd like to find my own place and take the Welbys off your hands. No need to leave them here. You got plenty to do. Angel's half grown and of a mind to keep Willie and Ida May close by. If she thinks she can find her family, I don't want to throw her out on the streets while she's trying. No reason to leave these kids out in the cold, what with this Depression hanging on."

At that moment, all breath left Fern. "You want the children?" She asked it flat as hotcakes. But a feeling of some sort came into her face and then a little into her words. "You're willing to go find a place to live, get a job, and be daddy to three children that aren't yours?"

"That's what I plan." When she did not respond he waved at Charlie through the glass in a way that told him to sit tight. "I'm going to speak with Ivey Long about that old house of his up near the schoolhouse. It needs some work. I'll exchange work for rent, if he's open to it. I'll let the kids know." The sound of small fingers shelling pecans drew him to lean back and peer into the kitchen. Ida May shelled the best of the three, her fingers small and reaching into the broken shell to bring out the pecan prize. She showed one to Jeb, but then got pulled back out of the doorway.

"You are a capable person, I'm not saying you're not. Work's scarce all over is all," she said.

That bit of warm coal from her caused him to confess, "Whatever you think of me now, I'm glad I knew you, Fern."

He turned to leave, then called for Angel who was hanging around the corner, listening to every word. "I'll be back for all of you kids as soon as I get us a house. Keep up with your studies and don't give Miss Coulter any lip."

Angel got up and stood in the door to watch him go.

"You're leaving," Fern said.

Jeb noticed how her fingers clinched atop the table. "I'll try and not leave the children with you too long. I know you have your own burdens, what with teaching at the school and all."

"The children can stay as long as is needed. You needn't hurry on account of me," she said.

Jeb backed out of the door.

"We'll have plenty of food for dinner. You may as well join the children here tonight."

When her eyes—the eyes that once fed him admiration—failed to welcome him along with her invitation, he said, "No need to fix a thing for me. I'll grab supper at the diner. Charlie and me need to catch up on things and—I wouldn't trouble you anyway."

"Always have more food than we need here." She stared out the window, her arms folded against her chest. "Bring Charlie if you want."

"I've been enough of a bother."

Fern sighed inwardly. She walked away from the front window. Her stance, elbows forward, chest caved in, made her look as though all of the stuffing were let out of her.

"I'm glad I found you home, at least." He could not look at her for a moment more without sensing the loathing he knew he saw when she looked at him. She was done with him. Jeb backed out of the door and closed it behind him. He walked down the path in the streaming light and it felt warm upon his back, nothing like winter. He heard the screen door slam behind him. Afraid he might turn and find anyone but Fern watching him leave, he drew his sights on Charlie. The engine sparked. Charlie made a victory fist when he got the old truck humming again.

That is when Jeb heard the deep voice, womanly and assured, the one he'd imagined before falling asleep on the hard jailhouse bed. The voice that sounded like the gulf winds blowing winter from the field.

"I'll see you then, maybe later," said Fern. She waited on the path just beyond the porch, her shoulders wrapped in a white afghan.

Jeb could not run toward her as much as his mind whipped him to do so. He could only open his mouth as though he tried to fill it with more words. He lacked too many of them in her presence, the good ones anyway.

She brought her hand to her mouth. With one finger she trapped a tear before it fell.

Philemon Gracie had set up more chairs around the front porch, a newly painted collection of ladder-back chairs rescued from the church storage shed. He was on his knees transplanting cedars from the woods to the front of the parsonage lawn. "So you want to be a minister, Mr. Nubey? What makes you think you can manage the study load and care for three children?"

Jeb took the shovel and tossed dirt into the hole around the cedar roots. "How do you manage, Reverend?"

"Not well, and I'm not earning a ministerial degree.

"You've not experienced the kind of pastorate that has you up all night studying only to rise before sunup to help a widow mend a fence. Or if the eaves of the church give way and no one else can help you fix it because the corn's come in—and even with your help, there's no money to do it. Or how tired you get when over several days you sit up with a distraught husband while his wife of thirty years takes her last breath. These things you should know. But if you're of a mind to do it, I can contact my old professors and have the work sent to you. If I speak up as your mentor, the accountable partner for your education, you might complete the courses by night. But that creates work for me." A thin smile hinted that Jeb's calling might be an interesting venture. "A challenge for us both." He poured dirt into the hole around the root. "I'd have to know my work was for something."

"I'll not quit on you, if that's your worry," said Jeb. He helped tamp down dirt.

"Jeb, as I've said, you've a tough road ahead. There is no pay in being an apprentice. Little pay after."

"It's a different kind of rich. I'm aware, Reverend Gracie," said Jeb.

"It's been interesting to see your climb from the pit, Mr. Nubey. You'd be wise not to ascend this journey by yourself."

"I'd never make it without you."

"Not me. I speak of Fern Coulter. The ministry can be a lonely life. I am thankful for the fruit of a family. My Ellen got me through many a worrisome night."

"Fern has not consented to join me. Her forgiveness could come at any time or not at all. But my decision's not based on Fern's belief in me."

"I agree. God's approval is all you need for now. I do believe that is her automobile pulling around the church, though, Jeb," said Gracie.

Fern parked beyond the new stand of cedars. When she climbed out of the vehicle, her arms were loaded with books.

"I've had these up in my attic, Reverend Gracie. I heard you were tutoring and thought you might use the extra books."

Even though he had been standing there all along, she suddenly seemed to notice Jeb, as though he'd come out of nowhere. "Hello, Jeb."

"Word spreads fast in Nazareth," said Gracie.

"If you don't want them now, I'll hold on to them," she said.

"Jeb, you're the one that'll be needing these, I believe." Gracie stepped away from Fern and dumped another shovelful of dirt around the root ball.

"Never had a library before. I'm grateful, Fern." He took the load of books from her. "We're planting trees. Reverend Gracie has an eye for landscape."

"Changes the whole look of the place," said Fern.

"Miss Coulter, your taste in authors is impeccable." Gracie stopped to take a look at the stack in Jeb's arms. "And I'm glad our apprentice here is such an eager student."

Fern answered him, "I know Jeb will learn many things under your tutelage, Reverend."

"He's introducing me to some of your local culture. We are going to visit an establishment called Fidel's for one of those chocolate malteds," said Gracie. "Do join us unless you're busy."

"We'd enjoy your company." Jeb stuck the shovel into the soil.

"Local culture. Fidel's is a good place to start in Nazareth. If you want to find a good meeting place for the locals, do try Beulah's café." Fern picked up a book Jeb had dropped. She carried it to the porch and left it where she and Jeb had once sat and read together.

"Reverend, you have to tell Fidel to give the ice cream an extra shot. He's a real chintz when it comes to the syrup." She still had not said either way whether she would join them.

Gracie excused himself to clean up.

"Your books mean a lot, Fern," said Jeb.

"I'm not a hard person. Not usually. Nothing wrong with a man trying to better himself."

"There's a singing over in Hope next week. Thought maybe I'd take a drive up. If you'd like to go, let me know. Invite Oz if you want."

"I don't know."

"Or just come with Gracie and me to Fidel's."

"If I do, I can't stay long. Papers to grade and such."

"Walk me over to the pump? I'm a mess," said Jeb. He carried the stack of books back to the porch and set them next to the one she laid down and then walked to the pump beside the parsonage, not knowing whether or not she would follow. She did. He cleaned his hands and asked her a question about Pascal and was relieved when she answered.

Finally, Gracie came out dressed in a clean shirt and wearing a hat like Jeb's. "I bought one when I saw yours, Jeb. Hope you don't mind. I like your tastes," he said. He had brought his cane—the one he'd used to quiet the enraged church folk—and used it to get himself out to his automobile.

Jeb walked Fern out to Gracie's sedan.

After Gracie had gotten inside, she waited for his door to close and then said, "Sometimes, I feel like I'm watching myself trying to get Fern to stop the attack and sound the retreat. I don't know if I ever told you that. I get it from my father."

Jeb decided not to agree or disagree. "Jeb, you've got a long ways to climb. I know you know that, but you can do this if you learn to trust. Nothing ever works well the fast way," she said.

By the time that Gracie had started the motor, Jeb had opened the door for her. Her hair brushed his cheek and it seemed she had deliberately drawn close to him, but then moved away like a boat that needed steadying. She climbed into the rear seat and offered the passenger seat up front to Jeb. He took it, respecting the distance she had set between them. He'd have some say-so about that in time. But this go around, Fern would get to know him as just Jeb. It unsettled him a mite.

He said, "The climb up is not so hard if I can see a smile every now and then coming down from the clouds."

Fern smiled.

"Ah, just like that."

The day was cloudless.

READING GUIDE

1. Are those like Jeb Nubey the norm in the ministry or are most ministers legitimate ministers who have studied and pursued a selfless life of service to others? How do you distinguish a charlatan from a legitimate minister? Do we tend to form our opinions from the study of religious leaders' lives or to draw our conclusions from popular opinion?

2. Discuss Jeb's internal conflicts as he begins to understand the legitimacy that truly exists behind the pulpit. From where does he seem to draw this new wisdom?

3. American families facing starvation during the Great Depression were sometimes forced to send children away to live with a relative. However, in cases where no relative was available, children/youths were put out on the streets to fend for themselves. Do you think such a circumstance could ever exist again in America? Do you believe there are needy people in your community? How do you know?

4. By the time the long-awaited Reverend Gracie and his three children supposedly appeared in the form of Jeb and the outcast Welbys, the members of the Church in the Dell had been a long time without a man in the pulpit. Do you think their desperation for a minister to attend to their spiritual needs caused them to overlook his lack of skill and education? Have

you ever known a church or other organization that made a mistake in choosing leadership due to haste/desperate need? Do humans ever choose to be blind to the truth in order to satisfy immediate need?

5. Jeb has a deep-seated need for feeling like he is part of a family. He finds that Nazareth's feeling of community and their acceptance of him fill this need. Do you think that some people who have an unfulfilled need might masquerade as someone else just to find acceptance? Once you realize this about someone, do you withdraw from them or do you encourage them to let down their guard and be true to self? Could you forgive someone like Jeb?

6. Discuss Jeb's guilt over the attempted murder rap from which he is running. How did his reaction to the crime change over time?

7. Jeb's infatuation with Fern Coulter, while causing him to want to be a better Jeb, also becomes part of the impetus for his gnawing need to confess. When we humans recognize a need for change, we often fight that change because of a fear of exposure. Have you come to believe that confession is good for the soul, or do you struggle with hiding your flaws/mistakes from others? Is this good, bad, or does it matter?

8. Jeb stops Clovis from making a bad choice that would have sent him to jail. Did Jeb help him only to further his own masquerade as a preacher, or did Jeb care about this man? Why?

9. While the devastating national conditions and lack of records allowed the Welby children to pose as the Gracie children, that situation would be less likely to happen in our modern information age. Do modern advances keep people honest?

Does a civilized and prosperous community guarantee a populace of good people?

10. Patricia Hickman seems to be saying that even a charlatan can find God. Do you believe that God is continually working to draw every person to him, even the ones we consider most wicked? Are you good enough to come to God? If for a moment we all agreed that no one is good enough to come to God, how are we made acceptable enough to come to God? In what state did Jeb finally come to God?

ABOUT THE AUTHOR

Patricia Hickman has written eleven novels, most recently *Sandpebbles, The Touch,* and *Katrina's Wings.* Her books have earned critical acclaim from both the secular and inspirational publishing world, including high reviews from *Affair de Coeur, Romantic Times* (Top Pick Gold Medal Rating), *Moody Magazine, Shine,* and the *West Coast Review of Books.* She is one of four authors selected to pioneer a line of high-quality women's fiction for the nationally popular Women of Faith women's conferences that are presented across the country. She has won two Silver Angel Awards.

Please visit www.patriciahickman.com for the latest updates or to email the author.

Look for *Nazareth's Song,* Book Two in the Millwood Hollow Series!